MR STEPHEN

MR STEPHEN

by

TERENCE DE VERE WHITE

LONDON
VICTOR GOLLANCZ LTD
1971

ISBN 0 575 00660 9

First published July 1971
Second impression September 1971

FOR

ROD GREER

PRINTED IN GREAT BRITAIN BY
NORTHUMBERLAND PRESS LIMITED
GATESHEAD

CHAPTER I

DINNER WAS OVER, and the men had divided into
groups round the table; a few were showing signs of having done themselves better than they were accustomed
to; but on the whole, as Stephen Foster remarked, they
were a decorous lot. So they should be, of course—the
chosen few at the head of their profession, and that profession the law. 'A decorous lot'—it would be nearer the
mark to say, 'a colourless lot'. In the old days—but he
was making a point lately of not harking back to the old
days. Perhaps, if he were to see them now through his
sixty-year-old eyes, those patriarchs would seem less impressive than when as a very young man he had been
admitted to their ranks. If he, at the age he was then,
had impressed them so much, it gave him a rod to
measure them with.

His colleagues did not always remember how early he
had got on. Even by his seniors he was regarded as a
survivor from the Golden Age. The old fellows he grew
up among had been giants to him. The names of their
firms used to conjure up an impression of permanence and
immutability. But his own firm was now forty years old;
and those once so impressive names cut very little ice in

Dublin nowadays. Some of them had melted away. And here he was, the doyen of the corps. Each speaker in turn had made a point of bringing up his name, expressing pleasure at his being with them; at which there had been a drumming of feet on the floor, cries of 'Hear! Hear!' and across the table he heard his name being called by one after another to draw his attention to a private toast. He had sat there beaming, taking it in, enjoying it rather. At the head of his profession, he had arrived without trampling on anyone's corns. He had worked very hard; but he had always tried to operate in a spacious way and to avoid the short cuts that earned the name of sharp practice. Nobody in the profession, so far as he knew, had a grudge against him; and he had outgrown jealousy. Except in Curtis's case. Curtis had himself come up at a meteoric rate, and regarded Stephen as his only rival. Curtis had big ideas. Typically, he had been too busy to come this evening. In Ireland a man is envied on his way up and solaced on his way down. At the top, Stephen discovered, old animosities seemed to wilt. Former critics came to prefer to bask in his shade. And he was always ready with advice or a helping hand. People really liked him. Not being married, of course, had something to do with it. A married man is a conspirator by force of circumstances.

Stephen looked at a young man who had been trying to catch his eye all evening. There was a wife and family there. He could always tell. Without them, what was to give the average attorney his drive? There was nothing creative about the life. All one left after one was the money that showed what you had earned and how you had looked after it, and a name that was forgotten in five years. A hall porter in a large hotel had more fame in life and as long in memory. Stephen smiled into his glass.

The idea of himself as a superior hall porter rather appealed to him. At everyone's beck and call. Their business your business. Their demands your duty. Their worries your care. And for this you were paid. Not very different from a prostitute; but there was less risk of disease; and advancing age did not threaten a loss of clientele, the value of experience outweighed the tax time levied on it.

Attorneys were invented to do other people's dirty work. Of course, the status of the profession had risen. With everything else. Everything going up as everything was coming down. There were bookmakers in clubs now; and time was when a solicitor would not have been let in, being regarded as ineligible for the same reason as a soiled-clothes basket; a necessary receptacle, but not something one wanted to look across a table at or stand beside at a bar or call in for a fourth at bridge.

The young man had moved up and was now at Stephen's elbow, waiting to be talked to.

"A very pleasant evening," Stephen said. "I never ate better lamb and this is a good claret. I've stuck to it. I see you are drinking whiskey."

The young man, thinking himself reproved, tried to look as if the tumbler in his hand had somehow arrived there by accident. Stephen noticed his uneasiness and went on: "There's a lot to be said for taking a whiskey and eking it out when fellows are trying to fill you up. You can spread a whiskey over the best part of an evening. I'd encourage you to try the claret; but I see you are a wise man who doesn't mix the grain and the grape."

The young man glanced round the table. Others, as ne was, were drinking whiskey; some had brandy in front of them; liqueurs were plentiful. Alone, old Stephen was sticking to claret. The odd man out. And for a moment he had felt guilty because he wasn't doing likewise. It was wonderful to get to a stage where one could make one's own rules and not have to bother with what was the proper thing to do.

As a rule these annual dinners were given in hotels; but this year Arthur Evans, the President, insisted that the Council and his other guests should come out to his home in Howth. It was like old times. Now seemed an appropriate moment to make the remark that had been mislaid earlier in the evening. The young man made it.

Stephen nodded in agreement. "Arthur Evans is a splendid fellow," he said. He always spoke like that of colleagues. It showed that he had succeeded. The young man was more accustomed to hearing criticism, and if any of Evans had been offered would have joined in. But he agreed that Evans—whom he had never met until he saw him at Council meetings—was an ornament to the profession. It was, as it happened, an ill-chosen compliment. Evans was uncompromisingly plain. But Stephen put the conversation back on the rails by saying that he had known him since he was a boy. The young man looked at Evans—very stout, very bald, very rubicund. Was it conceivable that he had ever been a boy? Then his uneasy glance ran over the great man by whose side he was sitting at last. His dinner jacket was a quarter of a century old, and he was wearing a white cotton shirt. His evening tie was frayed, and hanging out of his pocket was a large bandanna handkerchief. And yet he looked distinguished, the only distinguished-looking man among thirty or so present. The distinction was in his height, his broad brow, his wise calm eyes. Sitting beside him was like sheltering under a rock. The young man wished he could ask him for advice on several questions. Foster was benevolence itself; but he seemed to be relaxing to an extent that precluded references to anything approaching shop. Now he was off about the roses on the table. They were the decorative feature of the rather sombre room. The President, it appeared, had made a hobby of roses, and Stephen shared his interest in them. He discoursed at length about each specimen on display. The young man decided to plant roses next year, but found himself hard put to it to pretend to be attending to the conversation.

The party broke up spontaneously. Everyone was conscious that the Evans family was being kept out of bed for what was, in spite of the informal way it had been done, an official occasion.

Stephen kissed Mrs Evans—who had appeared from nowhere—on the forehead.

"Good night, my dear. I recognised your hand in the Charlotte Russe."

"Thank you, Stephen, dear. Always kind." She smiled rather shyly at the young solicitor, doing her duty.

"It really was a good dinner," he found himself saying, but in a rather reluctant tone as if to admit to any more was to let himself down. Success meant to kiss the President's wife on the forehead and compliment her on a pudding.

Stephen walked slowly, enjoying the night. He had waved genially to the young man to whom he had been talking, in token of farewell. One of the new recruits, anxious-looking and over-dressed—the sort that tended to charge too much and run into debt as well. He had noticed the effort to catch his eye during the evening and enquired what the newcomer's name was so as to be ready for him when he was run to earth. He wanted not only to know his name, but to make a point of mentioning it to show he did. That encouraged the young. And he liked to encourage them. Curtis was different. Curtis had an enormous practice nowadays, but he seemed to live in perpetual hostility to younger men, as if they threatened him. But, then, Richard Curtis was very vain and very jealous. He, thank God, had always been free of those pests. It derived a great deal from his good health. He never felt ill or nervous. His sanity and common sense were his best gifts. He had had them always. They were what had recommended him to his seniors when he was little more than a boy. "If you had been born in England, you would have been Prime Minister," someone had told him.

It was flattering, of course. If he had been born in England, it might not have occurred to him to put as high as he did among his maxims for the conduct of life, not to have anything to do with politics. Some men had used political connections to get on. Curtis owed a lot to them; but he had tended as he went up the ladder to take pains to shed the appearance of any party allegiance. He, too, saw that it was a restriction and shook it off when he could.

Curtis would have come tonight if he thought it might be helpful to his business. Ambition bit into him like acid still.

Why was he thinking about Curtis—spoiling the pleasure of the night? Because he was the only formidable person in his field. He thought of him because he had been absent as he would have thought about him had he been present. It was altogether pleasanter to think about Mary Evans. What a dear creature she was! How pretty still, and ever so little faded. She must be well into her forties now. A strange marriage. What had she ever seen in Arthur Evans? She might have married anyone. And so capable too. Did that dinner tonight with precious little help. Arthur was so proud of her. Hadn't got over his luck yet. Funny how a fastidious-seeming woman like that could face the prospect of bedding down with Arthur. He had always looked like some sort of genial sea monster, if a sea monster could be hirsute as Arthur was everywhere it wasn't wanted and nowhere that would have added to his beauty. But he was kind and dependable. He was President of the Law Society. He did well. Practice in the family for three generations. By no means bright. It was a comforting reflection that one could keep going as Arthur did and not be. Curtis now . . .

Stephen's house hove into sight. Little more than a cottage in his father's time, he had added to it by degrees; and nothing would ever persuade him to move. It was under the road, only the roof showed; he approached the house by a wicket gate in the wall instead of going round to the front. He locked the gate and walked down the flight of stone steps to the terrace. The light was on in the hall as he had left it, but he was surprised to see that his study was also lit up. When he left home it was still daylight. The servants must have been in there. He liked the decent couple that had worked for him for twenty years, but all the same, the idea of their pottering round his room disturbed him. They had their own comfortable quarters; why didn't they stay in them? With a sense of foreboding he turned the latchkey.

It was a sign one was getting older, the unease that so trivial an incident could produce. He took for granted a settled routine. Mr Clarke went round outside, last thing at night, to lock up, while his wife was putting a bottle in their master's bed, wrapping it round his pyjamas. A glass of hot milk and two rich digestive biscuits were laid on the side table. Stephen himself made sure that all doors and windows were locked inside before going to bed; then he went into the dining-room and helped himself to an apple from the bowl, never without its complement of fruit, on the sideboard.

The study door was open; the flood of light jarred on Stephen's nerves. He went to turn off the offending switch on the board inside the hall door. A woman's voice said "Oh!" Stephen switched on the light again and went into the study.

She was sitting in an armchair at the fireside blinking in the sudden light. A woman of no particular age with indeterminate-coloured untidy hair, in a cotton dress that revealed shapeless legs; a cigarette hung precariously from the end of her mouth. Its predecessors, with lipstick-stained butts, lay in ashes on a tray beside her.

"It's me," she said, and added, "Joan Joyce. You have forgotten me."

"Oh, Miss Joyce, I'm sorry. I was rather taken by surprise. I didn't expect to find anyone here at this time of night. We are early birds here."

He remembered her now. Ten years or so ago she had acted as his secretary for about a year without making any particular impression. Why had she gone? She had been submerged in memory by her predecessor, a loyal stalwart, and by the vital presence of her successor, a busy bee. Yes. Now he recalled that vague expression, which presaged disaster but somehow seemed to avoid it, the rather complaining voice, the lipstick on her teeth. She had been quite adequate. He had forgotten her existence.

"I thought you might be in. I would have called up but you wouldn't have known who I was. I told your house-keeper I was from the office. I had to see you. She gave me a cup of tea. Oh, I know you will say I should have waited and come to see you about it in the office; but I'm not made that way. When I'm really worried, I have to do something about it at once. You remember: I was always that way."

Stephen did not remember.

"It's about Miss Haggard's will I wanted to see you."

"Miss Haggard? Miss Haggard? She died about ten years ago."

"That's the one. She got ill all of a sudden, and you asked me to go down with you in a taxi to make her will."

"It was you, was it? I had forgotten."

"She had made no will, and if she died her nephew was to come in for it all."

"Well. What has that to do with you? And why should you want to come and see me about it at midnight?"

"I sat outside while she was giving instructions. She whispered to you, and I heard you say that there were several good charities, and you named a few. She left all she had to three of them. You acted for them all. They got about twelve thousand each."

"I still can't see what business this is of yours."

"If she hadn't made her will her nephew got everything. But instead it went to your charities."

"What do you mean by *my* charities?"

"Ones you act for."

"I act for a great many charities. Naturally I mentioned them when Miss Haggard asked me to recommend some. Her principal motive was to prevent her nephew from getting the money, if I remember correctly."

"I remember all that. He was wild. But then many a man is when he's young. An old lady like Miss Haggard wouldn't understand. She knew nothing about life, stuck down there in that gloomy old house. It gives me the creeps still when I think about it."

"You haven't yet explained why you came here this evening."

13

"Well, you see, I'm going to marry Sonny. We have been walking out, as you'd say, for ages. But he has nothing, and I am earning less than ten pounds a week. Sonny has his faults, like the rest of us. But we suit one another. What gets me down is the thought that those old charities have the money that by rights should have gone to him."

"Well, it's rather late in the day to discuss it. I'm sorry for your sake her nephew did nothing when she was alive to recommend himself to her."

"Sonny's too straight. He couldn't play up to anyone, even his aunt, just to get money out of her. I admire him for that."

"I still can't see what you expect me to do."

"Get on to those charities and explain the position. I'm sure you could persuade them to part with some of it."

"I'll do nothing of the kind."

"But you could put it to them that they might lose everything if it came to an action."

"An action?"

"If Sonny were to dispute the will they would lose everything."

"Rubbish! Nonsense! The will was admitted to probate at least ten years ago. The matter is closed. No court would entertain an action."

"It would if it could be proved there was something wrong with the will."

"There was nothing wrong with Miss Haggard's will."

"Oh, Mr Stephen! When the old lady signed it you told me to write my name as a witness; and you were going to write yours when she started to say something, and you went into a long explanation, and eventually she was satisfied. I wasn't paying attention at the time, but next morning I noticed that you hadn't witnessed the will."

"That's a lie."

"It's not. I noticed it; and I was going to tell you about it but there was so much fuss because Miss Haggard had died meanwhile that I didn't get a chance. And then I looked at the will again and your name was on it. I realised that you had seen your mistake. And I didn't want to make trouble."

"My advice to you, young lady, is to go home before you say something you may have cause to regret."

"That's all very well. I'm sure a court would accept your evidence against mine. That's how the world works. Who am I? But I have another witness."

The flash in the glass of Stephen's spectacles was a trick of light; but he looked menacing. The woman ground her cigarette stub in the ash tray as if she was repelling an attack.

"I showed it to Curran. I wasn't sure about it. I asked him what happened to a will if only one witness signed it. He said it wasn't worth the paper it was written on; but there was nothing to be done seeing as how the old lady was dead. He never said anything more to me about it."

"Naturally."

"But Mr Curran is a very honest man. If he's asked he's bound to tell the truth."

"Curran had nothing to do with the will."

"I showed it to him with only my signature on it. He was worried. He said the will was wrong."

"I won't listen to any more of this. It's rank impertinence."

"It's not my fault. Sonny wanted to see his solicitor about it; and I had a lot of trouble, I don't mind telling you, in getting him to agree that I should come and see you about it in private."

"And what did you think I would do?"

"Go and see the charities. I don't want to be unreasonable. If they fork up half, Sonny will agree."

Stephen stood quite still, then he took up the telephone and put his finger in the dial face.

"I'm ringing the Guards, Miss Joyce."

She did not react at once and he, after a moment's hesitation, turned the dial once.

"You can't threaten me like that," she said.

He took this as sufficient to stop, but kept a finger poised above the telephone.

"I know it must seem a mean thing for me to do. You always treated me fair, and I have nothing against you personally. But you know you shouldn't have done it. At the time I thought it was a slip that anyone could have made, and you were quite right not to let on; but now I see the matter from Sonny's point of view. His aunt shouldn't have cut him out like that; and if you made a botch of the will, then the money is his in law. You know that, Mr Foster. There's no need for me to sit here and tell you what the law is."

Stephen put down the telephone slowly. "Why, if you are in need of money, did you not approach me in a decent fashion instead of trying to get it in this preposterous way?"

"Why should you give me money? And, anyhow, it's not that. I'm only asking for what should be Sonny's. I'm not begging. He told me I'd get nothing from coming to you. And I see he was right."

"Anyone would have told you that."

She got up now, smoothed her skirt, patted her hair, and then shook it back into its previous disorder. She seemed to be gathering her dignity together after temporarily mislaying it.

"Mr Haggard won't like it when he hears the line you took. I wouldn't have expected it from a gentleman like you. Well, there's no point in my staying any longer."

But she seemed to be waiting for him to say something. He walked towards the door. She went ahead, assuming defiance. In the hall the ceremony was repeated. He shut the door behind her and stood, listening. The distance to the road was less than fifty yards. He smiled when he heard a motor engine starting up. Sonny had been waiting.

CHAPTER II

THE FIRM OF Foster & Foster, distinguished in Dublin, was Protestant in its provenance at a time when everything in Ireland—hospitals, banks, newspapers, shops, plumbers—had a clearly defined religious aura. The tradition of authority leaves its imprint. When Stephen began to practise, the Protestant community was able to give him all the business he could do. He became a director of banks, insurance corporations and public companies. But he saw the tide turn, and even though he had no children to follow him he was concerned for the firm he had built by his own efforts. It would be his only monument. He wanted to ensure its survival. In the course of his business as a company director he kept an eye out for a likely man to bring, as he put it, 'a touch of green into the office flag'.

Brian Fagan was the son of a partner in a leading firm of accountants. Their business spread over areas where the new men predominated. Stephen decided to take him into the office. He knew he would be met with opposition from his partners, and he knew he would have his way.

Stephen had two partners: his brother, Henry, reliable and without initiative, who walked in his shadow, and

Tom Murgatroyd, from the north of Ireland, whose father had been a clerk to Stephen's father in a much more modest office. Tom looked after all the court work and made no contribution to the collection of clients.

The partners had a Wednesday luncheon when, over cold meats and tea, current problems were discussed.

"How did the dinner go last night?" Henry inquired when the partners sat down in the tiny room in which the weekly ceremony was performed.

"Splendidly. It was very good of Arthur Evans to stage the show. I think everyone enjoyed it. Mary is a wonderful woman. I shouldn't be surprised to hear she cooked the whole dinner."

"Evans can well afford to employ a cook. Why should he leave it all to his wife?"

"She enjoys it, Tom. He's as proud as Punch of her. Not every man could throw a party like that for his colleagues nowadays. It was like old times. When I first got on the Council, the President used to entertain us, but not all together, so far as I can recollect. There was a series of dinners during the winter. Even then not everyone had the capacity of Mary Evans. I take my hat off to her."

"I have never seen you in a hat except at a funeral," Tom said.

Then Stephen got on to office business. He had been instructed to form three new companies. A well-known business was on the verge of collapse, he would be up until midnight helping to sort out their problems. "I'm afraid I can't cope. We need a wholetime assistant on the company end."

"Where are we going to put him? And in no time he will demand an assistant; and each of them will want a typist; and one typist won't be sufficient," Henry said.

"And by the time you've finished paying them all

you're no better off," Tom Murgatroyd said. He always said it.

Stephen shook his head. "We must either go on or go back; there's no use in pretending we can stand still. If we need more staff we must hire them. If we need larger premises we had better look out for them. I have someone in mind I would like to ask to join us."

At the suggestion Henry and Tom bridled at once; but Stephen pretended not to notice. "There is a very clever young fellow, Brian Fagan, in Curtis's office. I hear he is not too happy where he is, and I think he would come to us if we made it worth his while."

"I don't approve of pinching staff from other solicitors," Henry said.

"Nor I," added Tom. "We don't like it when it's done to us."

"Who said we were pinching him? His uncle is on the board of the bottle company with me, and he has made no bones about it: the boy is not happy with Curtis. He is never allowed to use his own initiative. The uncle, you may take it from me, has made it abundantly clear that the boy would jump at the chance of coming to us."

"How do we know he is any good?" Tom Murgatroyd said. He always said what Henry looked.

"I've taken soundings."

"If we are going to take in someone, what's wrong with Goodfellow's son? He is on the look-out, I hear."

Henry was making his effort, merely to keep up with Tom.

"He won't be new blood. Fagan is an R.C. I think we must face the fact that we can't remain exclusive. The banks are run by Catholics nowadays. Even Trinity College has a Catholic Chancellor. And they are becoming as like us as they can. They have the Mass in English, and

20

soon their priests will be no different from parsons."

"I don't like to see religion being brought into it," Henry said.

"We got on very well as we were," Tom Murgatroyd agreed.

"Well, I beg to differ. We are in danger of becoming stuffy. We must let in air. I'm not going to fall behind the times. Moreover the Fagan boy is much brighter than young Goodfellow, and more agreeable into the bargain. His uncle had him to lunch with us. I took to him greatly."

"We might as well take a look at him," Henry said.

"You put an advertisement in the paper, Tom, in the agony column. I'll see he knows where it comes from. We can have him to lunch with us, and if either of you two men don't like the cut of his jib, I'll not force him down your throats. I'm glad that's settled."

"Whatever you say," Tom said grudgingly.

"So long as it's not a woman I don't mind," Henry conceded.

"The office is stuffed with them as it is," Murgatroyd agreed, "and when they are not in the lavatory they are making tea."

"As we are on the question of staff," Stephen said—his mouth full of cheese—"I have had something on my conscience for a long time. Curran has been working here for donkeys' years. He is absolutely devoted to the office. I think I owe it to him to show we recognise his loyalty when we are introducing more young blood. New brooms are all very well, but we must remember the work the old ones did. And Curran is game for a good many years yet."

This suggestion was met in silence.

"Do you mean we should make Curran a partner?"

Henry said at length.

"I don't think we can when he's not qualified," Tom cut in.

"He could be offered a partnership on condition he qualified; but I wonder would he think the effort worth while now. He must be over fifty." Henry tried to convey by his manner that he was not opposing the suggestion. He never opposed Stephen when Tom was present. It was Tom who made difficulties.

"I'd like to delegate a department to him. He's a general dog's body at the moment. If young Fagan is coming in, perhaps I should tell Curran that he is to be my special assistant and raise him a few hundred a year."

"He will think you've taken leave of your senses," Henry said. He regarded himself as Stephen's deputy. After all, they were brothers and their father had set up the office.

"It will only give him ideas. He's perfectly happy as he is. And he has no children on his hands. I don't pity Curran." Tom had married late in life and held it as a grievance against the world.

Stephen began to get up; his bulk made this a slow process.

"There's nobody as trustworthy as Curran. I don't think we should ignore the fact. When he sees us expanding he may begin to wonder if he's going to be left out in the cold."

"Do whatever you like, Stephen. I'm very fond of Curran. But I don't believe he requires any boost to his morale."

Henry said that, but when his brother left the room, he told Tom Murgatroyd that he thought a young man of Fagan's type would get the office into queer street.

Later in the day he went into Stephen's office.

"What have you said to Curran? It's all over the office that he has had promotion."

"I dropped a hint to him this afternoon. This thing has been on my mind, Henry. I have felt that we rather let Curran down when we made our recent changes."

"But I thought he was only to be promoted if Fagan comes in. We haven't decided that one yet. We haven't seen him. We don't even know that he is coming."

"Don't fuss, Henry. I only put it that way. I was quite determined to do something for Curran before I even heard of young Fagan. I don't understand why there has been such opposition to my plan."

"It's all very well for you to talk," was all Henry could think to say. And having said it, he went.

He had hardly gone when Tom Murgatroyd came in, looking as always as if he was being operated on without an anaesthetic.

"Stephen, what did you say to Curran? My typist has just told me he has become office manager."

Stephen smiled, but Tom knew what it meant when he turned away from his desk. He was going to speak *ex cathedra*.

"Listen to me, Tom. I don't want to be taught how to run this office. Neither am I senile. I'll be going one of these days, and then you may all do as you please; but until that day I intend to act as I think best in my own department. I've taken Curran on. He's working for me. I wasn't going to do it without consulting you; but, frankly, I didn't expect any of you to raise difficulties."

"But you suggested a partnership. That would have affected us all."

Stephen raised a hand. "I dropped the idea when I saw it was not on. As to the news getting round—what does that matter? Half the pleasure of getting the rise for

Curran is telling about it. Of course he told Miss Poyntz at once, as a dead secret. She would never have forgiven him if he had let her wait to hear with everyone else. And she was bound to tell Miss Hall. And Miss Hall's sister is married to Robinson. And Robinson lives on the same road as Taylor. And Taylor's wife's nephew is the office boy. I must say the news has travelled rather faster than I expected. But I was sure it would have gone the rounds before breakfast."

"But Stephen, you seem to forget that it hinges on this young Fagan fellow's coming."

"Tom, don't you know as well as I do that his uncle has told him by now he has the job? I am determined to have him."

"You are an extraordinary man, Stephen. You lead everyone by the nose without fighting with anyone. I never ask for anything unless I am entitled to it, and yet I keep on running into trouble."

"That's because you keep your nose to the grindstone all the time. Why not give it a rest and keep your ear to the ground instead?"

"But you do both, Stephen, without seeming to do either. You make everything look so easy. I live buried under paper. I can't make you out."

"Well, we make a good team, Tom. I shouldn't last long if I hadn't you at my elbow."

Murgatroyd flushed. He had been feeling out of sorts all day, ever since the butcher's bill, kept out of his sight for six weeks, appeared unannounced at breakfast. By now he had forgotten what was the cause of his bad humour and sense of foreboding; whatever it was, Stephen had obliterated it. Tom left the room under a vague impression that it was he who had suggested to the others it was high time something was done to give Curran a lift. Going out he said a few words to Curran, which prompted him to remark to Miss Poyntz that Mr Murgatroyd (whom he had called 'a mean, old curmudgeon' not five minutes before) was really 'a decent class of man when you got to know him'.

CHAPTER III

"WHO WILL STEPHEN have for dinner? As well as Barbara, I mean. It's too much to hope we might get a rest from her."

"He muttered something about the Evanses. Stephen has a very soft spot for her."

"If Barbara notices that, I wouldn't give her long to live."

"Oh, leave Barbara alone. What's wrong with her? She keeps Stephen happy. We all owe her a lot."

"When Stephen dies and you find Barbara Preston has what ought to belong to your children you won't be singing her praises, if I know you, Henry."

Margaret Foster was settling her hair in front of the looking-glass on her dressing-table. Full view of her own appearance always had an irritating effect on her temper. She had been the prettiest girl in Mount Temple Lawn Tennis Club when Henry married her.

That was a quarter of a century ago, and her beauty, like wine of light grapes, had never promised to improve by keeping. Touched up, her hair had the heaviness of a helmet: it was once fair and fluffy. Her eyebrows had faded, but she insisted on calling attention to the fact with a pencil. Perpetual discontent with the way life seemed to break its promises was visible at the corners of the mouth, whose honey Henry had fed upon too long, one June night, at a dance in the Zoological Gardens. Her voice, as once her hair had been, was light.

"If you were any good," she proceeded, "you would talk to Stephen. Of course you think he's the wisest and most wonderful thing that has happened since Moses struck the rock, but I understand women. I know what they can do to men, especially at Stephen's age. Oh I know you hate me to go on about this"—she had caught her husband's expression of dislike in the glass—"I know you'd prefer to leave it to Stephen, as you leave everything."

"For God's sake, Maggie, can't you get off this eternal subject. I owe everything I've got to Stephen. He put me through the university. He took me into full partnership the day I qualified. He educated Frank and George. He has lavished presents on you and the children. It revolts me to hear you going on like this. I hope Stephen lives another twenty years at least; and by that time none of us will need his money."

"I'm not discussing your brother. Stephen and I have always hit it off. It's that woman. Quite honestly I don't know how he has got away with it. If anyone else were to go everywhere with another man's wife, he'd be in trouble. And so would she. But Stephen can do as he pleases."

"Johnny doesn't mind. It's been going on for years. And it's all open and above board. Stephen has been a wonderful friend to Johnny."

"I wonder how much it costs Stephen. It would have been much cheaper to have found a wife for himself."

"Isn't that his own business? He has never once tried to interfere with us. And when Doreen took up hunting, he gave her a pony, although I knew that he thought the whole idea an extravagance."

"If the daughter of a partner in a leading firm of solicitors can't afford to hunt, it doesn't speak much for the profession. My hairdresser's wife hunts regularly with the Brays."

"Well she may."

"What exactly am I to deduce from that?"

"You're awfully touchy, Maggie. You take everything personally."

"If that woman is wearing a new brooch, I'll spit in her eye. God! how my face depresses me. Would you mind hooking up my dress at the back instead of just standing there like a graven image."

Henry did as he was told, first kissing his wife in the centre of the little triangle made by her open dress.

"That won't do you any good," she said, but not harshly, not too discouragingly. Henry recognised the signs. He liked peace. To ensure it he was prepared to sacrifice every prompting of his will. When he kissed her neck, she dug him in the stomach with a friendly elbow. "I thought you were in a hurry," she said.

"That dress suits you better than anything you have," he told her as they went downstairs.

"I've had it about a thousand years."

"I've never seen you look so sweet. I'm sorry for women who put on weight. You've kept your figure. It's half the battle."

Barbara Preston had increased considerably in embonpoint recently. Even Stephen had remarked it. Maggie knew what her husband meant.

"That tie's nice," she said, settling it.

She was ashamed of her outburst. Whenever they were invited to lunch or dine with Stephen there was always the same quarrel. It had become, after twenty years, a ritual.

CHAPTER IV

"Mr Stephen asked me to apologise, but he won't be back in time for lunch."

'Mr Stephen' seemed a quaint expression for a partner to use. Murgatroyd sounded more like the family butler to Brian Fagan, who was disappointed to find himself alone with two grim partners. He came today without any feeling of strain because his uncle told him the lunch was a formality to meet the other partners. He knew them well by appearance, and did not relish the prospect of being alone with them without the catalytic presence of the senior partner. He had come to see Hamlet and found himself with the grave-diggers. The comparison occurred to him when he saw their baleful eyes fixed on the melon on the table. Nobody was prepared to carve it.

The two older men seemed to consider that Brian was standing between them and the melon.

"I suppose I'll have to cut it," Henry said with an air of grievance.

The melon was consumed in silence, Murgatroyd coming at length to terms with his slice. His face grew very red. Eating seemed to send his blood pressure up.

The cold meats that followed were already laid out.

"I should have offered you some sherry," Henry said. "We are not used to visitors."

"I never drink at lunch time," Murgatroyd added sharply.

He looked across the table at Henry. Henry returned his glance but with less emphasis. He seemed content to note the statement. It was intended for Brian's benefit and might be understood to imply that a charge of intemperance had reached their ears.

"What method of filing have you here?" Brian said to Henry. He could bear the strain of silence no longer and wanted to say something to show his mind was suitably employed.

"The files are numbered and there is a cross reference to every case," Henry replied, looking at his partner.

Murgatroyd gave a short laugh as a man might when he hears a child prattling of serious things. Then he said to Henry: "I hear that Lansdowne have a new centre three-quarter."

"They could do with one," Henry replied.

"But they will need more than that if they are to win the Cup. Trinity will have a good side next season."

"Not as good as National, judging by what we saw in the Cup."

"Trinity had bad luck. That drop goal in the first half was a fluke."

"You can never say that any drop goal is a fluke. You might as well say a try is a fluke."

"Sometimes they are."

"If that is the case there's no use playing the game. Why not toss up and save time and trouble?"

"You always go too far. I only intended to say that Trinity were worth three tries, and if there had been a replay they might have won it."

"But that is a ridiculous statement. The match was played and one side won. What is the use of saying that if it hadn't it might have lost another match that was never played. It's extraordinary to me, Tom, how you can watch matches year after year without ever understanding what Rugby is all about."

"I like that coming from the man who said Gibson was only a flash in the pan."

"I admit I was wrong about Gibson. I saw him on an off-day. Do you remember the way you went on about a certain full-back? I hear he is playing on their seconds now."

"He injured a thigh muscle."

"I don't care if he broke his ankle. He was as bright an international prospect at any time, Tom, as my backside."

"Do you follow Rugby?" Tom said to Brian, as if suddenly remembering his presence.

"Not really. I go to internationals if anyone invites me."

The silence after this was awful. Murgatroyd broke it by draining his tea cup rather noisily.

"I think it's a damned shame to give stand tickets for internationals to anyone who is not a regular follower of the game," he said, putting down his cup.

"I get mine from Wanderers," Henry said.

"So do I. But we are members. We pay an annual subscription. I tried to get an extra ticket for the English match and I had to go down on my knees for it."

Henry nodded. Brian felt as if sentence had been passed on him.

"If you will all excuse me, I must be going back to my office. I have only an hour, and it's now nearly two o'clock," he said.

He was given no help. Their joint expression seemed to say, 'Well, what are you waiting for?'

"We haven't discussed business," Brian said.

"Mr Stephen isn't here, you see," Murgatroyd said.

Henry nodded. "We don't do these things unless all the partners are together. You can find your way down, can you?" he added.

"I daresay Mr Stephen will be writing to you," his grimmer colleague said.

"I'll find my way. Thanks for the lunch."

Were he younger Brian would have been in tears going downstairs. Once again all his old doubts returned about the profession he had chosen. Was one destined to spend all one's life with such murky creatures? Better to be behind a plough in a field.

In the hall he met Stephen coming in.

"My dear boy. I can't tell you how sorry I was to miss our lunch. Did the others look after you? I hope they explained: it was in the nature of a Royal command. I had to go. Tell me what you agreed on, and when you are coming to us."

"We didn't discuss it. They said it couldn't be mentioned in your absence."

"That was very boring for you when you were good enough to give up your time. I tell you what: suppose I drop you a line and set out my ideas, you can then let me know how they appeal to you. We are a team here. We work together. I'm sure that's the way you want it to be."

Brian had seen the team in the captain's absence, but, somehow, Stephen's appearance had already made the last hour seem like a bad dream. But, for all his affability, there was obviously something else on his mind. He kept glancing in the direction of the stairs.

"Is that all right? And you do understand about today? Splendid. Are those other fellows still upstairs?"

Brian nodded.

"I want to talk to them. Goodbye, my boy. We are going to see a lot of one another before long."

He held the door open, waved to Brian and then made for the stairs like an excited elephant.

Tom Murgatroyd gazed long at the door after Brian left.

"He hasn't much to say for himself," Henry said.

"If he tries to interfere with the filing system he will have me to contend with," Tom said.

"I don't like the idea of an outsider coming in," Henry added.

"I don't know anything about that. I only know that if anyone thinks they can come in here and play puck with the filing system they have something coming to them. I think I ought to warn Stephen. I don't like that young gentleman one little bit. I don't know what Stephen sees in him."

"Oh, there you are," Henry said. He was facing the door, and saw Stephen coming in. Stephen sat down heavily and mopped his brow, as he always did nowadays, after climbing the last flight.

"I've something to tell you fellows and I might as well get it off my chest at once. Finnegan, the Minister for Economic Welfare, rang me up at home last night and asked me to lunch with him today. I mentioned it to you, Henry. I had heard various accounts of him but I'm bound to say I found him very frank and agreeable and intelligent. I thought he might have wanted to discuss the hotel project. I heard it was cutting across some of the Government's tourist plans; but he never mentioned it. He said he wanted to see me about the new scheme his Department has decided to try out as a possible solution to existing employer-labour relations in industry. He has set up a company to deal with the question of national housing. It will be run by a mixed board of workers in the industry and three 'wise men', as he called them. He said he must find people of achievement with no axe to grind whom the workers will trust, and he has picked on me as a suitable candidate. It means that I must give up all my directorships so as to ensure that I'll have no competing interest; but I can continue in my profession. He is also inviting an accountant; and he will second a senior Civil Servant to make the third."

"And what is he going to pay you?" Henry said, a vivid picture of Margaret at the looking-glass crossing his mind.

"Five thousand."

"A year?"

Stephen nodded.

"But you make twice that at least," Tom said.

"I know. But a man can't be thinking of his income all the time. I see this as an experiment that might have remarkable results. We must try to put an end to the antagonism between workers and management. It poisons our economy."

"That's all very well," Tom said. "But I don't see why you should give up half your income as a part of the experiment. I thought you were going to tell us you had doubled it. I don't think this is anything to be congratulated upon."

"You didn't commit yourself, I hope. You said you would have to think it over," Henry said, glancing suspiciously at his brother. Stephen became faintly pink under scrutiny.

"There's no point in beating about the bush. I accepted."

He looked at each of his partners in turn as if to confirm the statement.

34

"You must be out of your mind," Tom said.

"I accepted," Stephen continued, "first because I thought it was my duty; secondly because even if I lose by it in directors' fees, it will redound enormously to the credit of the office; and finally—and I think Tom, you and Henry will agree with me here—because the Minister said there was another lawyer whom the Cabinet had in mind, but they agreed to give me the first refusal. Can you see Richard Curtis hesitating if the offer comes to him?"

"If it did, he'd manage somehow to wangle the contract on his own terms," Tom said.

"Curtis is all right. He's a smart fellow; but I'm not going to turn down an offer that I know he will take."

Stephen set his face against criticism of opponents, even in his own office.

Curtis hasn't a brother married to Margaret. Curtis has no nephews. His only son is going to be a priest. Curtis can afford to indulge his fancies. These were Henry's thoughts. He regretted them.

"I suppose this is a secret," Henry said.

"Like Curran's promotion," Tom added. He could not make up his mind what to make of Stephen's news. All he was sure of was that it presaged change. And he hated change, on principle.

"We ought to keep it to ourselves. But I gathered from the Minister that he was about to publish it, and his interview with me was the last item on his agenda."

"You don't think Curtis turned him down," Tom said.

Henry flushed at this. "Who would ask for Curtis when Stephen was available?"

"He didn't invite you, by any chance," Murgatroyd said.

Henry swallowed the reply that was on his lips. Someday he would tell Tom just what he thought of him. Instead, he turned away and looked at Stephen; and Stephen said, "I don't like to see bickering between us."

It shut up the old fellows. It took away the sourness they spread in the air. It kept the peace. It was typical of Stephen.

"I don't know what's come over Mr Stephen these days. He's raised my salary by a hundred a year."

Curran was only telling his wife part of the truth. The raise was in fact five pounds a week. But he had his own reasons for altering the details of the encouraging affair. And one hundred was calculated to impress Mrs Curran without putting ideas into her head. She was for ever running out to the pictures since he had put his foot down on her attending Bingo sessions. They interfered with his evening meal.

CHAPTER V

THE ANNOUNCEMENT OF Stephen's appointment to a position with public responsibility might have been expected to damage his professional practice. He was going to have to give precedence to his new responsibilities, and his clients would suffer. But the world doesn't reason that way. A very few might, but, as Stephen expected, those who believe that influence is the only explanation of success read the signs and came to Molesworth Street. Anyone, they reasoned, could do legal work; not everyone was at a Minister's elbow. And even those who had no career to promote got a vicarious thrill from having their business done by a firm which was helping to run the country.

Stephen had not been installed more than a month before his partners began to complain that the pressure of business required more staff and more space. Curran needed help. Not everyone who expected to see Stephen was prepared to be transferred to a Dickensian law clerk, capable though he might be. It was hurtful to pride. One of these was Ernest Woodhouse. From the office point of view he was a most remunerative client; but Stephen found him personally offensive and, having put up with him for many years, was delighted to pass him over to Curran. Woodhouse was a land developer. He was practically illiterate and spoilt irredeemably any paper he tried to write on, but he had the same sort of gift that is claimed for water diviners where building land was concerned. Where to anyone else was a panorama, a wood, or a swamp, Woodhouse saw a sea of bungalows. A row of beech trees was a row of shops metamorphosed. In the twinkling of an eye Woodhouse made the trees disappear and the shops were found in their place. In the course of a decade he had changed the appearance of his native land as effectively as if an atomic missile had landed in its midst.

Stephen Foster was frankly philistine and suspected any values that could not be submitted to the order and precision of a balance sheet. He was suspicious of artists until they succeeded financially. He knew these were limitations; but they were helpful in business, as Woodhouse was. Nevertheless he found that worthy a trial to his patience, and rejoiced that now he could hand him over to Curran. He knew that Woodhouse would not take his business away from the firm. Nobody would set greater store than he on a Ministerial connection. And like the others he would not so much expect it to be operated in his favour as to derive satisfaction from a conviction that it was a power in reserve, a safety-net in case of spectacular falls.

Woodhouse accepted Curran (who in fact had been doing his business behind the scenes for years) but he resented the arrangement. He showed this by whistling when he went upstairs to see him and even singing, enlarging the volume as he passed Stephen's door. And he made a point of enquiring after 'the old fellow' as a preliminary to every conference with Curran. He implied that Stephen was declining rapidly in health and was shifting his work on to less senile shoulders. He developed a tendency to drag up for Curran's benefit his complaints through the years, the occasions when he was on to a good thing and lost it because Stephen hadn't moved quickly. He recalled prophecies of Stephen's that had failed to materialise. Curran found this very trying. He put up with Woodhouse—as Stephen had in his time—for the sake of the office, but it was a trial, and Woodhouse had become actively unpleasant. Added to Curran's other responsibilities, it was beginning to tell on his constitution. He was neither very young nor very robust.

"I'm afraid Curran is taking to the bottle," Henry told Stephen. But Stephen refused to listen. The Curran affair was an accomplished fact. He was not going to allow the partners to nag him about it, and he simply could not spare the time now for staff problems. His partners would have to take more on themselves. He abdicated from a benevolent dictatorship and declared himself president of a democratic republic.

Brian, revelling in a freedom that he had not known under a jealous master, threw himself into his work, and in the course of a few weeks found himself coming to Curran's rescue. When he came into his room one day and discovered the clerk crying over a pile of papers, unable to face the ever-increasing load, he offered to take Woodhouse off his hands; but Curran had no doubt that this was impossible. The tyrant would refuse to be pushed around. It would be the last straw. Nobody regretted his promotion more than Curran, except his wife. She started to make preparations for widowhood, and returned to her Bingo sessions.

One day Curran's patience broke. He had finished his business with Woodhouse, but the latter never removed himself when he saw his presence was not required. He liked to go in his own time, and in small matters show who was master. On this occasion, Curran had a case to get ready for the following day. It was six o'clock—after his time for going home—and Woodhouse was still sitting at the table; and in response to a valedictory message given by Curran's anxious eye-brows he drew out a pipe and filled it slowly.

"I was passing Haggard's place out at Malahide today," he remarked, pushing the tobacco well down. "I will never forget that old Stephen could have got that for me if he had lifted his little finger. The woman that owned it had got past looking after so much land. Her nephew was no good. And in the end it all went to charities. They put it up for auction."

"You could have bought it then." Curran hated these attacks on Stephen.

"I don't buy at auctions."

"Mr Stephen wouldn't have allowed Miss Haggard to rob herself on anyone's account."

"So that's the way the wind's blowing. We are getting very high and mighty all of a sudden," Woodhouse observed, smiling through the smoke.

"You've had the best attention this office can give you and I don't like to hear Mr Stephen being abused. I wouldn't take it from anybody." Curran was trembling. He was not a fighter.

"I don't think Mr Stephen—as you call him—has lost a great deal over my business, even if he has become too grand to attend to it."

"God! God! God! Can't you see I'm up to my eyes?" Curran put his hands to his face. His voice had risen to a scream.

Mr Woodhouse got up with elaborate slowness, knocked

his pipe out on the fireplace, and humming a patriotic tune, smiling as he went, he bowed to Curran and withdrew.

That night Curran came home very drunk. But Mrs Curran, although disapproving, inclined to see the bright side, for she had noticed that with his decline he had recovered the piety for which he had been remarkable in their courting days. He was constantly praying. It was depressing, but consoling. He confessed to her, as the result of an all-night questioning, that a man called Woodhouse was driving him mad. He had in general too much to do, but this was the place at which resolution cracked. On the way home he had called at the library and confided in a sympathetic girl that he was depressed and needed to be lifted out of himself. She withdrew, to return with a copy of *Carry on Jeeves* by P. G. Wodehouse. At the mention of the author's name he had cried out aloud and raced from the building. It was impossible for him ever to return. He was disgraced. Mrs Curran made him promise to put his problem before Mr Stephen who must not be allowed to drive him to his death. Why had he not been left alone when he was perfectly happy as he was?

But, closeted with Stephen next day, he could not summon up the courage to complain. Nor was he quite clear how to formulate his complaint. He could say 'I have too much to do', but not 'Woodhouse gets on my nerves'. And that was what he wanted to say.

CHAPTER VI

"Are you coming home for your lunch?" Barbara Preston in her dressing-gown addressed her spouse.

He never derived pride or pleasure from his wife's appearance. In bare feet, with the string of the garment pulled too tight, and her round eyes and hair in bobbles, she reminded him of a poodle they once had.

He was—to use his own phrase—'slipping out'. A desire to make himself as nearly invisible as possible may have accounted for it. Mrs Preston was not concerned; but he had a way of 'slipping in' and expecting to be fed. That, she resented.

"I'll get something in town," Johnny said.

"I wish you'd say. I never know when I'm to provide for you. It's not a great deal to ask."

"You know I never expect more than a boiled egg and a cup of tea."

"But who has to boil the egg? Who makes the tea?"

"I do it for myself when you are not here."

"And how often is that, pray? To hear you one would imagine I lunched out every day."

"Are you seeing Stephen today?"

"That's my own affair. I don't ask you who you are lunching with."

"You know perfectly well that I go to Bewleys for my bun and coffee. Anyone who wants to can find me there."

"You seem to imply that there is some mystery about my movements. I'm meeting Stephen at the Cosmopolitan Club, if you are interested. If you want to, you may join us. You know that perfectly well."

"I'll leave you to yourselves, but if you are talking to Stephen I think I ought to mention something to you. There's a little fellow who's always in the library—I'm not sure what he does exactly—but he holds everyone up to listen to him. I never met such a talker. He came up to me yesterday and said he had been having a drink with Henry Foster at his golf-club, and Henry told him that Stephen had distributed fairly large sums among his relations recently. It was impertinent of him to mention it to me; but he has a skin like a rhinoceros, and kept on repeating that it was something I would probably be interested to hear. I don't believe he was being malicious. I honestly believe he was tipping me off as a friend and fellow-student. The world takes a very practical view of these delicate matters. Of course I told him that it was no concern of mine; but I could see he brushed that aside as a face-saving device. It is easy to see I am an object of general contempt."

"If anyone had the cheek to talk to me like that I'd give him reason to be sorry."

Johnny laughed his patent laugh, it conveyed his long-considered judgment of his spouse, the reason, as he saw it, of the poor opinion in which the world held him.

"What was your friend trying to tell you?"

"Exactly what I said: Henry let drop that Stephen has begun to part with his money. He didn't say anything to you, by any chance?"

"Not a word. I'm astonished. Stephen tells me everything, and I have reminded him often enough that he has this horde of nephews and nieces waiting with their mouths open. Very little they ever do for him. But he will naturally leave them all something. It wouldn't be right if he didn't. I would personally be ashamed to face the family if Stephen failed to do the right thing by them when the time came. Are you sure this so-called friend of yours knows what he's talking about? He might be trying to draw you out. You're an innocent in some ways. Perhaps Henry put him up to it. That wife of his probably got at him to find out what Stephen has done. Naturally they'd expect me to know. But what a despicable way to go about it. Imagine a man in Henry's position talking about his brother's affairs to some drunk in a bar. I think I ought to let Stephen know. In his present position he can't afford to run any risk; and if Henry has become indiscreet in his cups, Stephen must do something to protect himself."

"Phil Deasy is not a drunk. You are making a mountain out of a mole-hill as usual. If Stephen gave money to Henry's children, why shouldn't he say so? Men get friendly and tell one another that sort of thing. No doubt it was a relief to Henry's mind. He may have thought you were getting everything. I'm sure his wife has told him so more than once. Don't you go trying to make trouble between the brothers. It won't help; but I thought you might like to mark your book. I'm slipping out. I want to catch that bus."

He always left his wife with a question unasked. Today she forgot about him at once. Her mind was racing. Stephen had not changed in his manner towards her; but he had become—in some way she couldn't define—elusive.

44

Not that he ever discussed business with her; but he used to give the impression of having laid it down to talk to her about herself and the children. He encouraged her to tell him her difficulties and took almost a delight in solving them. How well she knew that smile and the quiet manner in which his hand reached for the cheque-book in his breast-pocket. There was something indescribably benign and attractive about Stephen with his patient head bent over the table, writing in his copper-plate hand an order on his bank. He seemed to personify friendship and security. It was wonderful to have such a dependable soul at one's back.

Stephen met Barbara originally at a dance given to raise money for the lifeboat service. Her marriage was in a trough at the time and she made no secret of the fact. In the event he saw himself performing the office of a life-belt. After that evening Stephen had attended a great many similar functions in Mrs Preston's company. For all his prominence in his profession, he had always been the sort of man that husbands knew but did not bring home to their wives. He had no social ambitions and confined his private entertaining to his family. He owed nothing to social connections; and seemed too big in a drawing-room. He was satisfied to go home on most evenings to a chop, three hours' work brought back from the office and, in summer time, an hour's pottering in the garden. On Saturdays he took Mrs Preston to the races or some other entertainment, and they dined afterwards in town.

"He must save millions," Margaret had observed whenever she and Henry discussed the frugal nature of Stephen's existence.

On Sunday evenings he came for supper to the Prestons. Barbara and her boys accompanied him on his holidays and they went away together at Christmas, Easter and Whit and other weekends. Johnny Preston never took part in these expeditions. He had a car that Stephen bought for him; and he drove about in it by himself whenever he was not at work in the library. Genealogy was his passion. Looking up family trees brought him in a little pocket-money. He always paid the tax and insurance on his car and his club subscription. He spent all his spare time in the club, and whenever his spirits fell he wrote to Stephen suggesting that he should let his name come forward for membership. A conviction that when this did happen Stephen would be blackballed, kept Johnny Preston alive.

Nowadays Stephen had an abstracted air, as if he had not left his own concerns behind him. Frequently Barbara found that he was not listening to what she was saying and she had to repeat herself. Sometimes, when asked for a decision, he gave it without having put his mind to the problem—Leeson's golf lessons was a case in point. Should a boy be encouraged to concentrate on a game even if he did show promise? And who was to pay for the lessons?

Stephen pretended to consider and then said: "I think he has enough on his plate as it is." Later in the conversation he asked if the children had taken up golf yet.

She put it down to strain. This appointment was certainly a tax on his resources. Personally she could not see why he wanted to chuck the bank—where he got a free lunch—for an awful political job. And the idea of dropping money to take it sounded daft to her.

She humoured him, of course. The vanity of men takes unpredictable turns at times. But she worried in private. Was this a warning signal? Her own father at much the same age had started to help girls in the train with their school exercises. One thing led to another. He ended up in a looney bin, and very grateful they all were when

46

the magistrate took that view of it.

She took a bath and dressed herself carefully, using some of the expensive scent she bought in the airport the last time they were abroad. Stephen liked her in blue. He said it matched her eyes. These were, if anything, green; but she didn't argue. To please him she put on the blue blouse she bought in the Christmas sales. It was on the tight side. Every year she swore she would never go near the sales again. She was forever buying what she didn't want because the price was marked down a few shillings. She had to buy another blouse when she found how badly this one fitted. Today it served as a talisman. "I like the blouse," he would say. "It goes with your eyes." How often had he said it?

"You still notice those things. That is what I love about you, Stephen."

He would not bring the topic any further than that. He was not given to playfulness.

Or, would it be wiser to wash off the scent and wear black? That would bring home the message. But it was not the way to get round a man. A woman should be— approximately at least—the sunshine in his life. It was not always easy to keep it up; but no man enjoyed subsidising gloom. He got all he wanted of that commodity for nothing. Her contribution, she prided herself, was loyalty. He was willing to pay for that. She put more of the scent behind her ears and examined her lips. Sometimes, lately, she had not taken so much trouble as she should over detail. God what a struggle it all was! When the time came it would be a relief to leave off. It would be a comfort to be dead if one hadn't to die. Men could have children without paying for it in pain; women should be spared the horror of dying. No wonder people thought of God as a man. All the evidence pointed that way.

Barbara was often surprised to catch herself thinking about such deep matters. She had never been considered clever as a child. Johnny despised her intellect. He made no secret of that. Her looks had attracted him; and his ardour had made her lose her head. That was all so long ago. Stephen never seemed to mind about her having no brains to speak of. He talked about simple things. Johnny said he was a complete philistine; but then he wasted his own time reading books. He was capable of nothing better. And he had lost his looks. The false teeth were the final touch. They literally danced in his mouth. Nothing ever fitted him or went for him or worked for him. Without Stephen he would have sunk without trace. Never was one man so wholly dependent on another. And Johnny resented it, deep down he did. He did not know the meaning of gratitude.

Barbara settled herself at the table to which she considered by now she had a prescriptive right. She consoled herself for the unexciting setting in which Stephen was satisfied to place her by queening it rather. The club was a perfectly decent place to take a meal in, but strictly utilitarian. Nobody was drinking anything other than water. The decoration and furniture were eminently sensible. The waitresses had the appearance of having been recommended by clergymen and engaged for life. But over all lay heavily an atmosphere of women intent on the day's shopping, men eating now to save their wives the trouble of preparing a full evening meal, and members up from the country and not in the mood for a spree. At Christmas Stephen invited her to somewhere more glamorous. But it didn't suit him.

"He's a pragmatist," Johnny had said. She always remembered that but never mentioned it to Stephen because she thought it meant 'a rough diamond'.

Stephen arrived late for lunch, puffing a little after his encounter with the stairs.

"I'm sorry, my dear. But the Minister asked me to drop in on him, and one doesn't tell Ministers that one has a lady waiting."

"The same Minister will be the death of you. I ordered myself a glass of sherry. I hope you don't mind."

"Of course not. What's the menu? Have you ordered? I'll take the steak and kidney pie and carrots. No. I don't want any soup. And rice afterwards with a tiny spot of cream."

He was talking to the waitress.

"I think I'll have the chicken casserole," Barbara said with deliberation.

"I'm so sorry. I thought you said you had ordered."

"A glass of sherry."

"I am sorry. I didn't hear you properly. I say, I do hope you haven't been waiting for me for hours."

"You are only ten minutes late. Don't fuss. I am beginning to get very worried about you, my pet."

"Worried? Nobody need worry about me. I never felt better. Do you know I worked twelve hours in the garden on Sunday? If the worst comes to the worst I can keep myself very comfortably as a jobbing gardener."

"That's what you say; but look at you now—wipe your forehead. You are perspiring."

"Sweat, my dear. I took the stairs at the double."

"But that's what I mean. Since when have you started to rush? I always think of you as monumentally calm. Johnny goes rushing about, but that's because he is never sure where he's come from or where he wants to go to, and his main object is not to get caught."

"I haven't seen Johnny lately. He used to come in on

49

Saturday mornings; but since the decree that Saturday shall be a day of rest I hardly ever see him in the office. Henry meets him at their golf club. I'm always tickled at the idea of Johnny playing golf. It's out of character."

"Henry has a friend called Phil Deasy. He's in the library."

Barbara looked as if she had something momentous to communicate, then she concentrated on buttering a roll, smiling at it with her Mona Lisa smile.

"Well?"

"I merely said that Henry has this friend."

"But you said it as if you had something important to tell me. I expected to hear they exchanged blows."

"I don't see Henry in a fight. What funny things you say, Stephen. It's what makes you so sweet. At home I am accustomed only to hearing complaints. By the way, Leeson has started his golf lessons."

"Has he? Does he need lessons? I thought he knew how to play. Dammit, I've played with him since he was ten years old."

"Oh, Stephen! You know we had all this out, and you agreed that if he is to be really good at the game, now is the time to get him coached."

"Did I? I can't remember. I've a lot on my mind, my dear."

"I know. I can't make out how you do all you do; and I think you are very foolish to allow these politicians to make use of you, pick your brains, and pay you nothing for it. You are a baby in some ways."

"I'm not paid nothing. And even if I were, I should still be grateful for the chance to do something useful in the public domain. And do you know, I think I'm a success. I find that I get on much better with the workers than my colleagues do. I go and inspect the job in my shirt sleeves. They arrive with brief-cases and look owlish in their horn-rimmed glasses. And the Civil Servant goes by the book all the time. I am prepared to take a risk. There would have been a strike the other day if I hadn't given an undertaking which the men accepted. I said I'd resign if the Minister didn't back me up. My colleagues thought I was mad. That's what I was with the Minister about. I told him I had shoved my neck out; but there is no use in pretending we are running an autonomous body if in fact the Minister holds a whip over us. He was delighted with me. I've found my vocation. Would you like a glass of wine? Go on. It will do you good. You need a bit of bucking up."

Barbara shook her head and smiled sadly at the waitress who had heard the offer and was waiting to hear if it had been accepted.

"I don't need any 'bucking up', as you call it, dear. But what does worry me is you. Is everything becoming too much for you? I want you to know that if you ever think of coming and living with us your room is waiting for you. There was a time when that might have led to talk; but not now, not at our age."

"It would still lead to talk. Don't deceive yourself. The point is we would now ignore the talk. But I assure you —thank you for the offer—I have no intention whatever of giving up my house. I've shaped it to my ways. I would be lost anywhere else. When I leave, it will be feet first."

"Oh, Stephen, how can you speak of such things?"

"I don't as a rule. But only a lunatic thinks he is going to live for ever."

Barbara turned her head slowly from side to side—a gesture that she had seen in the cinema and thought becoming. Then she put on her brave look. Sporty, that was her line, unlike her sister-in-law, who attempted allure.

"I wonder if you had time, Stephen—I know how busy you are and I hate to bother you; but I would be ever so grateful if you'd turn your mind to something that has been worrying me. Time is passing so quickly. Soon it will be too late. I think I must consider now about making some provision for the future. I had two ideas: The first was to take a refresher course in hair-dressing. I suppose, even after all these years, I could get into it again. If I do that I'll sell the house and move into a flat. The alternative is to let the top of the house. If I could get a few students I could do breakfast for them. It would mean putting a shower into each room; but otherwise I don't think any outlay will be required. My trouble will be Johnny. But he must either lump it or leave it."

Stephen, bemused, stared at her.

"What's come over you, Barbara? Have you run into debt? Is Johnny in trouble?"

'No, my dear. But I have grown wiser. I cannot afford to live for ever in a rosy dream. You have been wonderfully kind to us all. I don't need to tell you that. Sometimes I tell myself that my life only began when you came into it, as surely it would end if ever you were to go out of it."

"Barbara, have you been drinking? What's the meaning of this nonsense?"

"It's not nonsense. Far from it. You know Johnny. Very soon the boys will have left the nest. Naturally they will want to make their own lives. They won't want to have an old mother dragging out of them. I must make myself independent."

Stephen stared at her. Women were unaccountable.

"Eat up your chicken. It's congealing on the plate. I've

looked after you for twenty years. Why should you think I won't continue to? Has anyone been trying to make mischief. If any one has, I will deal with him."

"None of us lives for ever. I pray—oh I pray every night of my life—that I shall be taken before you. But we are not allowed to arrange these things."

"I really think you must be bewitched or something. I'm nearly sixty-one. You're fifty. And as tough as they come. In the course of nature you ought to outlive me by twenty years."

"Stephen. Don't."

She took out a handkerchief that looked too tiny and fragile for her handbag and quickly applied it to the corners of her eyes. Then she smiled bravely.

"I'm sorry. I should keep these sad thoughts to myself. But you are so busy, Stephen, so sought-after, so useful to everyone. You don't know how long the days can be, and the nights."

"Did you ever speak to your doctor about that stuff I was recommended? What's the use of shaking your head at me like that? I told you it did the trick, and it's not habit-forming. No wonder you are blubbering like a baby if you are not getting your proper night's sleep."

"Blubbering. I hope I'm not blubbering." The word was an unfeeling one. It brought fresh tears to Barbara's not-so-large-as-once-they-were eyes.

"Listen to me, Barbara. I told you I was making provision for you in my will. I won't leave you in Johnny's hands. And I will tell you something else, although I shouldn't. I've left Johnny enough to give him pocket-money. He's as old as I am; but as he is less useful he will probably last longer. That's the way God disposes."

"I hate even to hear you talking about wills. I hate wills. They lead to so much unpleasantness. I was delighted to hear you had given your nieces their share now. They have it, and they have no interest in your death. They can think of you just as a loved one. But, of course, not everyone can afford to give away money like that. You're lucky. Then you've earned it. God knows you haven't spared yourself."

Barbara spoke with some chicken in her mouth and her eyes on her plate. When she raised them she encountered a blazing face and angry eyes.

"Who's been talking to you about my nieces? It's my own business what I do with my money. I want to know who told you this. And, by God, they are going to hear more about it when I do."

"Don't be cross with me, pet. I didn't ask for the information; and I supposed if Henry told his friend about it, he'd tell anyone."

"Henry told who? Are you sure of your facts?"

"I am. This man Deasy and he were playing golf on Friday. And when they were taking drinks at the bar afterwards Henry told him about it. I don't really see why he shouldn't. Naturally he was delighted; and I suppose he only wanted his friend to hear how grateful he was. And the friend told Johnny. It's perfectly simple."

"I'll let Henry have it plump and plain."

"Don't. For my sake. He will complain to Johnny, and Johnny—you know how he will go on. I'll never hear the end of it."

"Leave Johnny alone. There's very little harm in Johnny, if he wasn't such an infernal gossip. Henry is as bad. You've upset me by that piece of news."

"I'm sorry. It's the last thing I ever want to do. But it shows you what happens when that awful subject of money comes up. Johnny was talking to some man in a garage the other day who should have come in for a large estate if the lawyer hadn't botched the will. Everything went to charity. That's what I hate about wills, there's this element of uncertainty about them."

"There will be none about mine. And if I'm annoyed about it beforehand I'll tear it up and let everybody scramble. If you have finished that jelly, I must be on my way."

He had become remote, stiff, cold. She could not have chosen a worse day to bring up the topic. Trust Johnny. He suggested it. It was he who told her to tease Stephen, when her instinct was to leave him alone.

"You never noticed my blouse," she said as they went downstairs.

"What about it?"

"Nothing. It's very ordinary. I bought it at the sales because you are always telling me to wear blue. It doesn't fit actually."

"Well get yourself one that does." He took out his pocket-book and extracted two five-pound notes from a small bundle.

"No. No. Please, Stephen. I wouldn't have mentioned it if I thought you were going to do this. But you know how you say blue is my colour. It matches my eyes."

"Your eyes are green," he said, looking at them.

His own looked preoccupied and not especially kind. She took out her powder compact to look for herself at the same time as she dropped the two notes in her bag.

"I'll leave you," he said. And when she snapped back the lid of her compact she was alone on the pavement outside the premises of the National Society for the Propagation of Christian Knowledge. The window was full of a new book: *Strumpet City*. "I don't know what everybody is coming to," she said. She felt as if she had pulled a brick out of a wall and endangered the whole structure.

CHAPTER VII

"You've done so much, I hate to bother you Mr Fagan, but can you make head or tail of this?"

Curran, looking sadly seedy, stood in the doorway, holding a cigarette-packet between two trembling fingers.

"Let me see."

Brian took the packet—it was empty—and read the scrawl in indelible pencil on its face, "Watson give 20. Not more."

"Where does it come from? It looks like an order to a tobacconist for a re-fill."

"I wish it were. It will show you what I have to put up with. These are meant to be instructions from Woodhouse. He left it with the girl at the telephone and told her to give it to me. I'd know what to do, he said."

"Why not call him on the telephone?"

"I did. His wife says he's away. She won't help. She hates the sight of him. I don't blame her. He will pounce on me without notice and ask what I've done, and kick up a dust whatever I do. My nerves won't stand it."

"But can't you tell him that he must give lucid instructions. Nobody could do business this way."

"He does. Mr Stephen understood him. He's been putting up with the man for years. And between ourselves I think Woodhouse did this deliberately. He wants me to make a mess of his business so that he can go to Mr Stephen and say: see what happens when you leave my business in the hands of your assistants. I wish I could tell him to take himself and his business to hell out of here; but he won't. He sets too much store on the firm's good name. When you are as crooked as Woodhouse is it's important to have a respectable firm of lawyers to lend you countenance. Otherwise he would find it hard to get people to do business with him. But he has it in for Mr Stephen. He didn't like being passed over to me. I wish none of us had ever laid eyes on him."

Brian turned the packet over in his hands. It looked as if it had lain out in the rain for a fortnight. The writing had not only run, it had the look of having been made with the blunt butt of a broken pencil. He pictured Woodhouse in his mind's eye, writing his cryptic message with his tongue protruding slightly to facilitate the licking of the pencil, hands very dirty, hairy, and with close-bitten nails. Caliban.

He had been feeling gloriously happy. An envelope on his desk that morning had inside a cheque for a hundred pounds and a note—'Who helps Curran, helps me. Thank you. S.F.' And here was Curran, in need of help again. He had interpreted the cryptic pencil message to mean that something was to be bought from somebody called Watson for not more than twenty something. Whether pounds, hundreds of pounds or thousands of pounds might be guessed if one knew what Watson had to sell. He put all this up to Curran. Was he quite sure Woodhouse had not mentioned anyone called Watson?

"I can never be sure with him. He talks to himself most of the time. He wants to tell you as little as possible and to catch you out if he can. Did you ever read Dickens, Mr Fagan? I love him myself. I've read all his books three or four times over. Well if you know Dickens, Woodhouse is like Quilp, the dwarf."

"In *The Old Curiosity Shop*."

"Oh, you know."

Brian was rather vague about Quilp, but anxious to get on with his work.

"I'll ask Mr Stephen," he said. "He may have an inspiration."

"I don't want to go bothering him."

"I have to see him anyway. I'll tell you what he suggests."

Stephen answered his knock. He was sitting at his desk, looking tired, he thought. But he smiled at him.

"I came to thank you. I'm overwhelmed."

"I don't want to hear a word about it. I like young people who are kind to old people."

"I'm afraid we have more trouble. Woodhouse left this for Curran. It's supposed to be instructions of some kind. We can't make it out."

Stephen took the packet and looked at it.

"I recognise the handiwork. I've had instructions on even more unlikely paper from the same gentleman. Watson? Watson? Let me think. I'll ask Henry." He picked up the house telephone.

"Henry. Didn't we have a transaction with someone called Watson of recent years? The name seems to ring a bell."

Brian could hear the voice on the other end of the telephone. Whatever was being said seemed to depress Stephen. His mouth curled with distaste. When he put down the telephone, he said in a flatter voice than usual, "Henry says that someone called Watson bought the Haggard property in Malahide. Your old employer acts for him."

"So he does. I'll ring up and find out. Perhaps it's for sale."

Stephen nodded absently and took up a sheet of paper. Brian took the hint and withdrew.

A telephone call confirmed Stephen's guess. Watson had thought of disposing of the place. He had hoped to build on it but had run into difficulties.

"That means it's going cheap," Curran said. "Trust Woodhouse."

It was even as he said. The offer was accepted over the telephone. A contract for sale at nineteen thousand and five hundred pounds would be delivered within an hour. Curran was ecstatic.

"It's a curious coincidence," he told Brian. "Woodhouse was going on about that place last time he was in here, saying that Mr Stephen slipped up in not getting it for him at the time and allowing it to be sold at auction. I flew at him, lost control of myself, I did. I can't stand here and listen to a crook like that abusing the likes of Mr Stephen. Now he's going to get it for less than half what Watson gave for it. He ought to be pleased. But he never lets on. I bet you he will say that if he'd done the business himself he'd have got out of that five hundred pounds and try to make us feel we owe it to him."

Stephen very seldom came near Curran these days, but that morning he looked in as he was passing. Apparently a casual call, but when he sat down, Curran knew there was something on his mind. He waited and learned what it was when Stephen said, "I hear Woodhouse is after Miss Haggard's place."

"We bought it for him today for five hundred pounds less than his top figure."

"You don't mean to say you've *bought* it."

"Subject to contract, of course. That's on its way. I want to have everything ready for his lordship when he calls. Did you ever see anything to equal his instructions. If you hadn't caught on, I wouldn't have known what to do."

"Be careful, Curran. You know I have an instinct about these things. Watson bought the place at the auction and found out too late that he couldn't make a road to join up the two parts of the property. That meant the better part of it was useless for building purposes. Curtis acted for Watson—it all comes back to me now—and did his damndest to get him out of his bargain. But we had him sewn up in the Conditions of Sale. Between ourselves, I think Curtis slipped up that time. I don't want to make the same mistake. Woodhouse only buys land to develop it, and he can't develop this until he gets permission to build a road across a field that belongs to somebody else—I can't remember who. But I do recall that she was a very tough lady who was quite determined to prevent building so near her own house if she could prevent it. And she could. Watson offered her some astronomic figure for permission to put a road across her field."

"Woodhouse may have got round her. If he had he'd never talk to us."

"But we must find out first. He's quite capable of signing the contract knowing the difficulty and then threatening to sue us if he can't get out of it. The place is a tremendous bargain at the price; and he may be gambling. I want you to consult me before you commit Woodhouse to a contract. I have a presentiment about this transaction."

"Why do we act for him? Can't we afford to tell him to take his business away?"

"I never like to lose a client, and we make a great deal out of him indirectly. If he gets permission to build on Miss Haggard's farm it will mean five hundred houses. That's a lot of business. It would keep some firms going for a few years without anything else. No, Curran, we won't get rid of Woodhouse; but we will watch our step very carefully."

"I'm glad I can talk to you about it. That takes a load off my mind."

Stephen had always been able to leave his troubles behind him in the office. It was part of his strength. He fed the powerful computer of his mind with the material of his own selection. But this evening when he wanted to think about his new appointment—there were so many problems to be considered—he found himself unable to forget the farm in Malahide. And at night he had a dream. He was making his will, leaving everything to Curran. He wondered who to get to witness it, someone who would not argue with him. He felt guilty about what he was doing. He shouted to Brian Fagan to come in. He called again and again. He tried to get up, but he was paralysed. Then the door opened and Woodhouse came in. He was looking inexpressibly evil. Behind him came Miss Haggard. They advanced, coming closer and closer. He tried to hide his head under the sheet. He tried to call. If only young Fagan would come. He shouted for the last time.

He woke up shouting. He was damp with sweat. It was four o'clock. He was relieved to find he had been dreaming. It had all been so real, so real and so terrifying. He had never liked old Miss Haggard. She had always some cause of complaint. If nothing else she would comment acidly on the firm's stationery. She liked to be addressed simply as 'Miss Haggard', when a new typist put 'Miss D. Haggard' on an envelope, the old lady came straight in to Dublin—eight miles—to complain. Nothing would appease her. She recalled the occasion when a letter arrived with the gum-flap open. It was a ten year old grievance but resurrected whenever occasion served. Little wonder her nephew went to the bad. She put off making her will until the last possible moment. She disliked so much the idea of anyone enjoying her money; and her whole concern was to make sure her nephew got none of it. In default of taking it with her, she was indifferent as to who got it so long as her nephew did not.

And now Woodhouse—one of the least attractive characters he had ever encountered (not excluding the criminals he defended in his early days)—was stepping into Miss Haggard's shoes. It was a bad omen. Perhaps Curran was right. Perhaps it would be wiser to tell the fellow to take his business away. He would put it up to the others and see what they had to say. The trouble was that nobody who hadn't to do the work and deal with Woodhouse would see the reason for throwing his business out. But he couldn't keep Woodhouse on his hands and do his new job properly. The man was so damnably inconsiderate and time-consuming.

CHAPTER VIII

Ernie Woodhouse left home early. It was the first day of the children's summer holidays, and their presence in the house gave him no pleasure. His wife got up, as usual, at seven o'clock to get breakfast ready for the household. After breakfast she would start whinging about money. She seemed to think he was made of money. One way to avoid that was to get out. He could hear her north-of-Ireland voice raised in remonstration upstairs; under its cover he retreated by the kitchen door.

There was no comfort at home: brown linoleum on the floors; green colour-wash on the walls; chairs and sofas without covers and with broken springs; the bottle of stout he drunk by himself last night still on the mantelpiece. The contrast provided by his car was extraordinary. He grudged expenditure on everything else. But a posh car had been his boyhood dream. His first large purchase, as he hoped it would be his last. At the wheel he was transformed, a creature in its proper element. His habitual grin softened into a smile when he gazed at the world through a windscreen. He had a powerful car, but he drove rather slowly, exulting in the sense of power that could be unleashed by the pressing of a pedal. He liked to see and be seen when he was driving. It was his only relaxation.

This morning he was on his way to Malahide. He had left a message with old Curran to buy Watson's place. He wanted to find out what he could get it for. He never expected Watson to part with it at the figure he mentioned. He put that down to tease Curran, to give him something to think about. The fellow needed a bit of a shaking up. Not that Woodhouse really wanted to buy land at present. But he had heard someone else was after this place, and he didn't like even to hear that. When someone else wanted land he did his best to see he didn't get it. He considered it was his right to have first refusal of any building land there was on the market; and he had another reason for looking after this property—he should have been offered it by Stephen when Miss Haggard died. Instead of that it was put up for auction and sold at a huge price, as prices went ten years before. He would never forgive Stephen for that; and now he had shipped him to Curran—a clerk! He didn't forget that sort of thing. Someday he would get his own back. Stephen thought he was God Almighty. Nobody slighted Ernie Woodhouse and got away with it. Ask his wife.

He had an instinct about property. He could smell its potential. And his luck was extraordinary. He was able to score where everyone else had tried and failed. It was sufficient to hear that Watson was in difficulties to know that this was his opportunity. However casual he had been in his instructions about the purchase, when he came to the turn near the Castle and saw the farm, smiling in sunshine, he knew it was meant for him. Those beech trees would have to come down. He felled them in his mind, and visualised the terrace of semi-detached villas that would replace them. He could squeeze twenty in. But that was a poor frontage. He drove on to see what other space was available beside the road. A lane separated the field from a high wall. Further investigation showed that this bounded another property, and it ran as far as the next road. He had assumed that it was part of Miss Haggard's place. He came to a gate. He decided to clear up the mystery, and drove in.

The house that came into view was a large Regency-type villa, and at one time it must have stood on quite a modest site; but now a path at the side, beyond the stables, led to a gate. Woodhouse drove as far as this and found the path ended here. But there was a track across a field on the other side.

The mystery was soon explained: the gate on the opposite side of the field was the entrance to six other fields of reasonable size; on the far side of these was a stream. No wonder Watson's plans had broken down. All this part of Miss Haggard's property was an island, land-locked. The only entrance was the track across the field belonging to this other property. If this could be turned into a road the problem of access was solved. If not, the only alternative was to acquire the dividing field and if necessary the property to which it belonged. Otherwise the greater part of the Haggard property was of no use for his purposes.

Woodhouse's first thought was whether in the circum-stances he had offered too much. This was a farm, not building ground. A hundred acres at two hundred pounds an acre. A bargain, but not a fantastic bargain, not a Woodhouse bargain. If Curran had acted on his instruc-tions he would make life unpleasant for him.

Fifteen thousand was all he was prepared to give on the chance of joining up the property eventually. If the road difficulty could be got over, it was the best bet he had ever made. And the breath in his nostrils told him it was. He felt a glow in his heart. When a skylark spiralled up into the blue, singing its little heart out, he responded. It expressed what he felt. A stone was lying handy. He picked it up and pitched it at the bird. The throw fell short by a mile, and landed in a cow pat. This delighted him. He was enjoying his trip to the country.

Now, what to do? A telephone call to Curran to reduce his offer to £15,000. That was at the top of the agenda. Then he would prowl round and see what luck offered. He wanted to learn what he could about the people who owned the property which was interfering with development.

He was not afraid of meeting anyone on the premises. There is no effective method of dealing with a trespasser so long as he keeps out of the house. This he had discovered long since; and he always entered when he wanted to inspect a likely property. He was impervious to abuse. He enjoyed it. His grin met every situation and, by the undiscerning, was put down for good-humour.

Nobody was astir. He drove out as he came in, but left the gate open, reasoning that it saved him the trouble of getting in and out of his own car and performed a similar service for the next person who wanted to use the gate.

He liked to telephone at someone else's expense and gave thought how this could be accomplished, deciding finally to call at a garage and pretend to be interested in the purchase of a car and willing to trade in his own. The garage man was impressed by his car, as well he might be, and gave delighted consent to the free use of lavatory and telephone.

Mr Woodhouse dialled the familiar number.

"How's tricks?"

He never announced himself, and was amused to catch the anxious displeasure in Curran's voice. "Who's speaking?"

He knew very well. "How's tricks?" was a signature tune.

"I'm out in Malahide."

"Oh!"

"Have you got that place for me?"

"You will be glad to hear we have. And I knocked five hundred off your price."

"I don't understand."

"You gave instructions to go to twenty thousand. I got it for nineteen and a half."

"If you did, I'm ruined."

"Mr Woodhouse! You said—"

"Ruined. The place is a paddock. I wouldn't give half that for it."

"A hundred acres. Close to Dublin."

"That doesn't interest me."

"You needn't sign the contract. There's nothing to bind you."

"You don't need to tell me that; but you've thrown away my chance to bargain. You've put a figure in their minds. You've let me down very badly, Curran. I'm surprised at you. But this is what I might expect."

Silence. Curran couldn't know his persecutor was grinning.

"Mr Woodhouse. You must listen to me."

"I'll be coming in to see you at six. Don't get me into trouble in the meanwhile."

He rang off, well pleased with the conversation. Curran would be at his wit's end now.

He agreed to buy a new Rover if the garage proprietor would give him fifteen hundred pounds for his present car, three hundred pounds more than its market value.

No business was effected. But they parted on good terms, and he got air in the tyres as another small recompense for the time involved in acting the little play. He learned also—which by itself justified the visit—that an elderly couple, Major and Mrs Bramwell, lived in St Anne's, the place beside the one he had decided to buy. They were the owners of the interesting field. An old-fashioned, reserved couple, reputed to be well-to-do, they inherited the estate from Mrs Bramwell's father. He had been a brewer. They were interested in charities of a Protestant character, particularly the Society for the Prevention of Cruelty to Animals. Mr Woodhouse took a mental note of this.

He drove back to 'his own place' and sat outside the gate in the car. Then an inspiration came. It always did. He started up his car and drove to the Bramwells' house. This time he shut the gates after him and made for the front of the house. His car looked well with the sun gleaming on the flawless paint work. He rubbed a speck of dirt off the bonnet with his pocket handkerchief and then, to save himself the trouble later, blew his nose with it. The knocker had a friendly appearance. His knock would have aroused the dead.

A bashful girl in maid's uniform answered it.

"Is anyone in?' he enquired.

"Who did you want to see?"

"Either of them will do."

She glanced behind him at the glossy expensive car and tried to reconcile it with his appearance.

Seemingly carved out of bog oak, the head took up a disproportionate amount of the material. It was narrow at the forehead; under black brows, the eyes were bright with calculation passing off as amusement. The mouth was a trap set in a rectangular block of chin. He was dressed in a blue serge suit, bought once for best wear;

his shirt was off-white under a patched yellow wool cardigan, the only garment to relate to a very new pair of golfing shoes. An open fly-button drew attention to grease stains in the vicinity.

A fund-raiser, no matter how well he was faring, would not have arrived in that vehicle. He might be some sort of official. That meant trouble. An inspection. The service of notices. An increase in annual expenditure. She was a shrewd girl. If this was such a one she would say her employers were out. Then light dawned.

"You are the plumber. They were expecting you."

Mr Woodhouse always grinned and there was no alteration in his expression at the girl's mistake. He had never qualified as any sort of tradesman when he set up as a builder and had to hire skilled labour. But his vanity was hurt. The girl had seen the car. Only the plumber of a Maharajah had ever driven about in so splendid an equipage.

"Did you ever see a plumber in a Mercedes?" he said.

The girl looked confused.

"What did you want to see the boss about?"

He might, she decided, be a superior sort of beggar, working on a commission basis, for a political party, perhaps.

"The Cruelty crowd."

She stared, uncomprehending.

"The crowd that collects for cruelty to animals."

"You are collecting."

Mr Woodhouse shook his head and winked.

She looked hesitant. The business of protecting her employers from importunate callers taxed her inexperience. At home the door was open to everyone. But not here; and yet there were sometimes rows when she left people standing at the door instead of inviting them in. But if you left a tinker alone in the hall you might come back and find he had pinched everything in sight. What was a girl to do? The Bramwells sighed over her deficiencies and calculated whether, like one of their friends, they could afford a foreign couple; but it seemed a wild extravagance. They were careful of their money.

A stout, bald, almost ovoid figure in tweeds emerged. Major Bramwell had decided to inspect the visitor. He had been left inside the door, but a safe distance from any valuables in the hall.

"You wanted to see me about something." The voice was stern. Woodhouse knew the type. One had to penetrate this outwork, and then the next defence wall, and then the next. He had overcome them often enough; and the land they once protected nobody would now recognise under tarmacadam and concrete and tiled roofs with their television masts pointing to Heaven.

"I'd like a word with you. About the Cruelty."

He pronounced it 'croolty'; and the master, as the maid, found him unintelligible. Mr Woodhouse was disappointed. He expected the fat man to say: "Ah! the Cruelty. I would be delighted to discuss that."

"That field of yours," he said. "I'd like to hold a gymkhana there. For the Cruelty."

"Cruelty?"

Major Bramwell had caught the word, but not its significance in the context.

"Cruelty—you know—to animals."

"Oh. You must be from the I.S.P.C.A.* I beg your pardon. When you said 'cruelty' I couldn't make out at first what you were driving at. If the society wants to hold a gymkhana here I'm sure my wife will be delighted. We must ask her. But its surprising that nobody mentioned it

* Irish Society for the Prevention of Cruelty to Animals.

70

at the meeting on Friday. Who's idea is it?"

"I only thought of it today when I was passing. That field would be ideal for a gymkhana, I said to myself. And then I thought of the Cruelty."

"It's an extraordinary coincidence. My wife is very devoted to that charity. Very curious how these things happen. Makes you think there are forces at work we don't understand. Come in, Mr—"

"Woodhouse."

"—Mr Woodhouse and talk to my wife. What position do you hold in the Society?"

The Major knew a great many of his wife's friends on the committee, and this visitor did not strike him as typical of workers in the good cause. They were apt to be more genteel.

He led the way across the hall into an unexpectedly spacious room, at the end of which were french windows into the garden. A woman of somewhat dehydrated appearance in a cotton dress, unfashionably cut, was seated bolt upright beside an empty fireplace, crocheting.

She looked up over her spectacles. Her dryness depreciated the value of her husband's rubicund appearance, raised doubts as to the strength of the solution of good cheer in his composition.

"Mr Woodhouse has called, my dear, to know if you would let the I.S.P.C.A. hold a gymkhana in the big field. What date had you in mind?" He turned to the visitor, but Mr Woodhouse's attention was wandering. He was struck by the lady's withered condition. His own wife was heading that way. One ought to be able to trade them in like cars.

"What date had you in mind?" Major Bramwell raised his voice.

"Oh. Whenever it suits. This is June. Say August. Some

Sunday. It won't give you any trouble. I'll hire all the gear."

"I think we ought to enlist helpers. We want to make as much as possible. If we hire anything, there will be no profit for the I.S.P.C.A."

Mrs Bramwell spoke as one who was accustomed to good works. Mr Woodhouse recognised the tone. These people were out of his line.

"Whatever you say. I only wanted to save you trouble."

"I don't think I've met you before," Mrs Bramwell said. "I don't remember any Woodhouse in our list of sub-scribers since the Brigadier died. But I'm sure I have seen you somewhere."

She looked round the room over her spectacles. "There," she said. "The treasurer's report is on my desk, Brereton. Give it to me."

Mr Woodhouse hadn't thought of this. "You won't find my name there. I always give money anonymously. A man like me would be skinned alive if he gave something to everyone who looks for it. As it is I have to tell the wife I'm out if anyone calls at the house. They'd take the clothes off my back."

Mrs Bramwell's spectacles roved quizzically over the garments in question.

"What business are you in? If you don't mind my ask-ing," the husband enquired, reading his wife's mind.

The question gave Mr Woodhouse pause.

"I was in the building business; but I've retired. I look after a few properties. It takes me all my time."

"I bet it does. I can't get the carpenter to mend the gates here for love or money."

"That's it." Mrs. Bramwell nodded to her husband not to mind the interruption.

The Major's voice was cordial. Mrs. Bramwell left off

her scrutiny. The mystery was solved. A builder who had done well and was content to remain in his natural setting. It all fitted together. The too-grand car, the finger-stains at the fly-buttons, the generous impulse, the 'croolty'. A simple-hearted, unspoiled, useful member of society, prepared to give his time to organise a gymkhana, too modest to push himself on to the committee of a charitable organisation. The salt of the earth.

"We have been having coffee. Would you like a cup?" Mrs Bramwell said.

"I wouldn't mind."

"Ask Christine to bring us in another cup, dear. Won't you sit down."

Mr Woodhouse let himself down on to the straightest chair, the one from which he could detach himself with least delay. If the Bramwells were at ease, he was not. He had breached the first wall of the fortress. The heat of the battle lay ahead.

"Do you often organise gymkhanas? Are you particularly interested in horses?"

The question put an idea into his mind. He must let these people know he was a Protestant. It would be another bond.

"I am thinking of getting one up for our clergyman, Mr Vokes. Do you know Mr Vokes? He never leaves me alone. I often tell him he will have me in the poor house before he's finished."

"It must be an endless struggle for parsons. Even in our own church, people don't subscribe as they used to. Planned-giving is a leaf our priests have taken from your book."

Mr Woodhouse's grin wobbled. He might have made some terrible gaffe. Who would have thought this pair were R.C.s? In the North, where he came from, it could never have happened.

The Major returned.

"Coffee's on its way."

He was all smiles. "I was thinking, dear, that Julia will get a tremendous kick out of a gymkhana."

"Julia is our grandchild," Mrs Bramwell explained. "We bought her a pony last season. She hunted with the Fingals and had tremendous fun."

"We must see she gets a prize," Mr Woodhouse said.

"I don't think she can. The pony was sold to us as perfectly safe for a beginner. But it's touched in the wind," Mrs Bramwell said.

"And the wrong height," her husband added.

These were sore points, but Mr Woodhouse could not have been expected to know the saga of how Lady Coddingham stuck the two trusting Bramwells for twice the market value of the brute. It was a dirty trick; and they would have cut her if they ever met her; but they never did. She lived in Kilkenny and had failed to find a home for the pony where its form was known.

"We can fix it," Mr Woodhouse said.

Mrs Bramwell smiled at her crochet work. He was rather a dear. Out of his depth. But meaning tremendously well. His wife really ought to talk to him about his trousers.

When Mr Woodhouse left the Bramwells he had fixed the gate in the yard for them, and relieved a pipe from the kitchen sink that was stuffed. He had also walked the grounds.

"There's a right of way across that field," the Major said, as they came out of the garden and walked in the direction of the sea. Mr Woodhouse had expressed a desire to look at the water. "I love the sea," he said. "I should have been a sailor."

74

He knew that to satisfy his boyish longing would involve a tramp across the property. An opportunity to inspect the land. He had found that out.

Major Bramwell opened his mind to his charitable new friend.

"It's a damned nuisance, but it has its advantages." They were traversing the track that led from one part of the neighbouring property to the other. "We were able to stop them from building. They wanted to put a road across the field. Slap in the middle of it; and then build a colony of dreadful bungalows on my door-step. But we put a stop to their little game. Our man was a match for them. The fellow who bought the place burnt his fingers over it. I hear the Bank is selling him up. We played with the idea of trying to buy it. What do you think it would be worth? Our solicitor tells us we are quite safe. Nobody can build on it unless we agree to give them access; but one has an uncomfortable feeling all the same. We live in such bolshy times."

"You are right there. I'd be afraid the County Council might take it over. It would be a pity to have a crowd of council houses on your door-step, as you said yourself."

"Good God!"

Major Bramwell halted, shocked by the thought.

"They couldn't do that."

"Of course they could. And if you buy Watson's place it's my opinion that's what would set them off. Why? First of all there would be local jealousy. Second, you have enough land as it is. And best of all; once you bought the place next door the trouble over the road disappears. As it is, when the engineers look at a map they see there's no access to those fields. They forget about them. But if there's a straight line to the road, man—I'd say the

Council would be on top of you with a plan for two hundred houses within a twelvemonth."

"If my wife hears this, she will get ill. The place is hers, you know. She was brought up here. She loves every inch of it. You've put the wind up me. But I'm grateful. There has been talk about building on the shore side. But I thought we had put a stopper to it, once for all."

"If I were to buy the place next door, we would make a team. I wonder what sort the house is."

Mr Woodhouse caught a fleeting glance of dismay in those bulging eyes.

"It would be wonderful to have you as an ally," he said.

He meant it, too. After the first shock of disappointment—the Bramwells had hoped for socially congenial neighbours—he realised that a tradesman like this who would not expect to be on dropping-in terms would be better than some of the awful pushing new rich from Dublin.

"If the Bank is selling it, they will only be concerned for themselves. It might be got cheap."

"That's what we were thinking," the Major said.

Mr Woodhouse ignored this. He had decided to close the purchase at once at the agreed figure. It was probably the amount of the bank debt. He would call in on Curran, complain, and then sign, leaving Curran under the impression he was dissatisfied with the way he had handled the transaction. Then he could concentrate on getting the better of this old fogey. Not that it would be easy with that wife. There were no flies on her.

He waived the pleasure of looking at the ocean when he heard that it involved a departure from the estate. Major Bramwell was surprised. Having walked so far, it seemed foolish to throw up the idea for the sake of a short scramble through a thistle field. However, it was Mr Woodhouse's affair; he had suddenly become anxious about the time, having given the impression of being singularly free from its tyranny. He became silent and preoccupied, not listening to the Major's free-running discourse until he mentioned Miss Haggard. Then he paid attention.

"Did you know the old lady?"

"Very eccentric. Fell out with her nephew and left the place to charity. We were worried about it at the time. However, nothing happened. Then this Watson man bought it, and we heard he had ideas of building. He paid a lot, at the time. Prices have gone up since then. We have had anxious moments. My wife isn't very strong. It's not good for her. Why can't we be left in peace? That's all we ask."

"If I were you, I'd clear out. I'd sell this place and find myself some nice little house where there was a view and not too much to keep up. Down in Kerry, or in the West. That's what I'd do if I were in your shoes."

"Between ourselves, it's what I'd do, but Mrs Bramwell wouldn't hear of it. You know what women are."

Mr Woodhouse did. Only too well. If his spouse stood in the way of his plans for half a minute she would get his fist in her face. But he realised that not everyone had such command of the domestic situation. What puzzled him was why this man should put himself out for such a wizened old trout. But, there, he was forgetting, she had the money. Mrs Woodhouse didn't even have that to recommend her. At the time it looked like a lift to marry her. He hadn't known his powers.

The Bramwells had a quick consultation while Mr Woodhouse was freeing the pipe whether they should invite him to lunch; would he expect it? In the old days he would have had it with Cook and Christine in the kitchen.

"He is the image of the Carpenter," Mrs Bramwell said.

"What carpenter?"

"Oh, you know. The Walrus's friend."

They invited him only after he expressed his determination to leave; then they said he must come again.

He had decided to go into Malahide to see what more was to be found out. When the bars opened, he would drop in for half pints of Guinness. There was usually something to be learnt in a pub, even at noon. The hardest drinkers began when the doors opened. And the regulars were the best for gossip. In a small place like Malahide, it would not take long to find out what was going on and the prospects for enterprise.

His first call was a failure. A very old man sat in a corner under the darts board with a half pint of Guinness in front of him. Nobody would ever talk to him. A radio was playing, mocking the absence of customers. The old man wasn't listening. He hadn't heard anything for years. The 'pop' tune introduced a tinny note to the fly-blown appearance of the surroundings. A thick-set man with ginger hair and freckled flaming skin was washing tumblers behind the bar.

He turned to serve Mr Woodhouse, looking at the ceiling as he did so, operating mechanically, waiting while his customer felt in his pocket for money.

"Ta," he said, when ten shillings made its reluctant appearance. He slapped the change on the counter and returned to his task. Throughout he treated Mr Woodhouse as if he wasn't there. A man who minded his own business.

Nobody could make a drink go further than Ernest Woodhouse. He appeared to take large gulps, but contrived to let only so much through his lips as might seep

78

through a crack in hard wood. In half an hour the level had not dropped appreciably, nor would it in twice the time. When the porter had served its purpose, he would toss it back. He looked at the clock. Half-past twelve. Another quarter of an hour; then he would make a purchase at the chemist's or in one of the smaller shops where a conversation across the counter passed muster for civility. If nothing came of that, he would go to the hotel for lunch; but he resented hotel prices, and that would be only his last resort.

The minutes dragged on. The old man seemed to be dead. When Mr Woodhouse had given up hope and was on the point of tossing back what remained in the tumbler, a sharp-faced man in a shiny blue suit, a clerk of some kind, came in. An habitué, Mr Woodhouse felt. If there were a newspaper in the village he would have said a journalist. He lacked the processed look a bank employee acquires. A bookmaker's clerk, perhaps. Sharp but shabby. He said "Morning" to the barman, and the barman said "Morning", and took his hands out of the water. Having touched them with a towel he proceeded to mix samples from several bottles, and put the resultant concoction down, looking away while the customer felt in his pocket. Mr Woodhouse shifted at the bar.

"Nice day," he said, when the barman went back to his slops. The man in the serge suit stared stonily into his strange drink and grunted.

"Live round here?" Mr Woodhouse said.

The man continued to watch his drink. He might have been engaged in a chemical experiment. He did not seem to have heard Mr Woodhouse.

"Down from Dublin like myself?" Mr Woodhouse enlarged his grin, as if they had now something in common.

The man took up his tumbler and swallowed the contents.

"Quick work," Mr Woodhouse said admiringly.

The man took out a clean but worn white handkerchief, wiped his lips, and walked past Mr Woodhouse. The door into the street slammed.

Mr Woodhouse finished his stout, belched thoughtfully and said "Good day to you" to the man at the bar. *"Slainte,"* he replied, without looking up.

For whom were all the glasses being washed? When had they been used? It was hard to picture the premises as other than deserted. The old man in the corner was contemplating the froth on a fresh pint. He was a fixture.

The summer day, the faint cool breeze floating up from the sea, greeted Mr Woodhouse on the pavement. He did not notice that. He was on the scent. At the end of the street, the hotel beckoned. It would be full of visitors at this time of year, and local labour was recruited. He should have gone there at once and not wasted the best part of an hour in a derelict pub at noon. But he never cared very much about time. He always preferred to wait. It was his strength. He had the somnolent quality of a snake or crocodile. When he moved it was to some purpose. He conserved his energies; and if any bustling had to be done, he let others do it. Every day, for instance, he made a point of putting through a leisurely call to his lawyer, architect, estate agent and bank manager, enjoying their discomfiture at his very personal style in which threat and cajolery were equally mixed. Their exasperation at being kept up to the mark and having their own time wasted gave him macabre delight. Just now he knew his bank manager would be going to lunch; a public call box gave him the idea. He entered and pressed button B to see if the last occupant had been careless. He had.

Mr Woodhouse re-inserted the sixpence. He knew the bank's number by heart. He would ask if Curran had lodged any money to his account yesterday. Then he would ask Curran the same question when he saw him. If he had forgotten to, and tried to lie, he had caught him out. It was a little game. In any event, he would let him know he was being checked.

It was five minutes past one when Mr Woodhouse left the telephone booth, having had good value for sixpence. He had spoilt the manager's luncheon, now he must think about his own. Would he be able to get sandwiches at the hotel? Or would he be press-ganged into a set-price menu?

He entered somewhat defiantly, keeping on his cap, humming to himself. All round him were people whom he could buy and sell if he called upon his resources; his appearance was a camouflage; it entitled him to do hard bargaining, and was a reproach to anyone who, with the advantages of soap and water, tried to stand up to him. In the bar, fathers in holiday clothes were miming affluence for a fortnight, imitating the coloured advertisements in Sunday newspaper supplements. Mr Woodhouse looked out of place in their charade; but he went up to the bar and ordered his half pint of stout, pulling out, at the same time, a packet of the cheapest cigarettes. The boy behind the bar glanced at his cap, but lacked the authority to tell him to take it off. A rather starved young man, in a blazer, who was comparing the hotel to its disadvantage with one he had stayed at in Jersey last year, for the benefit of anyone within earshot, kept glancing at Mr Woodhouse's yellow vest, as if he was adding it to the items on the debit side of the hotel's account. Mr Woodhouse took out a pencil and started to clean an ear. He would have liked to ask the young man if he was sure that he could afford the two aperitifs he had just ordered, although he had known at first glance that he could not. The sort of smartness he affected was a public announcement of lack of capital and insufficient income disguised behind an aping of affluence.

"That will be three and a penny," the bar boy said.

Mr Woodhouse produced a wad of five-pound notes, and handed one to the boy. That would put them all in their places, he told himself, conscious of stares. More money than any of them had ever had in their pockets in their lives. He always carried a lot of money about with him in large denominations. It was a way of saving and he had it there if an opportunity arose. He could slap down a deposit on a likely property while someone else was communicating with banks and lawyers.

This crowd, mostly from abroad, or remote parts, were of no use to him. He gave the bar boy a shilling for himself and asked if he was from the locality. The boy, not impressed by the shilling, said he came from Dublin. A shilling thrown away. But God never shuts one door that He does not open another. The boy's surly reply was followed by the appearance of a newcomer, a once good-looking, down-at-heel, world-worn, individual. His frayed collar and cuffs, stained check suit and weather-beaten face were all very pleasing to Mr Woodhouse. He greeted him at once and for the first time that day met with a civil response. The stranger talked with the accent of the upper class but, like his suit, it was somewhat in need of repair. His teeth, like his fingers, were brown. His movements were swift and slightly uncertain. He dropped everything he handled and knocked over anything he touched. Mr Woodhouse was reminded of the action of a road drill. There seemed to be one at work inside the stranger.

"I was going to have a half pint. Will you join me?" Mr Woodhouse said.

Perhaps his new acquaintance had seen that wad of money. He did not repulse him. "I stick to whiskey."

Mr Woodhouse's grin was proof against the blow.

"Whiskey," he said to the bar boy. "Irish?" to his guest.

"Irish," he replied.

"Large or small," the boy said.

Mr Woodhouse stopped breathing.

"Large," the man said, "with water."

"Well. Here's to you," he said, knocking over the glass containing cocktail pickles with his leather-covered elbow.

"What are you doing here? I've never seen you in Malahide before." He was glancing at Mr Woodhouse's pockets as if looking for the gun that would betray a bank robber. The idea pleased him. It corporealised a fantasy.

"I'm looking round," Mr Woodhouse said. "Do you know of any properties for sale, anything with a bit of land?"

"My aunt's place is in the market. I don't know what the man who bought it wants. He got stung over it."

"Can it be seen?"

"I'll bring you up there if you like. I've time to spare. But what sort of money had you in mind? This is quite a large farm. Watson gave forty thousand for it ten years ago. He thought he could build on to it."

Mr Woodhouse nodded at the bar boy.

"Another Irish for my friend. A large one."

"I ought to pay for this," Miss Haggard's nephew said.

"It's on me."

Mr Woodhouse had put aside his grin. His benevolence was expressed in action. His eyes were more noticeable now. They were like a parrot's, wise and fixed and bright and hard.

"I know the place," Mr Woodhouse said. "I wouldn't mind getting hold of it."

"It should belong to me."

"Your aunt left it away, did she? You can't have played your cards properly."

"I couldn't stand the old faggot. She was as odd as they come; but I was her only relation, her brother's son."

Mr Woodhouse nodded. Relationships meant nothing to him.

"But that's not the whole of it. Her lawyer made a botch of her will, and I should have got anything there was, in spite of her. But they faked up the will, and the place was sold and every penny went to charity. Every sausage."

"That's hard. I must say. I think that's hard. What do you mean when you say 'faked up the will'? They couldn't do that. Nobody can fake a will. Not, that is, if anybody knows about it."

"That's the trouble. Her old lawyer did it to cover up his own mistake. When I heard about it the damage was done. But I haven't given up. Not by a long chalk. The hell of it is that it's the devil to get one of those lawyers to go for another. When it comes to the point, they're as thick as thieves."

"And who is the lawyer?"

"Foster. Stephen Foster, a director of this new property company the Government has set up. All things to all men, the same gentleman. I only heard about the will by a fluke. My fiancée spilled the beans. She used to work in the office."

"I'm surprised at what you tell me. I think Foster ought to pay up. He can well afford to. I mean it's unfair to have you left with nothing because he made a mistake. I wonder what he got out of the charities."

"I don't suppose he got anything. My old aunt was determined I shouldn't get a penny. It would have been the joke of the century if I had, in spite of her. Foster forgot to witness the will and put his name to it after she died."

"I bet you, all the same, he got a handsome whack from the charities."

"Why do you say that?"

"For what other reason did he do it? A man like him. He could have come to you and explained the position about the will and done a deal with you. That's what a decent man would have done. I'm sure you would have made it worth his while."

"You bet; but I can't see a man like Stephen Foster engaging in that sort of transaction. He's as respectable as the bench of bishops, even if he does keep a doxy. But he can get away with that. He's established. He's not afraid to be seen with her. But I'm not going to let him rob me for the sake of his reputation. If he wants to keep that he will have to pay for it. Am I unreasonable? I want to get married. I haven't a rex. What do charities want money for? It's a terrible waste. And it would be a treat to spite the old aunt. She made me miserable when I was a boy. I'd like to think of her squirming in Hell, or wherever she is. I can't think they were anxious to get her in either place. She would cast a gloom over a tinker's wedding."

"And have you said anything to Foster?"

"My fiancée has. But he wouldn't admit to anything. He threatened her with the police. Oh, he's tough. He won't be pushed about."

"Why didn't you set your lawyer on him?"

"I did; but he tells me I haven't a chance. It's Joan's word against Foster's; and when the Court hears that she is going to marry me and kept her mouth shut for ten years, I haven't a ghost, he says."

"Nobody else knows about it, I suppose."

"Joan swears that she showed the will to a clerk called Curran. But when my solicitor spoke to him he refused to admit anything. I suppose he's afraid to. I wonder if we could let him know there would be something in it for him. But that's tricky. He might tell Foster."

"Curran, did you say? I know Curran. Leave Curran to me. I might be able to do something. I won't promise."

"Are you serious? If you can help I won't forget you. I don't expect you to interest yourself in my business for nothing."

"I like you. But I'm not in business for my health. If I can get round Curran, I'll talk to you. We can come to an arrangement. I'm doing a bit of business with Curran at the moment. I'm seeing him at six as it happens. Would you like another spot of whiskey?"

"These are on me," Mr Haggard said.

"It's a small world," he remarked as he finished his third whiskey. Mr Woodhouse, not given to philosophy, left the observation in the air.

"I never got your name?"

"Haggard. My friends call me 'Sonny'."

It was not until he said 'Sonny' that Mr Woodhouse determined his age. He would never see forty again.

"Ernie Woodhouse. If you need me at any time, leave a message at Mooney's in Baggot Street. I don't want any business talked about at home. My wife has become very nosey lately. It's her age, I expect. They all get that way."

"Here's my card," said Sonny.

It had been printed when he represented a firm that sold paint, and the address was altered in ink.

Mr Woodhouse read it slowly and then transferred it to his pocket-book, seeming in the process to change the colour of the pasteboard from white to grey.

CHAPTER IX

BRIAN HEARD A timid knock and Curran's head came round the door.

"Oh, I'm sorry, Mr Fagan. I looked in about this contract for Woodhouse. He will be in at six to sign it, and to tell you the truth I'm scared. I smell trouble. It has all been too easy."

Brian looked through the contract. It was on a ready-made printed form with the minimum of special conditions. There was nothing in it to arouse apprehension. The price was amazingly low. It was, on its face value, a desirable document.

"I can't see anything to worry about."

"Woodhouse was on the telephone, complaining about the price, said I was too easily persuaded."

"You tell him there are at least three clients in the office who will take over the bargain if he hesitates. That ought to fix him."

"You don't know him. He will say it's no concern of his. He goes on as if he was the only client the office had. I never met such a man for putting one in the wrong. I wish Mr Stephen was still looking after him. He's driving me out of my mind."

"You mustn't let him. I wish you had seen the way Curtis used to treat his clients. They were in terror of him. You try that on Woodhouse. Tell him to take his business away."

"Can you see me doing that? Of course, Mr Stephen took no nonsense from him; but between our two selves I think he resented it; and he will never forgive Mr Stephen for passing him on to me. I wish I had seen the last of him."

Brian, in his new-found strength, felt capable of everything. "I'll talk to Mr Stephen. I don't suppose he understands the extent to which you've allowed the man to get under your skin."

"Would you really? I'd pray for you. I'd do anything to get shot of him. Anything."

But, as timid people so often discover, the reality did not justify the apprehension. Woodhouse was grinning, but neither humming nor whistling when he arrived. This was a favourable omen. He glanced at the contract. He never read one. It weakened his hand if, later, he had to take an action for negligence against his solicitor, a resource which he would never hesitate to avail of in the absence of compensation. He did not question the price—and seemed not to care when Curran pointed out that the greater part of the property had no access to the road. It was only when Curran mentioned the deposit that any of the good humour was dissipated. "I think the firm might at least put that up for me. It will only be for a month. You must have a lot of my money here as it is. Did you lodge anything yesterday?"

"I did. Every penny we had without even deducting what was due to us."

"They told me that in the bank."

Curran went white. He had very nearly forgotten to

make the lodgment. He might have lied and been caught out.

"I'll have to ask permission. Five thousand pounds is a lot of money to advance," he said flatly.

"I shouldn't have thought it was much for a firm like this. You are very busy these days, aren't you? Or so I have been given to understand."

Curran winced. This was a reference to the shifting of his own cases away from the senior partner.

"I'll see the old man myself. Is he in? I want to talk to him about a personal matter, nothing to do with business."

"I'll enquire."

Curran rang Stephen's secretary, aware that the message would not be well received, but longing to get rid of his visitor.

"Is Mr Stephen in? Would you tell him Mr Woodhouse wants to see him. A personal matter."

Curran looked up into his tormentor's face—Woodhouse never sat down—"He'll see you now."

"That's very good of him. I met a friend of his today, a nice class of a fellow. Haggard was the name. He was talking about this office. You used to do business for an aunt of his. Made her will, I gather."

He looked at Curran as he spoke, with his parrot eyes, grinning. But Curran had turned to a side table and was busy searching for something. He had not found it when Mr Woodhouse's grin disappeared behind the door. It surfaced without announcement—he never knocked on doors —in Stephen's office. Stephen saw the grin appear, but continued to read the letter he had been asked to sign. When he turned to greet his visitor he left a doubt whether he had in fact been aware of Mr Woodhouse's unheralded presence. But he was perfectly genial.

"How are all your affairs? I keep in touch. Curran tells me you have made a marvellous bargain. How do you manage it? Land can't be bought for love or money; and yet you pick it up virtually for nothing. Of course there is a difficulty about development. The contract makes that clear. There's no proper access to the road."

"I'll get over that."

"If anyone will, you will."

"I hear you've become grander than the President himself these days. I never expected to be allowed to see you."

"That sort of talk doesn't go down with me. I am sure Curran is looking after you properly. I had to ask him to take over your cases. They require constant attention; and I'm so placed at the moment that I just can't give that sort of work the time it takes if it's to be looked after properly. Of course, Curran knows I am here if he has a problem. I hope you understand. I've had to do the same with other clients. I must say they have all been wonderfully decent and understanding."

"Of course. Of course. Why not, to be sure."

Stephen understood silences. They did not embarrass him. Not even the one that now took place, which was, he knew, intended as a reproach. He knew Woodhouse must break it. He wanted something. It came out at last.

"Will you put up the deposit on this purchase? I'm at my limit in the bank."

"Very well. How much is it? I suppose the sale will be closed soon. It will be, if I know Curran. He's a beaver."

"About five thousand. And, by the way, I want to touch you for a prize. I'm organising a gymkhana for the Cruelty."

"Croolty? What is the croolty?"

"Animals. You know the act. I.S. something, they call themselves."

"I.S.P.C.A. That's very good of you. I didn't know you were interested in them. You used to dislike them, if I remember rightly. There was that trouble about the horse."

"They reported me to the Guards once. I had forgotten that. If I had remembered, I'd have told them where to put their gymkhana. But I said I'd organise one, for an old fellow called Bramwell. He has a place beside where Miss Haggard used to live. I believe you used to act for her."

Stephen did not return the sharp glance that followed; he was feeling in his pocket. "How much do you want?"

"Twenty pounds will do. It's for the old fellow's niece. She has a pony he gave her that's gone in the wind and is too big to compete in the regular competitions."

"A sort of consolation prize."

"You could say that; we must fake up something. Would a competition for winded ponies look all right?"

"Not under the auspices of the I.S.P.C.A."

"Let's say for ponies not qualified for the other competitions. I'll give the judge a few quid and let him in on the secret. You wouldn't come down would you and present the prize yourself? You are well known in those parts. You used to act for Miss Haggard, didn't you? Made her will, I'm thinking."

Stephen put back his cheque-book. "I give a subscription to the I.S.P.C.A. as it is. My friend, Mrs Preston, is on the committee. I don't really feel like giving this prize. I don't know the child; and I'll be doing the pony a kindness if I ensure it a rest."

"Please yourself."

Stephen's face remained, as usual, imperturbable. Mr Woodhouse changed his tone.

"I wanted to put myself right with the old pair. That

place of theirs will be worth getting when I have the other beside it. It will be a nice piece of business for this office. I could get a few hundred houses in there if the drainage will stand it."

"You don't let the grass grow under your feet, or anywhere else for long, for that matter. Well, it was nice of you to look in. I'll see a cheque for the deposit goes with the contract."

With anyone else Woodhouse would have stood his ground and refused to be shoved out. But he could never, he learnt long ago, 'get a rise out of the old fellow'. The best he could do on this occasion was to go without thanking him for the loan. It saved him bank interest for a month. Not a great deal. But every little helped. And the prize, now he came to think of it, was a daft idea. He'd slip the child a fiver; better than trying to bribe a judge. Mr Woodhouse never expected anyone to act except under threat or for a bribe. In his veins ran the blood of Vikings.

When he took himself off, Stephen rang for Curran.

"I had a visit from Woodhouse. He stuck us for the cheque for the deposit. He prefers that we should pay overdraft interest. Wise man. I gave him the bad habit when interest rates were low. You don't look well. What's the trouble?"

"It's the nerves. I'm all right really. Just the nerves."

"You need a holiday. When are you taking one?"

"I always go in September. I don't know why. We stay in Arklow. I don't know why. I'm always glad to get back."

"Why not take a fortnight at once? Go somewhere else for a change. Have you ever been abroad? Treat yourself to a decent holiday."

"Mrs Curran won't go abroad. She couldn't stand the food, she says. And she won't go by sea, and she'd be afraid to fly. I'll be all right. We've booked our room in Arklow."

"Are you doing too much? If you want help, you must tell me. There are two new assistants coming at the beginning of next month. One of them will take some of the weight off your shoulders. You wouldn't like to be deprived of the conveyancing, would you? You're such a dab at it."

"To tell you the truth: the only thing I dread is Woodhouse. I'd give up half my salary if I could get shot of him."

"Very well. I'll tell Mr Fagan to take over Woodhouse's work."

"But you know, Mr Stephen, it's you he wants. He doesn't like being handed from Billy to Jack. He's very proud in his way. I'm afraid of him. Could we not afford to tell him to take his business out of the office altogether?"

This was a desperate plunge. Curran was so alarmed when he made it that he leaned back in his chair to ward off the abuse he felt he deserved. Stephen remained very calm. He considered. He rubbed his chin with a forefinger. Curran knew the sign. He held his breath. Was it possible. Was deliverance at hand?

"Did he say anything to you about Miss Haggard," Stephen said at length. He continued to mime the act of shaving his chin and looked into the distance. Curran recognised that mannerism also. It meant that Mr Stephen was showing foresight.

"He did. He said something about meeting Miss Haggard's nephew. A regular no-good as far as I can remember."

"Did he say anything else?"

"He said we made Miss Haggard's will. I suppose the

nephew was complaining. The old lady cut him out, I seem to recall."

"He didn't mention the nephew to me."

"I suppose he thought you wouldn't be interested."

"He did refer to the will."

"It's no business of his."

"It certainly is not. I don't think we will shift Mr Woodhouse just at present. If he manages to buy the adjoining property—and I don't put it past him—we will be making leases galore for the next few years. We need the money, Curran. I can't drive business away at the same time that I am taking on so much extra staff. And you know the rent we have to pay for the new office?"

"I heard. We live in terrible times. I sometimes wonder what the future has to offer. I wish I had been born fifty years earlier."

"Then you'd be dead now. That wouldn't help you. Hang on. Don't let that fellow get you down. He's only trying to bully you to gain his own ends."

"Very well, Mr Stephen. Whatever you say."

At the door he turned to say something, but Stephen, speaking over his shoulder, anticipated him: "If he has anything to say about the Haggard will, tell me. Woodhouse could do mischief; we must keep an eye on him."

Mr Stephen always got his way—with everyone.

CHAPTER X

MRS PRESTON SAT up in bed in the bed-jacket she had admired one day with Stephen beside her outside Switzer's window. Her expression of pleasure had been as spontaneous as Stephen's reaching for his wallet. They were 'very close together' in so many ways, like a singer and her experienced accompanist.

"I shall die," she said, "if someone doesn't bring me my breakfast."

"Wait, woman. Can't you wait. I can't do a hundred things at once. No chance that one of those fat sons of yours will get his mother a cup of tea, I suppose."

Johnny was making his bed. He resented having to do it, but not as much as coming up at night to find it left undone. He made it every morning and kept Barbara waiting for her breakfast in consequence. Once or twice he had slipped out without bringing his wife up her tray and had returned to no dinner. Her defences were always one move ahead of his attempts to assert himself.

"You've no right to talk like that about the boys. Herbert was late at his grind last night and Leeson is not well lately. I think he ought to see Dr Mayne. Would you suggest it?"

No answer was forthcoming; she looked across the room to see why and saw her husband sitting on the bed laughing like an idiot.

"What's up with you? What do you find to laugh at?"

"It only occurred to me this moment, after all these years, that your sons are called after the parks of Dublin. Pity there wasn't a third— Phoenix. Phoenix Preston would have been a fine name, whether he was entitled to it or not."

"You will be laughing on the other side of your face one of these days when you hear that you have to support your wife. And you'll only have yourself to thank. Why did you bully me into worrying Stephen about his will at this time, when he has so much on his mind? I never saw him angry before."

Johnny stared. He was genuinely puzzled.

"Don't play the innocent. You said that someone had been jeering at you because Stephen had settled money on Henry's children. You told me to bring up the question or all the money would be gone. Well, I did, and he bit the nose off me. I think he felt I was doubting him. I felt so ashamed. And it was all your fault. You are constitutionally incapable of understanding a nature as noble as Stephen's."

"Hell and damnation. I'm not going to be preached at. I told you what Henry Foster said. You didn't need any encouragement. You should have seen yourself and Maggie Foster that day at lunch, spitting at one another across Stephen's table. A nice pair. She won that round. I'm off. I'll rouse whichever park is awake and tell him his mother is waiting for her breakfast."

"Don't think you are going to find dinner here when you come back this evening."

"I shan't be back."

"Where are you going?"

"To Milltown, if it's of any interest."

"Where you will drink and hear more gossip."

"Precisely."

"There's the telephone."

Johnny listened, then sighed. "I suppose I must answer it. I've no doubt who is the dogsbody round here."

He went out and came back to say that some Miss Joyce wanted to know if it would be all right if she called at five o'clock. Barbara bounced on the bed.

"I hope you said 'yes'."

"I did. I didn't want to have two journeys."

His wife wasn't listening. "I wonder why she is coming now. I laid myself out to be neighbourly when she arrived on the terrace and I must say she was as impudent as she could be. I suppose she didn't know who I was."

Johnny laughed. His laugh had been perfected by practice. It was finely orchestrated. It carried every shade of meaning by a nice variation of tone. It was the way in which he insulted his wife; his only means of fighting her, of getting his revenge. Words were messes that had to be cleaned up. A laugh left no trace. It said everything that needed to be said, and could not be produced afterwards in evidence. Johnny's laugh conveyed everything, except mirth.

"Would you please stop laughing and drop in on Mrs Dunne on your way to the library and ask her if she would oblige me by coming this afternoon instead of to-morrow. I don't want to have to answer the door to Miss Joyce on her first visit."

Outside the house Johnny laughed again. The Miss Joyce who had spoken to him on the telephone was not, by a long chalk, the daughter of the former Chief Justice in the Bahamas.

97

"Did she mention a time?" Barbara called out. But Johnny had disappeared. That was how he always left the house. It saved him from being loaded with errands or saying where he was going or undertaking when to return.

Stephen stood in the hall, and called out "I'm off" in his cheerful voice, and waited in case there was any farewell message. He was as solid as the door frame. Johnny was like the draught that blew under it.

Johnny had escaped without making her breakfast; but he would call at Mrs Dunne's. He was reliable on that sort of errand. It seemed to amuse him. She got out of bed with a rolling motion. It would be nice to have someone to run a bath for her. She would have to go into that uninviting room—she meant to do it up—and turn on a tap, and then go down to the kitchen, filthy with yesterday's leavings not put away, and make breakfast for Herbert and Leeson—poor boys with such a father or no father or whatever way you liked to consider their unnatural position—then the house to settle for Miss Joyce. If she called Stephen on the telephone, he would send flowers. He did so much. If only he would do a little more. She had hoped and hoped that he would say someday she was to come to the cottage. He had once intended to share it with the Henry Fosters. He told her that. But he gave up that idea when he met her. At first, with Johnny and no children, it was prudent not to make such an emphatic gesture. But now that pair of old servants were robbing Stephen, and he would enjoy the company of Herbert and Leeson. He put up with Johnny. Johnny was out all the time anyhow. It would suit everyone if they came to the cottage. But Stephen seemed to be dead against it. Perhaps, when the boys were off her hands...

Mrs Dunne came at two and hoovered the hall. Stephen,

rather abrupt on the telephone, sent a bunch of irises. She had hoped for roses. When the bell rang at half-past five, Barbara, on edge from the delay, found it hard to remain seated in the lounge while Mrs Dunne went to the door.

Barbara was proud of her lounge. It was modelled on the private one in a good hotel in West Cork she had stayed at with Stephen. Johnny always laughed when she referred to it. He was sneering, of course. Johnny was always trying to convey that he had taken a nose-dive socially when he married.

"This," he said to the parson when he called, "is what my wife calls her lounge." Then he laughed. The parson didn't know where to look. Naturally."

"Miss Joyce," said Mrs Dunne, at the door.

Barbara rose and advanced with her right hand stretched out. She dropped it when Mrs Dunne gave place to a woman in a cheap mackintosh, stubbing a cigarette on the cover of a cigarette packet.

"I was expecting someone else."

"I'm sorry. I couldn't explain on the telephone. It's very good of you to see me."

Barbara gesticulated with her fat arms, summoning the various pieces of furniture to support her. She could not conceal her disappointment.

"You don't remember me; but I remember you. I was Mr Foster's secretary. 'Mr Stephen', they used to call him in the office."

Barbara brought down her circling arms. Her vagueness vanished.

"Joyce. Joyce. I don't remember anyone of that name in the office."

"I was there for eighteen months, after Miss Parkes had her trouble."

"I remember Miss Parkes very well. She worked for Stephen—Mr Foster for many years. Then Miss Bradley came."

"Pardon. Miss Bradley was after my time. I left the law. It's dry, I found. I went into an advertising firm for a bit. Then I worked in London. But I didn't like it over there. A girl can't even sit down on a bench for a rest without some strange man coming up and making suggestions to her. I'm with film distributors here in Dublin. I don't like it much, but it's a job."

Barbara was not attending to the history of Miss Joyce's career, and had she possessed that ability would have received it with unconcealed irony; but her range was limited and did not run to nuance or the subtler shades of expression. When she felt anything her inclination was towards action rather than words. Miss Joyce now assumed a wholly different appearance. Barbara's inattention was not due to lack of interest. Rather the reverse. Where Stephen was concerned, and more particularly when women came into the picture, she was thrown at once into a defensive posture; a she-bear whose young is threatened was not more watchful or apprehensive.

"What can I do for you?"

There was no mistaking the expression accompanying the question. If she had been armed her finger was playing with the trigger.

"Well, it's like this—by the way, may I sit down? My legs are giving way under me. I had to stand all the way in the bus."

Barbara nodded. But it was a concession. She let Miss Joyce sit on the chair that gave least support, and enthroned herself in 'Stephen's chair'.

"It's about Mr Foster. I hate bothering you; but I know

how great a friend of his you are. And somebody must speak to him."

She stared pathetically at Barbara, asking to be let off too long a recital. Her hair had fallen round her face like a disintegrating piece of matting. A ladder in her stocking had grown since she sat down and now showed the way from knee to navel. Her fat thighs had a certain pathos as if born out of their time. She lit a cigarette. "Sorry, do you smoke? I should have asked you."

"I never interfere in Mr Foster's business. He is our oldest friend; but my husband and I make it a rule never to discuss business with him in any shape or form." She was going to invite the visitor to put her question to Johnny; when an alarm sounded in her brain. Suppose what this woman had to say gave Johnny a lever—how would he use it? Now, she wanted to hear, and to hear at once, before Johnny came in, what this Joyce person had to say.

"As you have come all this way perhaps you would tell me what it is you want me to hear, not that I can promise to do anything about it."

"It's hard to explain. You see I'm getting married to Sonny Haggard, whose aunt in Malahide, was a client of Mr Foster's. She cut him out of her will. It was only when I met Mr Haggard I remembered there had been something funny about the will—"

"Funny?"

"Yes. Not right. Mr Foster forgot to witness it, and when he discovered his mistake it was too late; so he had to put his name to it after Miss Haggard was dead. That's illegal."

Barbara fancied herself in the queenly pose which she now adopted.

"Miss Joyce, let me tell you one thing: Mr Foster is incapable of a wrong action. Whatever he did, I'm sure it was the right thing to do and was done with the best motives. I shall not sit here and listen to any insinuations to the contrary. Mr Foster's reputation is second to none."

"I know all that. He was very decent to me. I've nothing against Mr Foster. That's why I'm here. At the time I thought it was very sensible of him to put things right and avoid fuss and confusion. Besides it was what the old lady wanted. It is only since I met Sonny that I see it from his point of view. If Mr Foster made a mistake, that's Sonny's good luck. He shouldn't be done out of it. Not by nobody. The law says he is entitled to it."

"Whatever your fiancé is entitled to he'll get if he leaves himself in Mr Foster's hands."

"That's what I said. I thought he could explain to the charities—"

"I can't follow this. What charities?"

"Miss Haggard left everything to charity."

"I see. Why didn't you say so in the first place?"

"I didn't get a chance. Anyway I thought Mr Foster would tell them the story and get them to give back something to Sonny. He would be satisfied with half."

"I really can't go into this. I don't know why your fiancé doesn't call on Mr Foster. Why drag me into it? It has nothing to do with me."

"But can't you see—I called on Mr Foster. I explained it all. He wouldn't listen. And Mr Haggard isn't prepared to let go. He will stop at nothing he says. He's talking about the will to everyone he meets; and it doesn't do Mr Foster's reputation any good."

"I don't think anything *your* fiancé would say could hurt Mr Foster. You'll excuse me for putting it bluntly."

"He is going to bring him to court. As soon as he finds

102

a solicitor who will take the action for him. There's no time to lose."

Miss Joyce was not more attractive than her message, but she was obviously not a bad woman. She lacked guile. What her fiancé proposed to do she deplored; but she couldn't prevent it; and insofar as she had brought it on, she wanted a compromise that would not hurt anyone. The charities were the obvious solution. One didn't feel any pang for them. Everyone, Miss Joyce, assumed, was at one about that.

Barbara was thinking. She had always seen Stephen as a rock, a tower of strength—every cliché ever uttered to express invulnerability and solidity rang true for him. It was of his essence. She had always been alive to the possibility of peril to her relationship with him. No matter how often she repeated 'I have given him the best years of my life', she knew it would convince only a stranger, and an ingenuous stranger at that. Nobody so shrewd as Stephen had ever given so much for so little, and she had as much security as she could possibly expect. If 'anything happened' between them now, she stood to lose his company—a rationed commodity always—outings which nobody else would provide her with—holidays in hotels—and, in the heel of the hunt, a fat present in his will. It was a considerable stake; and she would not put it to risk. If she made a wrong decision, she might. From what she heard she had come to the conclusion that an insignificant couple were 'standing up for their rights', regardless of the inconvenience occasioned thereby to their betters. An instinct informed her that a sum down was the solution. She saw no ethical problem. It was a matter of business, unpleasant business, as business sometimes can be when one is trying to back out of a contract or retrace a too-hasty step.

Stephen would know what to do better than anyone; and nobody was going to get at Stephen through her.

She rose to her feet.

"I'm afraid I can do nothing for you. If you have anything to say, say it to Mr Foster. I don't think my husband would approve of this at all. I expect him home at any moment."

Joan rose wearily to her feet. She was an old ball that children kicked around and then discarded on a dump heap. She had no ill-will towards anyone. Life's play, so far as she was concerned, had always been at the other end of the field. The woman standing there, like an old-time film extra, had managed her life better. But luck hadn't made her kind; and she should have been. She had nothing to recommend her. Like the room, she lacked warmth or taste or distinction of any kind.

Sonny would never have proposed to Barbara, even at his lowest ebb. She was like a madam in a superior knocking-shop. Not that Joan had ever seen one; but there are a host of conceptions in the furniture of our minds that are based on nothing more substantial than guesses such as this.

She did not relieve her feelings by being rude. She shrugged her shoulders, and dragged herself out. She might have been inquiring for lost property with no strong hope of finding it there. And she had grown tired in the search.

CHAPTER XI

WHEN JOAN JOYCE left—Mrs Dunne, who had been attempting to listen, met her in the hall and let her out— Barbara sat in Stephen's chair, trying to imagine what he would advise her to do now. She had made a tactical error, ringing him up this morning and hinting that he should send her flowers. He responded. He always did. But he was quite curt on the telephone. She had hoped, by making a so natural call on him, to show that she had forgotten the unpleasant lunch; but it hadn't worked that way. It would have been wiser to let things settle and to have left the initiative with him.

The situation was urgent. But she was unaccustomed to thinking out a problem and coming to a solution. She acted instinctively in the ordinary business of life. When she wanted advice, she turned to Stephen. Of recent years most of their conversation was a sort of desultory consultation. And now she was faced with something she couldn't ask Stephen to solve. There was no one else. It was a terrible position to be in. Other women had husbands; she had Johnny. The idea of consulting Johnny was out of the question. But—she had hardly said this to herself than she thought again: her present position vis-à-vis Stephen was entirely Johnny's doing. He must realise that. More significantly, Johnny was concerned with the outcome. If Stephen's aid was withdrawn, Johnny stood to suffer. He was a broken reed to have to lean on, but he was intelligent in his irresponsible way. He despised her mind. He told her so soon after their marriage. He resented her being a shopkeeper's daughter. He thought no end of his academic attainments and his descent from a Cromwellian bishop. That was the meaning of his persistent laugh. It was to remind her that he might be undependable and impotent and incapable of keeping a secret or a penny piece and unable to hold his liquor— but he despised her for all that.

Nevertheless he was the only person who could help her now, if only by listening. The boys were too young. And, anyhow, they were kept in the dark about everything at home. There was too much that it was better they shouldn't know about. Once she began where was she to leave off?

She went to the telephone and rang up the library. Johnny kept strange hours, and was usually to be found on the premises before they opened or after they closed. He was never anywhere when he was wanted.

He sounded surly when the caretaker eventually dug him out; he disliked, more than anything, a call from home.

"Johnny, dear. I'm sorry about our tiff. I have a chop waiting for you."

"You may eat it yourself."

"Oh, Johnny!"

"What do you want? You know I don't like being rung up. What are you up to?"

"There's something I must tell you about. A woman called. She is threatening."

There was a pause. Johnny was examining what his mother called his conscience.

He decided to brazen it out. One comfort in life was that Barbara had forfeited the right to complain of infidelity. He swam in those treacherous seas in a permanent life-belt. Perhaps he had been too complacent. There were possibilities of trouble in every situation in which a woman was involved. He thought of ten pounds borrowed and not returned, a slanging match outside the Metropole cinema, the spree in Dunboyne when he was uncertain afterwards whether he had done the trick. A fog had descended on the evening. That woman came from Cork. Her husband was in the fish business. It had been the subject of a witticism.

"Johnny, are you there?"

"I am."

"I thought you had gone. I can't tell you over the telephone, but I must do something about S. Do you catch on? If he isn't safe, who is? I'm frightened."

Relief was Johnny's portion. If Stephen was involved, not he, if there was a chop at home, why sulk? Why spend money on a bad meal? And, for once, Barbara might have something to talk about as well as her stomach aches and the cost of things.

The idea of Stephen being in trouble worried him not at all. If he needed help he would turn to Stephen in perfect certainty of getting it; but Johnny did not feel for people or against them.

Out of the window of the bus he saw a dirty-looking youth carrying a bundle of placards on poles. DEFEND RIGHT OF FREE SPEECH AGAINST FASCISTS was written on the one that caught his eye. There were always people like that. He remembered them in his time. And before that. One derived comfort from reading history. Nothing was new. But it reminded you that turmoil and violence and slaughter were, on average, the norm. Peaceful streets, policemen on the beat, tea and tennis—they marked an abnormal interlude, the high holiday of the middle classes. In his day nobody asked questions if they were kicked downstairs or cared how hard they hit the street. But how did you protect yourself against these boys?

Johnny was conservative in his political opinions. He disliked puritans, and disapproved of permissiveness. Nowadays, when one was not bawling in your ears the other was rolling at your feet. Johnny was in favour of the old rule, to which he was a conspicuous exception.

Barbara met him in the hall, wearing her mysterious expression. She liked drama. He would have to endure an impromptu five-act tragedy to learn a few details that a sensible woman would reel off before she had finished her first cigarette.

"Is dinner ready?" was his first question. He wasn't particularly hungry, but he wanted to establish a proper order of priorities. She knew the tone, but for once overlooked it.

"In a jiffy. You'll have time to wash your hands."

That was masterly. Johnny was for ever reminding her of his superior antecedents, but an addiction to soap and water was not one of his inherited characteristics.

"And don't leave black marks on the towel," she called after him.

When she heard her own voice she decided to change her tune.

"You look nice," she said when he returned.

He gave his laugh.

She was not a bad cook, and there was nothing to complain about the dinner. Because of the presence of the boys, nothing was said by the parents. Leeson talked all the time, unlistened to, and unreproved. His presence at meals was one of the reasons Johnny liked to stay out as often as funds would allow. He could not stand Leeson; but he had no objection to Herbert, an esurient and self-contained boy.

"Wash up, boys," their mother said when the meal was over. Leeson groaned aloud. But Herbert, who in fact would do less, began to clear away.

"Good son," Barbara said.

Johnny followed her into the sitting-room. He noted the flowers. He disliked this room, Barbara's 'lounge'. It was a temple to everything he most disliked in his wife. Their bedroom, which was sparsely furnished, reflected the truth of their marriage. The sitting-room was what Barbara had got from Stephen and put her stamp on. The dining-room furniture came from his own home. It was, he considered, in its old excellence, a standing reproach to his misalliance.

"Don't," he wanted to say when Barbara put on again her cinematic manner, but he decided to sit back and hear her out. She kept on talking for an hour and nine minutes. He timed her. Sometimes his mind wandered. Had Stephen made a fool of himself with this woman whose name Barbara had not had the intelligence to remember? He often wondered about Stephen: had he confined himself to Barbara for these last twenty years? Was it conceivable? Really, considering how long he had known him, he knew next to nothing about him. Not even what happened between Stephen and his own wife, could not even be certain about the children. It was technically possible that both were his. Neither resembled Stephen or himself. Herbert was a facsimile of Barbara's father, the Rathmines milliner. Leeson had an absurd resemblance to the British Prime Minister, and none to his mother or either of his possible fathers.

What satisfaction had Stephen obtained for his money? Was the poor fellow lonely? Living in that house in Howth, perched on the hill, with that predatory pair in charge, wasn't most people's idea of fun. True, he loved the garden, and he did carpentry, and he was on good terms with his neighbours. But that seemed a small return on all he had put into life. He might as well have taken it easy. He only entertained relations or the friends from the past who turned up occasionally. On the servants' night off he went to the Evans's. He had a soft spot for her. It drove Barbara nearly mad when the two of them met.

Would she ever stop? He had built up over time a resistance to that voice, and switched off whenever it began, but its message reached him eventually as if relayed by his inner ear. When at last she shut up it began to percolate through.

If Stephen had done what sounded such an un-Stephenish thing he would pay anything to have it kept dark. That was the pith and marrow of the story. Haggard and the lady were after his blood. Having been regarded as a moral invalid for years, Johnny could not help enjoying the spectacle of Stephen caught with his exemplary trousers down.

"I'll talk to Henry," Johnny said suddenly. "The brothers are as thick as thieves. I'll leave it to him."

"But Stephen was furious with me yesterday when he heard that Henry had been talking about family matters to outsiders."

"Well it's tit for tat. He will now see the advantage of our hot line. But you will have to be ready when he tackles you. What are you going to say?"

"I'll manage Stephen," Barbara said. Stephen suffering;

Stephen in trouble: their relationship after twenty years would take a new turn. Now his 'secret' would bind them close.

"I might catch Henry alone if I went into the office in the morning. I don't like the idea of waylaying him at the golf club. It looks too casual," Johnny said.

Neither mentioned the matter to the other then or in the watches of the night. Barbara as always went to bed early with a book; Johnny fell asleep in his chair, woke in the early hours and found his wife asleep when he went upstairs. The arrangement of their beds was peculiar. Barbara slept in a double bed and Johnny on a divan in the corner. The arrangement was accidental and dictated originally by economy, but it told the history of their marriage.

In fact nobody could share a bed with Johnny. He jumped about like a fish at the bottom of a boat. But a prouder man would have insisted on a less symbolical disposition of the furniture. Johnny was not proud, neither was he physically lazy. He was a busy person, for ever immersed in futilities, and conscientious in whatever he undertook outside his duties.

He was up at seven, rather early to expect to find a Dublin solicitor of Henry's age in his office, but Johnny busied himself copying in an exquisite hand a quotation out of Shakespeare over which he had involved himself in a dispute. The solution lay at hand on the library shelves; but neither he nor his antagonist had any inclination to spoil the fun by such peremptory measures. It would be shooting the fox.

The argument arose when Johnny described himself as not only witty but the cause of wit in others. His colleague recognised Falstaff in this, pointed it out, and said the correct quotation was: the cause of wit in other men.

Johnny begged leave to differ—they were engaged at the time in compiling a catalogue now three years overdue at the printers. The argument went on so long that Johnny succeeded in shaking his adversary to the extent that he lost faith even in his attribution and doubted whether Falstaff had said the thing. It was Touchstone, he was beginning to remember. The rest of the passage was coming back to him. Johnny demurred. It was certainly Falstaff, somewhere in *King Henry IV*.

"You won't find him anywhere else," his colleague said crossly. He had lost his head, and when Johnny put him right on this, began to sulk, and said he didn't give a damn if it was Shylock, grasping—Johnny could see— even then at the possibility that this was a fresh inspiration. Now, up early to see Henry about Stephen, Johnny was writing in his copperplate hand:

The brain of this foolish-compounded clay, man, is not able to invent anything that tends to laughter, more than I invent or is invented on me: I am not only witty in myself, but the cause that wit is in other men. I do here walk before thee like a sow that hath overwhelmed all her litter but one.

It took time. He had to find the quotation. Then the pen failed. When he had everything in trim, it blotted at 'I do here walk', and as he was a perfectionist in a matter of this kind, Johnny had to begin all over again.

He looked with pleasure on his handiwork. Very few people of his acquaintance wrote such a perfect script. It was a sign of a buried self that he would never discover now, for which he would never get credit. He would like to show Stephen this example of his art and impress him with the true nature of the man he thought of as an insignificant item in the list of crosses he was doomed to carry.

Barbara discovered her husband at the kitchen table, hard at work—she had grown tired of waiting for him to appear with her breakfast.

"I was up at cock crow," he expostulated.

"Well it's after nine. What are you doing there? Shakespeare! Well, can you beat it? A crisis in your family, and you can only waste your time on nonsense!"

Johnny laughed, the laugh he had patented.

At ten o'clock precisely, in his funeral suit, he arrived at the Foster office to learn that Mr Henry was not expected in. He had a sore throat. It was, Johnny thought, typical of Henry. While he was standing in the hall deciding what to do, he felt a large hand on his shoulder.

"What brings you in here?"

"Hello, Stephen. I was looking for Henry."

"He won't be in. Can I do anything for you?"

"I didn't want to bother you. It was just something I wanted to tell Henry."

"Well, tell me. I'm going to see him this afternoon. I promised Maggie I'd leave her out some cuttings from my carnations. I pass the house. I suppose you are tempting him to neglect his business for the golf links."

Johnny always looked shifty; but there were fine shades of difference in his expression. Stephen knew them all. He had come to the rescue too often. Johnny knew something that he didn't want Stephen to know. *That* he read in Johnny's red-veined eyes.

"It's absurd to trouble you. I'll wait until he comes back. I might ring him up this evening. It's nothing."

Nobody had ever set store by a communication with Henry. He was the sort of man that people talk to about the news on the front page of the evening paper. Johnny knew that and Stephen knew that there should be nothing Johnny wanted to tell Henry which couldn't be sent by any messenger. There was some mystery, and Johnny had lost the right to keep his mysteries to himself. They cost too much.

"Come in," Stephen said. He had a presentiment. Barbara had annoyed him by revealing anxiety, greed and lack of confidence; she had also annoyed him with the knowledge that Henry couldn't keep his mouth shut. Henry had discussed Stephen's business with some friend of Johnny's. This visit was in some way connected with that. In what way, Stephen decided to find out. He sat in a chair beside Johnny and turned his massive head towards him and looked at him with his eyes that were kind and could, as Johnny knew, be formidable.

"Barbara tells me you have been talking to some friend in the library about my business. I was put out. Don't do it, old chap. Gossip is for old women. I don't like to have my affairs discussed by every Tom, Dick and Harry."

"I wish Barbara would learn to keep *her* mouth shut. Henry told Phil Deasy, a friend of mine—I see him every day—that you had settled money on his children. That's all. I told Barbara."

"Why?"

"You know how it is. Man and wife. One drops out what is said during the day; and whatever has to do with you is naturally of interest to her."

"Henry is to blame. I'm ashamed of him. Such an example. But I would have expected you to have more sense. I look after everyone I should look after; but I'm not going to be badgered. I am telling you that plump and plain. I do what I want to do with my own money."

"I don't know why you have to get at me, Stephen. I'm

not in your confidence."

"I'm very busy, Johnny. I don't want any more bother than I can help having. I want to know what it is you were going to tell Henry. I know it has something to do with me. And I'm not going to be discussed behind my back. By God, if I get any more trouble, I'll make some people jump. There's a limit to my patience."

Threatened, Johnny stung.

"If you want to know, some woman called Joyce has been bothering Barbara. She says you did something to a will that lost her fiancé a fortune. The man's name is Haggard. I remember the family. They lived somewhere on the north side."

Stephen's expression didn't change. His eyes never left Johnny's face. They showed no alarm, only a close scrutiny, warning Johnny to be accurate.

"Barbara didn't know what to do."

Johnny looked hopelessly round the room. The volumes in the cases gave him no comfort. This was the literature of Stephen's world, not his.

"She knew jolly well that she should have come to me. Why did she send you? And to Henry—dammit—that's the limit. To send you to Henry. What's got into you all? Why is everyone treating me like this? God knows I've carried the can pretty well until now. Is this business to be discussed first at Milltown golf club bar and then re-tailed to me? I have a good mind to— No. What's the use? You keep your mouth shut. Do you hear me? I'll talk to Henry if I think anyone should talk to Henry. Tell Barbara I want to see her in here at five o'clock. I'll send her home in a taxi. And if anyone else calls at your house on my business ring me up then and there. Leave Henry out of it. He has enough to attend to."

Johnny had often to acknowledge humiliations to

Stephen, who had always soothed him in the past, never taken advantage of his weakness or patronised him. This was the first occasion when the boot seemed to be on the other leg, yet it was Johnny who left with a metaphorical boot in his apologetic-looking backside.

He derived some satisfaction from his telephone conversation with Barbara—at the library's expense. "Stephen is in a rage. You are to go in at five o'clock to see him. Watch your step."

Barbara had asked innumerable questions, but he answered them all with the laugh he had perfected over the years. They were back to normal again, Barbara and himself. He would have liked to be a fly on the ceiling at five o'clock. It was time Barbara got her comeuppence.

But in fact the interview did not take place.

"It's no use trying to explain," Stephen told himself, and asked his secretary to ring up and cancel the appointment.

CHAPTER XII

CURRAN LEFT THE office at ten minutes to six. If he walked briskly he would be in the chapel of the Marist fathers in Leeson Street before the Angelus rang. Then he would call next door for a port and peppermint, a drink which he had discovered answered his pressing need.

As he proceeded along Kildare Street, a motor-car which had been parked near the corner cruised up to him and his hunted eye saw Mr Woodhouse's grin at the window.

"Can I give you a lift?"

Curran knew that instant what a coursed hare feels like.

"No. Thanks. I haven't far to go."

"You might as well jump in. It's going to rain."

The hare made its first circle to escape the descending jaws.

"I don't mind. I'm only going to the corner."

"Let me stand you a drink."

"Not now. Not today. I haven't time."

"Come on, now. I'll drive you wherever you have to go afterwards. You've had a long day."

The hare takes a second swerve.

"I never drink at this time of day. Mrs Curran is expecting me for my tea."

"By the time you get your bus, you will be able to throw back a few balls of malt. I'll have you home at your usual time."

The hare took its third turn.

"I have a call to make on the way."

"So much the better. My time is my own. My missus expects me when she sees me."

"Please don't put yourself out for me."

"Jump in, man. We are holding up the traffic."

Horns were sounding. There was a queue of cars in the street. "Drive on to hell and get out of their way" was what Curran wanted to say. Instead he found himself climbing in the door that Mr Woodhouse had already opened. He was in the jaws now.

"That's better," Mr Woodhouse said. "Where did you say you were bound for?"

"You might drop me at the top of Leeson Street beside the hospital."

"Someone sick belonging to you?"

"No. Thank God."

At the hospital, Mr Woodhouse said, "Don't hurry. I'll be here when you come out."

"I didn't want to go to the hospital."

"I thought you said—"

"I asked you to leave me at the corner."

"But what good would that be to you. You live out in Ranelagh."

"I get a bus here."

"But I'm driving you, man. You are going home in style."

"I wanted to slip into the chapel for a minute or two."

Why had he been ashamed to mention this? His religion was something he kept to himself in the office. The clients were mostly protestants. Theirs was the prevailing atmosphere. His port and peppermint and his prayers to the Blessed Virgin were his own business. He needed them. He didn't have to share them. They gave him strength to go on. And it was in them he found his only solace now since this cloud had descended on his life. He wanted to protect this private kingdom from Woodhouse. He threatened it.

Inside he couldn't pray. He saw women saying the stations of the cross; would he do likewise? The devotion took a long time. Woodhouse would get tired and drive away. He was tempted to, and to offer up the exercise for his intention, that somehow he would be saved from Woodhouse soon, before it was too late; he had come to personify every terror, every evil that life held. Here he could take sanctuary, here he was safe. He took his place in the queue at the first station. As he proceeded from one to another, tracing the footsteps towards Calvary, the nearer he got to the end, the harder he found it to concentrate. Two thousand years separated him from the Passion and Crucifixion of his Saviour, but less than fifty yards away Woodhouse might be waiting for him, and if he was then it meant a crucifixion for him, one he could not hope to make intelligible to anyone. It sounded irrational, the mere impact of a personality. Even Mr Stephen, who knew the man, couldn't understand. He prayed very slowly—an edifying example. When he had finished his prayers before the last station, he went back to the altar steps and kneeled down and uttered a simple prayer: "Please God, let him have gone away. Please God."

When he came out it was raining. The car had gone. He didn't need a port and peppermint now. He would go straight home. He went to the bus stop; the queue had diminished. But he didn't mind having to wait. He didn't mind the rain. He lifted up his face towards it; part of a cleansing that began when he had had the courage to pray. He had prayed; his prayer was answered; and he had forgotten in his blessed relief to thank God. How typical! Back he was going to go and offer up a special prayer of thanks. Then if she felt like it, when he got home, he would suggest the cinema to Mrs C. As a rule, the request came from her.

The chapel was not so full. People had to go home to tea, which in most houses was at six o'clock. He knelt down and prayed. He usually prayed to the mother of God as somehow more accessible than the deity, whom he found too remote and too vague in outline. But, after this signal act of mercy, and her successful intervention, he thought it only fitting to thank God in person. He found himself talking to Him on the altar. He never felt so close. His protection clothed him like armour when he walked back, down the aisle. The rain had stopped. He saw a bus coming round the corner of the Green. If he ran he would catch it.

"There you are," said a voice at his elbow. Mr Woodhouse was grinning into his face. "I was getting a packet of fags. I thought you had taken root in there. I was going to go in and dig you out if you hadn't come just then."

Curran stared and trembled. He could not even run away. He got in beside Woodhouse.

"If you don't mind my saying so, I never like to see a man running into chapels at all hours of the day. It doesn't look good somehow."

Curran made no reply. If he were in a church now he would stay until morning.

"I don't like bigotry. The women on our road are terribly bigoted. In and out of the chapel from morning till night. Upsets the wife. She's not used to it. She was brought up on the Bannside. Father had a nice little business in his time. Never gave credit."

Curran gave no directions but let himself be driven wherever the other pleased. Will had gone. Mr Woodhouse pulled up outside a public house in Donnybrook.

"We can get a jar here. Better than your chapels, I'm thinking." He winked. He was grinning.

"I am going into Hell," Curran told himself.

"What is yours?" Mr Woodhouse said.

"Whatever you are having."

"I'm taking whiskey."

"Port and peppermint, please."

"I don't know how you can drink that stuff," Mr Woodhouse said. Curran's hand was trembling. It was the first time that Mr Woodhouse realised where his weakness lay. Chapel-going and port and peppermint. It all fitted in. Merely a matter of time. No hurry. He had no small talk. And they drank in silence; Curran rather fast, as if it was a preliminary to escape, Mr Woodhouse slowly, as if it was a chain holding him fast.

"Have another."

"No. Thank you. I must be on my way. Mrs Curran—"

"The wife must have your number by now. Here. Boy. Another port and peppermint."

Curran tried very hard not to drink the second so fast as the first; but it was of no avail. Down it went. And Mr Woodhouse had scarcely begun. A third drink came. Then a fourth. He had lost any power to refuse. He felt giddy, but better; not in acute distress; in a dream now. Mr Woodhouse's face had lost its contours. It was floating and far away. His voice, too; that seemed to come from somewhere inside Curran's head. Everything was blessedly vague. And then an age passed. Mr Woodhouse was very close now, looking into his eyes, and the voice inside Curran was saying: "About the will, Miss Haggard's will. Foster forgot to sign it. That girl showed it to you. The will was no good. He put his name to it afterwards. That was wrong. Very wrong for a man in Foster's position. Didn't Curran think it was wrong?" *Say it was wrong. Say Foster's name was not on the will. Say it, and be done with it. Say it and escape from here. Say it and get back to Mrs Curran. Say it and go home.*

"It was none of my business. Mr Stephen knows best. There is no one like Mr Stephen. If he did put his name to it, what of it? Anyone can make a mistake. The best of us can make a mistake. And who was to know? Why had that girl to be talking about it? She did show it to me. I didn't see the signature. But it must have been there. It might have been. I didn't see it. The girl said it wasn't there. I saw the will afterwards. It was there. He might have put it on. Who was to blame him? Anyone can make a mistake."

Mr Woodhouse's face had been very close and one eye bored into Curran's brain. Now the face began to spread out, getting larger as it retreated. Like a toy balloon. It would burst. Mr Woodhouse's face would burst. But his grin came to the rescue. His grin tied it up. His grin became a band of iron round the balloon. And he was saying that if Curran didn't want another drink he thought he ought to be taking him home. Mrs Curran might be wondering where he was.

He had forgotten about time. Had they been in the pub for five minutes or five hours? It didn't matter. He was going home.

He was standing at his door. It was raining again. Raining cats and dogs and he was being sick. He was all alone in the street. He felt better when he had been sick. He wanted to hide somewhere. To hide and be left alone and asked no more questions. Never again. Never asked about tonight. Never asked to tell what had happened with Mr Woodhouse. He had said—what had he said? He wanted to find out. He wanted to see him once again just to say that nothing he said about Mr Stephen was true. To tell Mr Stephen's secrets to Mr Woodhouse. Not for anything in the whole wide world.

The whole wide world: Mr Curran turned back to the railings.

CHAPTER XIII

"Stephen was on the 'phone," Margaret Foster said. "He's dropping in. You had better put on a tie."

"I'll put on a tie if I feel like putting on a tie," Henry replied, but to the air. His wife had left him. She had gone upstairs to settle herself. Then she came down and settled the cushions in the drawing-room, and lit the fire although they did not have fires in summer. She was waiting for Stephen when he arrived.

As always he had something to give. Plants for the garden, expensive cigarettes. But he didn't kiss her on the forehead today. She missed that.

"How's Henry?" he said.

"He wanted to go back to the office; but I thought he should let his throat clear up completely. No sense in spreading it round the staff."

"He's in his den, I suppose. Don't worry. I'll find him."

There was something unpleasant in the air. Margaret knew when Stephen wanted to talk to Henry alone. She knew his every gesture. If she had married an equerry, it would have been much like this. Since Henry came home and said Stephen proposed to settle ten thousand pounds on each of the children she had lost the nagging feeling about him, the feeling that he was something of which she didn't get a fair share. But it was remarkable; although it was only a matter of days since the news about the money, the sense of pleasurable surprise had gone. Ten thousand each was much better than nothing. But did it mean that Stephen felt free to leave all the rest to the Preston woman? She might come in for a fortune. It was hardly fair. And those boys of hers, called after the Dublin parks—were they going to get what should have come to nephews and nieces? Were they Stephen's? Was that the tie? What a deep one he was. Had it been Henry everyone in Dublin would know every detail. And nobody would care.

She got tea ready. Pity about the bought cake. She liked to hear Stephen admire her cooking. But when he emerged from Henry's 'den'—a tiny room in which he hid—Stephen was in a hurry to be gone. He couldn't wait for tea. He was late as it was. Whatever she was to learn about his visit would have to come from Henry, who was communicative to every stranger but close with his wife, grudged her even gossip. It was his revenge. She was parsimonious with her favours; he denied her gossip. He had become more difficult of late. The changes in the office were upsetting him. It was an evil day for everyone in Foster & Foster when the Minister sent for Stephen.

Margaret took a cup of tea into Henry. He did respond to little gestures of that kind, she found. He liked her to wait on him. It satisfied a frustrated longing to be master somewhere. It explained his passionate devotion to his ill-favoured, ill-tempered Kerry Blue.

"Something was upsetting Stephen," she said.

"He's worried."

Henry was devoted to his brother, but he resented Margaret's attitude towards him and her open acknowledgement of Stephen's superiority to the man she married.

"Some relation of old Miss Haggard is raising questions about her will."

"I don't know anything about that. Who is—was—

Miss Haggard?"

"Just a client; but they are trying to say Stephen didn't witness her will. It's blackmail."

"Can't he prove it?"

"Yes. Of course. But he doesn't like the aspersion on the office. He's so much in the limelight. It wouldn't do."

"I'm afraid I don't understand."

Margaret did not bend her brains with a good grace towards any subject which bored her. She was a bad listener. Henry, when they first married, tried to discuss office problems with her; but he soon gave it up. She would cut right across his narration with an irrelevant remark or a question. She hated detailed answers. 'How much?' she would say, or 'When?' She wanted a reply in a word. If Stephen's trouble was some long office complication, she couldn't be bothered listening to it. Blackmail had an ugly sound. She thought at once of Barbara Preston and the two boys. If the wind blew tidings of all that, she would have been prepared to listen. But who could be bothered with Miss Haggard and her silly old will?

Stephen had told Henry about Johnny's visit. "I am not going to have Johnny discussing my business. Do you hear me, Henry? And I don't want the affairs of Foster & Foster brought up at the bar of Milltown Golf Club. What came over you to mention to anyone outside the family what I did for your children?"

"I only said how decent you had been. I didn't know it was a secret. Everyone is aware of what you have done for your family. It's part of your legend."

"I didn't know I had a legend."

"Of course you have. You're news. Not like the rest of us. When we get a legacy or win a round of golf, we want to tell someone about it, after the game. Why not?

I like people to know what a hell of a good brother you are. Can you blame me?"

"I must go. For Heaven's sake keep your mouth shut about this Haggard business. It wouldn't suit me at all if it were to be talked about at the moment. If this fellow got to know I'm vulnerable, he would stop at nothing. And I'm damned if I'm going to be mulcted of my savings by a common blackmailer. Do you remember the girl— Joyce? Stringy-looking. Reddish-haired. Whiney-voiced."

"I think I do. She left for some reason. You used to complain about her spelling."

"So I did. She got everyone's name wrong. It comes back to me. She nearly lost me a client over it. Funny how someone like that can slip completely out of mind. Perhaps one wants to forget them. I'm sure one of the psychiatric chaps would come up with a reason in exchange for a few harder-earned guineas."

Stephen left in better humour. Recalling Miss Joyce's bad spelling made her seem somehow less sinister—like a ghost speaking with a brogue. He straightened his shoulders before he stooped again to get through the door of the waiting taxi. With that gesture he placed the trouble from the Haggard's in perspective; his shoulders could take that burden on them as well. Now he had put the talk with Henry behind him. He was on his way home. He planned to spray his roses, having seen ominous signs of black spot. He hoped the Evans had escaped it. They were rivals in rose growing; but the roses mattered most; it would give him no satisfaction to hear they, too, had seen the blight in their garden. And they would sympathise with him. Last year they had their troubles; lack of frost the previous winter, someone said. Frost killed off rose pests, and should be endured cheerfully for that good reason.

CHAPTER XIV

HIS APPOINTMENT WITH Curtis was at a quarter past twelve; Sonny had time to slip in to the pub at the corner of Leeson Street and take a stiffener before he faced the solicitor. He liked to brace himself in this way before any encounter, and if a day were full of them, Sonny, at the end of the day, was noticeably the worse for wear. Joan had suggested that he should abstain on this occasion. A smell of whiskey off the breath at midday made a bad impression, she said. Sonny agreed. But habit was too strong; and as he downed the whiskey he thought sentimentally of Joan. She was a splendid companion. Slovenly in her person and round the house, but not irascible, not a barger. They would be happy if only he could raise the brass to keep a home and the luck to keep a job. Joan made about ten pounds a week; but that was not enough for both of them.

Once the Bramwell's property was in the bag, Ernie had promised to let Sonny Haggard have a newsagent and tobacconist's shop in the subsequent development scheme. These were the most sought-after of all shops— the chemist came next, general grocer third—and Sonny if he minded the business was safe for life.

Ernie was Sonny's America, his new found land; and Ernie's grin warmed his heart. A rough diamond, a tough customer—all these timeworn phrases fitted Ernie like a glove—but he was something more, not easy to put in words, sufficient to say—Sonny's last chance. In spite of his jauntiness, Sonny was not self-confident. He was dreading the interview with the solicitor; a ridiculous state of affairs when it was merely a matter of giving him instructions to act. But Curtis was a successful member of his profession, and, confronted by success, Sonny always became conscious of failure, and bluffed.

In the present instance he was led on by need of money; and Joan had not succeeded in assuring him that what he was doing was right. His aunt did not intend him to get her money. She took every step to prevent it; and in Stephen's place he would have done what Stephen did without hesitation. He had no moral objection. But fate had dealt him a card and he was going to play it. If Stephen was prepared to compromise or to get the charities to compromise, so was he. It would make him feel better. He was not tough; neither was Joan. She was unhappy about the whole business, inclined to natter about it. The sooner it was settled, the better for everyone.

He played with the idea of a second drink, a small one, a quick one, and felt in his pocket. Only two shillings there. No use. But he felt that he had won a moral victory and kept faith with Joan. It was a minute to a quarter past twelve.

He had to wait for a quarter of an hour before Mr Curtis could see him. Ready, with his gambit on his lips, he was discouraged by the delay; and when, eventually, told to go up to Mr Curtis's office on the next floor, he had forgotten how he intended to begin.

He knocked and a testy voice said 'Come in'. For a moment he thought he was back at school and was tempted to run away. In his nervousness he knocked again, as if hoping to educe a more encouraging welcome.

The irritated scream which it provoked put Sonny's

business out of his mind. He came in, embarrassed and guilty, as if to face a trial. At the end of a long room a pair of spectacles stared at him from behind a desk. He walked towards them, blinking in the sunlight.

"Will you sit down over there."

The chair to which Sonny was directed left him facing the light. His legal adviser remained in shadow. Afterwards Sonny had no recollection of anything except hair of the lavatory brush type, once fair, now grizzled, enormous spectacles, and a mouth like a rabbit-trap.

"I would first like to know who recommended me to you."

"Ernie Woodhouse."

"I don't know anyone of that name."

"He's a developer. Buys property for housing schemes. I'd have thought you had come across him."

"He is not a client of mine." Mr Curtis said this crossly and decisively. It was impossible to escape the implication that if he had been worthy of note he would have been.

"He's with Foster & Foster."

Mr Curtis made no reply.

"I don't think he's too happy there. He said I should give you my case. I think he has an idea of transferring his own business."

"Foster & Foster are an excellent firm. I know them well," Mr Curtis said.

Sonny tried again.

"They haven't been very lucky for my family. That's why I have come to see you. Stephen Foster made a mess of my aunt's will."

Mr Curtis sat very silent. Sonny was not quite coherent, but he was not interrupted. By degrees his nervousness subsided or, rather, took a new turn. He became confidential. He spoke of his approaching marriage. He mentioned the promise of a shop. He had never encountered such an attentive audience. He spoke for three quarters of an hour. Just as it had been difficult to begin, so forbidding was the solicitor's mien, he now found it impossible to stop. He was in full career, running downhill, in a car with no brakes. Powerless to brake, he might, at any moment, crash into a wall. Not only that; he had an inner terror of what would follow if he once drew breath. His narrative kept Mr Curtis at bay. Drop it, and he was at his mercy. And he had never in his life felt so frightened of anyone.

When he started to repeat himself, the solicitor cut him off abruptly.

"Mr Foster is a very old friend of mine and beyond reproach in his profession. I shall certainly not take any proceedings about the will unless I am sure that the witnesses bear out what you have told me. I must see Miss Joyce and Mr Curran, and I shall arrange a consultation with counsel at which you will have to see they are present. Before that I must ask you to leave twenty-five pounds with my cashier; and if I decide to take the case I shall ask for a thousand pounds on account of my costs before proceeding."

Sonny had not seen twenty-five pounds together at the same time for so long as he could remember; a thousand pounds was as remote as the summit of Everest, and less attainable. But he had taken Ernie's advice; he had come to the man who could take Stephen on. It had never occurred to him that anyone paid costs in advance. They were what lawyers took at the kill. Nor had Ernie mentioned the possibility of having to pay. In his case—but Sonny could not have been expected to know it—law costs were, like death, something that came to other people.

At the beginning of the first world war a recruiting poster showed the fierce and martial features of General, Lord Kitchener, pointing an accusing finger. Such was the aspect of Richard Curtis; and it proved too much for Sonny Haggard.

'I'll have to make arrangements. I'll write to you. Do I owe you anything now?"

The last was a desperate throw. In his pocket was only the two shillings which would not have been there had it been enough to buy the smallest measure of whiskey.

"That can wait," Mr Curtis said. He smiled—the gleam of the moon on the brass plate of a coffin—and was out of his chair, at the door, holding it open, taking leave of Sonny Haggard, who had forgotten he was the man's client. Sonny had lived through the experience of a prisoner in the dock.

But he went away impressed. The Kings of Ireland at one time used to have to pay tribute to the outrageous Vikings; they hated the obligation, but they must have respected the power that was able to exact from them a rent for their thrones. In a fight they would have preferred them as allies than enemies. And that was precisely how Sonny Haggard felt when he left the office of Richard Curtis, and exactly how Richard Curtis intended he should feel. He took no cheek from his clients. He inspired awe. But of his formidability there was no question. The problem now was to raise twenty-five pounds and to sound out the ground for a further thousand. The last seemed to make the prospect of a law action fanciful. But it did not occur to Sonny to try any other lawyer. He needed the strength of this man, and he pictured Stephen Foster confronted by those spectacles, like the headlamps of a pursuing motor car in a spooky film.

CHAPTER XV

"IF YOU CAN spare the time, come and lunch with me."

Brian was getting used to the formula. Whenever Stephen had something special to say he put his head round the door at precisely ten minutes to one.

"I am beginning to see something of high life since I decided to dedicate my life to the welfare of the race," Stephen said as they settled themselves in a comfortable corner of an expensive restaurant.

The waiter had recognised him and dropped his name.

"That's fame. Real fame. Next stage is to be able to address jockeys by their christian names. Already I do that to the Ministers of State. I'm coming on. Over there I see a Socialist deputy having champagne and oysters. Must I go that far to prove I am in favour of the era of the common man? It's a curious thought, that when I was solely involved in private enterprise I lunched off bread and cheese. But now!"

He was in high spirits and refused to be deflected into any office talk. However, when they came to coffee, the stage at which he usually glanced at his watch, he settled into his corner. He had something to say. Brian recognised the symptoms. He never made heavy weather or drama-

tised for the sake of effect. His method of lending significance to what he had to say was a lightning change of
manner and elaborate care in the choice of words. Nobody
was ever able to make the excuse that he hadn't understood Stephen's meaning.

"I wanted to mention Curran again. My great mistake.
You must pass on whatever you can to Miss Martin, who
is very capable, and take over Curran's work whenever
he has to meet the public. Get him back to his conveyancing. He's good at that. I'm afraid it means saddling
you with Woodhouse. But I shall make it worth your
while. I must consider how to deal with that gentleman.
He will pretend that the change-over is to his detriment.
And it may well be. He is probably pulling all the wool
he can over Curran's eyes."

"Why don't we get rid of him? Is any client worth the
trouble he gives?"

"I used to boast that I had never lost a client. But that
is not the reason we must put up with Woodhouse. Apart
from the fact that he brings in a few thousand a year to
the firm, I have my own reasons for wanting to keep an
eye on the gentleman in question. He was trying to get
a subscription from me, which I was quite willing to give,
but he saw fit to hint that he could make trouble for
me, so I withdrew the subscription. I wanted to show him
that nobody can intimidate me."

"But how could he, sir?"

"He has heard a story about a will I drew up for an
old Miss Haggard. A disappointed nephew is spreading a
rumour that there was something wrong with the execution of the will. Woodhouse has heard it; these are the
ladders by which he rises. I wouldn't put it past him to
try to exploit the situation. I've good reason to believe
that he owed his extraordinarily preferential terms in the

bank to once having caught the manager *in flagrante delicto* with his typist after banking hours. An illegal lodgment. The man is vile; and I would like to be rid of him. I should have shaken him off, but I rather enjoyed our relationship. He was forever putting up improper proposals to see if he could seduce me with the prospect of easy gains, and I resisted all his temptations. Had I once succumbed, he would have used the occasion as a source of moral blackmail. He stays with me because he knows he can trust me. And, therefore, he enjoys testing my steel. I can't tell you all the various propositions he has put up to me in the past; but I must warn you that he will try his tricks with you. His first question will be, what is your salary. And when you tell him, if you tell him, he will say it is inadequate and will undertake to supplement it. One of his suggestions to me, to give you an example of his methods, was that we should put five guineas on every bill for mapping fees, give the architect three and divide the balance. Afterwards he told me he had raised the architect's fees to five guineas, but I heard the young man complain that he had to hand two of them back.

"That's the sort of man we are dealing with. And I was very much at fault in leaving him in Curran's hands. Knowing Curran for years I felt perfectly safe; but I can see he is under strain, and I surmise that Woodhouse is persecuting him. And one final thing, if he mentions the will matter to you—"

"If he does, sir, he will get it from me on the nose."

"That would be foolish. Listen. Say nothing. Tell me. Tell me everything. Don't spare my blushes. I am particularly vulnerable at the moment, and Woodhouse knows that. If he is in touch with the nephew he may well be arranging to frighten me into a settlement of his claim.

Woodhouse would then levy a handsome commission. Oh, I know him!"

The prospect seemed to gladden Stephen's heart. He fairly glowed. The younger man found it hard to understand how a formidable and sordid threat could have so stimulating an effect.

"I never shirk a fight; if I never look for one. I'm a match for Mr Woodhouse. I've met better men. I could settle this business by drawing a cheque for twenty thousand pounds. That's what it amounts to. I can do it. It would not alter my way of living in the least. But I shan't. It would be defeat. It would be an admission of guilt. Woodhouse is not going to get any of my money. But what would a young man do if he were in my position? A young man with a wife and family to keep? I can see Woodhouse drive someone like that to suicide. One has to learn to be self-reliant, Brian. In our business one is sometimes faced with unpleasant decisions, and has to do things that one can never tell to anyone, not even one's own wife. And when you do those things—and you will have to do them sometimes in your life if you are the head of an office, if the ultimate responsibility is yours—don't confide in your office staff. They go elsewhere. And don't confide in your barristers. They may get on the Bench."

This was said as with utter trust out of deep experience; it left Brian flattered and puzzled.

"Can you give me an example of what you have in mind, sir?"

Stephen pursed his lips—a habit he had when he was considering. Then he looked at the ceiling for inspiration and gently pinched the end of his nose between thumb and forefinger.

"I can't at the moment think of an example. But you

will know what I mean when you meet one. Take my father—a conscientious, industrious solicitor—he was lost if he could not refer to the book. And what happened to him? He died at less than my age, leaving a widow and three sons, whom I, the eldest, had to support and educate. I don't complain. I accepted the challenge. It partly explains why I never married. But my father was incapable of giving the impression that anyone was safe in leaving his destiny in his keeping. He could tell you the law and consult barristers for you and keep cases up to date, but he never became what nowadays they call 'a father figure', someone you can always rely on, someone who is not afraid to play at being God."

"How-ya, Stephen?"

It was the Minister himself, dressed to kill, coming in to lunch with a Japanese. He winked and passed on.

"You see, Brian. This is what happens when I come here. I charge up these luncheons to advertising expenses. Don't forget I am a man with a Minister's ear. A public figure. What a nonsense it all is. And, my goodness, what a waste of money!"

He had glanced at the folded bill on the plate the waiter had laid on the table as if administering a caress.

CHAPTER XVI

"It was that man on the telephone," Mrs Bramwell said.

"What man?"

"Oh, you know. What other man could it be? Since we told him to come down whenever he liked he's practically taken root here. Now he wants to know if it would be all right if he brought someone with him this afternoon."

"We haven't to put up with it for very much longer, dear. Presumably he will have no excuse for haunting the premises after Sunday. You must give him credit for taking a load of trouble on himself over the gymkhana."

"To tell you the truth, Brereton, I wish we had never heard of the damn gymkhana. I never contemplated anything on this scale. It will be a regular Donnybrook Fair. I thought we would simply put up a few fences and have seats round them and refreshments in a marquee. I saw it as a manageable thing; but I never thought we were going to have the world and his wife tramping round the grounds. I hesitate even to think of the damage they will do. And it's goodbye to our flowers."

"Nonsense, dear. We can have the garden locked. My

only regret is that Julia doesn't seem to be getting any kick out of it. The idea was to put on an entertainment for her. Where is she, by the way?"

"Up in her room, as usual, reading one of her dirty books. I can't think how Marina allows her to read the sort of stuff she has in her trunk. I insisted that she shouldn't leave it lying round the place. We have enough trouble with Christine as it is. Fortunately they are not illustrated."

"You know, dear, part of the trouble is the pony. I think our Julia considers herself to have outgrown Trixie, and she feels that she won't be able to do herself credit on Sunday. But I really cannot afford to buy her a show pony. If George can't rise to it, I can't. If I could, I'd be hunting myself."

"I've no patience with the child. Trixie is a topping little pony. If Julia would get some weight down she would be exactly right for her. We have decided to put her in for the under fourteen two class. We can't be having our grand-daughter disqualified, in spite of Mr Woodhouse's promise to square the judge."

"That's a marvellous story. I told it to them in the club, I thought Charles would have apoplexy, he laughed so much."

Woodhouse arrived when the Bramwells were in the middle of lunch. He had an unerring faculty for disturbing them at their meals, and they wondered at what times he refreshed himself.

"Carries his own hay bag, I fancy," Brereton Bramwell said, and laughed immoderately.

He was, on this occasion, accompanied by an unimpressive individual whom he introduced as Sonny Haggard. Remembering the austere lady of unrelenting pride of ancestry, who used to live next door, the name—an unusual one—struck them both as surprising. But nobody in his right mind could connect this seedy specimen with their former neighbour.

Mr Haggard's excuse for being present was not explained. He confessed to not having had 'a bite since breakfast' and had to be fed. Surprisingly, he animated Julia, hitherto unresponsive. He was coming, he said, to see her jump on Sunday.

"You won't see anything," she said, looking sulphurous. "She's up against big ponies. Granny is afraid to let me jump her in her proper class."

"Now, that's unfair, Julia. You know there is always a doubt about her height, and I don't want to have her disqualified as she was at the Rathfarnham show."

"That was because she was standing on a slope. The vet confessed as much afterwards."

"We asked Colonel O'Flaherty about it."

"That old stick-in-the-mud. I'd have told him he could humph himself."

"She's a great kid." Sonny turned to her grandparents, nodding for emphasis. They ignored him.

"Anyhow, Trixie is gone in the wind," she added.

"Only *touched*, dear. We had all that out with Lady Coddingham. The Colonel was good enough to make enquiries, and he was assured that so long as she wasn't over-ridden she would be sound. Trixie," Mrs Bramwell turned to Sonny, "was going to be sent to England for the Queen's youngest. We wouldn't have had her if it hadn't been for this little flaw."

"Little flaw! She blows like a whale," Julia snorted.

"What a kid!"

Mrs Bramwell gave Sonny a look of supreme contempt,

but he assumed it was her normal expression and read no rebuke.

"I'd like to show Sonny round the place, Major," Mr Woodhouse said.

Mrs Bramwell caught her husband's eye. This, she decided, was the time at which to draw the line. What possible excuse had this blackguard to make so free; the full horror of the prospect of him as a neighbour dawned on her now. Brereton must put his foot down.

"Oh, do come, Mr Haggard," Julia said.

"Do you use these?" He produced a packet of cigarettes as he rose in answer to her invitation.

"Have one of mine," the child replied, groping in her skirt.

Under her auspices the two men withdrew. Mr Woodhouse grinning; Sonny paused on the threshold to wink at Major Bramwell. "You have a wonderful kid there," he assured him.

The trio left behind them a silence, as after some great convulsion of nature—a reverberating silence which Mrs Bramwell was the first to break. "Her mother all over again. Where does she get it from?"

"Ask me another. But Marina did all right in the end."

"Hm."

"Now, there's nothing wrong with George, as people go nowadays."

"I didn't say a word about George. What I do say is that the sooner the gymkhana is over the better. How did you ever agree to give a man like that the run of the house?"

"I? My dear! You told him to go ahead. The place is yours. I expressly told him to ask your permission."

"Don't waste time arguing about that. Do you realise he will soon be living next door; and how are we going to cure him of the habit of showing his friends over our grounds."

"Talking of friends, what did you make of that one?"

"You don't need me to tell you. Out of the question. I found it very hard to keep my temper when he assured me for the tenth time that I had a 'great kid there'. And what is he doing here? He hasn't anything to do with the gymkhana. Why is he being shown over our grounds?"

"I put that down to the other's not knowing his place. He acts as if we had adopted him."

"It's bad enough his not knowing his place. What worries me is how well he is getting to know ours. You don't think—"

"What?"

"We know nothing about him. He couldn't be *up to anything*, do you suppose? Consider for a moment: he bought Miss Haggard's place; he haunts ours. Now he is bringing shady-looking customers down to inspect the premises. Watson tried to develop Miss Haggard's property, and would have if we weren't in a position to prevent it. And it only now occurs to me: is there any significance in that man being called Haggard? Miss Haggard had a nephew who went to the bad. He would be about that sort of age. Suppose that pair were in collusion."

"My dear, you are letting your imagination run away with you. We are not concerned with Miss Haggard's place; we have our own. We know that it is impossible to develop that property without our permission. God bless whoever arranged that crazy pattern of fields, I say. We stopped Watson. We know we can stop anyone. And we have all our neighbours behind us. I'm sure the Castle doesn't want a colony of bungalows under its windows."

"Well, they are not suitable companions for Julia. I wish you had stopped her going out with them."

"That was your job, my dear. How could I have prevented her?"

"Oh, don't just stand there, Brereton. I have enough to put up with."

Out of doors, the men walked together with Julia tagging on behind. Mr Woodhouse explained the lie of the land to Sonny; and the latter took the keenest interest in the field in which the gymkhana was to be held. "I don't know how it ever got separated from our place. A family fight, I suppose."

Julia heard. She heard everything they said. Sonny gave her a cigarette. She was forbidden to smoke, and accepted it gratefully.

"That's where the road should be," Mr Woodhouse explained to Sonny, pointing out the track, which the passage of carts and cows through the year left clearly defined.

"I've decided to let the Council have the top fields for a graveyard," Mr Woodhouse continued. "If the old folk won't allow a road, they can't object to hearses so long as they keep to the right-of-way. It will make a lovely graveyard. And the Council is leppin' to get it."

"It will be depressing for the houses round," Sonny said. "I wouldn't like it myself, to be shaving in the morning and to have tombstones to greet you before you had properly faced the day."

"I'd rather build houses there, but what am I to do?"

Julia's curiosity could no longer be controlled. "Do you really mean to turn the sea fields into a cemetery, Mr Woodhouse? Granny will have your life when she hears about it."

"What's this, long ears?" Sonny said, but not crossly. "I can't stop the Council. I could if I had a plan to develop those fields, but that is out of the question so long as the old people refuse to give permission for a road. I'm sorry for them. I know they will take it hard." Mr Woodhouse stopped grinning for a moment as a mark of respect.

"Look at me," Sonny said. "Would you ever think that by rights I should be living over there"—the roof of Miss Haggard's house had come into view—"but my friend here has bought it. It's his. He can make a cemetery in the grounds. I can't stop him. And it should be mine. When you think of that, how little your granny has to complain of. An odd funeral going past will only remind her that we all end up in the same place. But I must admit the view of the graveyard from the drawing-room window will be depressing until they get used to it. They will. People get used to everything in time. I was at school at Portora. And look at me now."

Julia listened with an absorbed attention that was wholly flattering. When Sonny asked her to contemplate his degradation, she looked in Mr Woodhouse's direction. It was the only evidence, so far as she could make out, that Mr Haggard had fallen on evil days, except his clothes; they were cheap and shabby. Generally he seemed in need of repair: his hair was in rat tails; his teeth were as many coloured as Joseph's coat and full of gaps and broken edges. He had been faithful for too long to the same razor blade.

Mr Woodhouse changed the subject. He thought Sonny had had a more than sufficiently long innings. Now it was his turn.

"We want to fix Julia up for the gymkhana, Sonny. Do you know any of the judges?"

"It's no use," Julia said. "Everyone can see when you hit the fences."

"It never does any harm all the same to have the judge in your pocket," Mr Woodhouse said.

"Granny says you know nothing at all about gymkhanas or how they are run or anything. Colonel O'Flaherty will be in charge on Sunday. That's the worst of it. He knows Trixie was disqualified on account of her height at the Rathfarnham show; if he wasn't coming I could have taken a chance and put her against the smaller ponies."

"Put her in," Sonny said. "I'll have a word with whoever is measuring them. I know the jumping crowd pretty well. We can make sure she is standing on soft ground when the measuring takes place. Don't have her shod."

"Sonny knows his way round," Mr Woodhouse said.

"But Grandpa has sent in my entry."

"I'll look after that," Mr Woodhouse said. "The programme isn't printed yet."

"But what will I say when Trixie's name appears in the wrong class. Granny is frightfully strait-laced."

"Tell her it's my fault," Sonny said. "I don't think she has too high an opinion of me."

"It's touch-and-go. Trixie used to be eligible for the under 13·2 hands; but she was definitely over that at Rathfarnham. Ponies don't grow after ten years, do they? She was sold to us as under 13 hands. But the old bitch who owned her would have robbed her mother, I'm told. Granny was taken in by her title. If you have a title you can get away with murder, it seems to me."

"Ernie gets away with it and he hasn't a title," Sonny said, and broke into laughter. It ended up in a fit of coughing, no less violent.

Julia, fascinated by her company, looked at Mr Woodhouse to see how he had received this doubtful compliment. He was grinning, but, then, he was always grinning.

When they drew near her grandparents' house, Sonny

145

said, "It might be as well to keep that business of the cemetery to yourself until after the gymkhana."

"I was thinking that," Julia said.

At the back-door, through which they were re-entering the house, she gave a conspiratorial wink at the others. "May I tell *after* the gymkhana?"

"What do you say, Ernie?"

Sonny looked at his mentor.

"It won't matter then," he said.

"Let *me* tell her." Julia's face became almost pretty in anticipation. "I'm longing to see her face when she hears."

"You're a wonderful kid," Sonny said admiringly. Mr Woodhouse who seemed to have had something on his mind ever since they climbed the first gate, slapped her behind. It lifted her from the scullery into the kitchen.

CHAPTER XVII

"WE HAVE TO close the sale of the house in Ailesbury Road at four." Brian was going over the day's appointments with Curran. They found that they worked together splendidly as a team. Curran had at first been anxious at the prospect of so young a collaborator. It was hard after years of deference to men older than himself to be under the direction of a boy young enough to be his son. But it was the road of escape from Woodhouse, and worth whatever it cost.

"I have the cheque marked 'good' for the purchase money and our requisitions on title. We still lack replies to 10 and 18. The searches are being made this morning. I wonder if you would be good enough to go to Curtis's office and close it for me."

"I'll be glad to do that for you," Curran said. "Who's looking after the case in Curtis's office?"

"Delaney. The red-haired assistant with the cleft palate. I can never understand what he says, but he is formidable on paper."

"Oh, I know him. We have often done business together."

Curran's plan was to go early so as to make sure of not

running into Woodhouse should he call. He didn't mind having to wait if he was too early for the appointment with Mr Delaney. After the sale was closed—a very short ceremony if both sides had done their work properly—he would slip into the Marist church in Leeson Street for a few minutes. Then he might treat himself to a port and peppermint when the pub at the corner opened and be back in time to look after the post.

When he arrived in the Curtis office, ten minutes too soon, he was aware at once of an atmosphere of flurry. He had not personally encountered the proprietor of the business for many years—since his eminence had put him out of reach—but he saw him every other day in the street and wondered whether he was as absent-minded as he contrived to look (nothing in his successful career supported it); but Curtis never recognised and had probably forgotten him. Curran accepted this philosophically. He had no pretensions. Such men as Curtis were planets out of the ken of his kind. He asked only for a quiet life.

He had heard that Curtis was a martinet in his office. The serenity that Stephen Foster spread around him was unknown here where everyone lived in dread of the unapproachable chief. 'I wouldn't work here for anything,' Curran told himself.

At half-past four Mr Delaney had not yet appeared. Curran had no complaint. The longer he was kept legitimately away from his own office today the better. He dreaded to return and find his persecutor waiting for him, had even contemplated feigning illness and going home when he had completed the business here.

The girl on the telephone, whose activities had been engaging Curran's attention, dropped the rather cinema-style manner which was her wont and became like a frightened child.

"Yes, Mr Curtis. No, Mr Curtis. He hasn't come back from court yet. He hasn't sent a message. Someone is waiting here for him from Foster & Foster. Yes, Mr Curtis. I'll tell him right away."

Resuming her rôle, she called out to Curran. "Mr Curtis will see you. Sorry you've been kept waiting. You know his room. First front. Hello. Curtis & Co speaking. Who shall I say?"

Curran was forgotten on an incoming call. He set off to find the stairs, shivering now with nerves—if he had known he was going to have to deal with Curtis instead of his assistant he'd have fortified himself with a port and peppermint, and a prayer (if there were time to fit it in).

He knocked on the door marked PRIVATE, got no response, knocked again, waited, knocked, turned the handle gently, slowly opened the door, and found himself contemplating a water closet. He shut the door hurriedly and knocked on one facing it.

"Come in," shrieked a voice.

Curran almost fell in his effort to respond to its frantic tone.

This was a large room, lined with cupboards; at the end —a mile, it seemed—a pair of the largest spectacles he had ever seen glared at him.

"I've come to close the sale," Curran said.

"What sale?"

"Lindsay to Fitzpatrick, Ailesbury Road."

"Come over here."

He was put at a table at Curtis's elbow; it was covered with legal documents. The solicitor picked up one bundle and went through it with an air of fastidious distaste.

"Mr Delaney has been looking after this. My client wants to get the matter finished today. Are you satisfied with the replies to your requisitions?"

"I think there are only two outstanding. I've marked them on my copy," Curran held out a sheet of paper helpfully. Curtis did not take the offer, but he looked at the document.

"The first requisition is absurd. I'll give you my personal undertaking about the income tax."

Curran was an experienced conveyancer, something of a perfectionist—it was the only art to reach his life—and it hurt him to hear one of its refinements described as absurd.

"We haven't been given any evidence that Miss Holmes never married. If she had had a child, it would have altered the whole title."

"Miss Holmes was sixty when she inherited the property. That's stated here."

"All the same."

"Do you seriously require us to go to the trouble and expense of proving that a spinster of sixty didn't marry and didn't have a child. Do you?"

"Someone else may raise the question. Our client may be looking for a loan on the property."

"Well, I refuse to believe that anyone in his sane senses would require such a matter proved."

"I've met the same question in my time."

"I hope you refused to have your time wasted with it."

"I'm afraid I have no authority to waive any of the requisitions."

"I'll ring your employer up. I can't see Mr Foster making an issue of the point."

"It's in the bible."

"What's in the bible?"

"Women having children past the age of sixty."

Curtis took up the telephone. "Get me Foster & Foster. I want to speak to Mr Stephen Foster. Hurry."

Waiting for the call to come through, the men sat in silence, hostility moving like a real presence between them. Curran noticed that one toe-cap was coming away and needed stitching. Curtis employed the interval in a scrutiny of the papers. The telephone rang. Curran's heart jumped. Curtis picked the receiver up as if it was a revolver. Then he put his hand over it.

"What's your name?"

"Curran."

"I didn't catch it."

"Curran."

Curtis hesitated, then said into the telephone, "Don't disturb Mr Foster if he's busy. It really isn't necessary."

Then he replaced the receiver.

"Would you be satisfied with a declaration that Miss Holmes never married? I will make it."

"Certainly. It would tie the title up. That's all I want."

"Very well. I'll include that in my undertaking. I see that you owe a balance of £15,000 on the house."

Curran handed over the cheque. Curtis examined it carefully.

"Here are the deeds, the key, and the authority to close the search. I suppose you have examined it."

Curran nodded.

"I needn't have asked. It's a pleasure to see a case so competently handled. How is Mr Foster? I haven't seen him for some time. He has flown out of the reach of common attorneys like myself."

"Mr Stephen is very well. We see him in the office nearly every day."

"I thought he was always closeted with Cabinet Ministers."

"Not all the time. We couldn't carry on without Mr Stephen. This isn't my case. I am only doing it to oblige.

It's Mr Fagan's. He's a partner now."

"So I heard. As you are here, Mr Curran, there was a little matter that I wanted to mention to you, and we might as well dispose of it now. Have you got a few minutes to spare?"

Curran opened and shut his mouth without saying anything.

"Good. I've been instructed to act by a Mr Haggard in a rather embarrassing matter. I'd have refused to have any part in it had I not considered that if I had passed it up Mr Haggard would take it elsewhere; and it struck me as a matter that was best dealt with between friends. I understood from Mr Haggard that you saw his aunt's will after she had signed it and remarked that it was incomplete because there was only one signature by a witness."

Curran stood up. Curtis smiled. The sudden and unexpected charm was magnetic. Curran sat down.

"You were shown the will by a Miss Joan Joyce who is prepared to swear to the fact. She was the only witness to the will. Subsequently, and very naturally, you forgot the incident, but you recalled it lately and confirmed Miss Joyce's account in a conversation with Mr Ernest Woodhouse. He has made a statement to that effect. Miss Joyce and Mr Woodhouse are both prepared to swear. Now we come to the delicate part of the case—and this is why I decided not to allow the story to be carried to another lawyer's office. I have the highest regard for your employer. But if a breath of scandal were to affect him, it would reflect on the whole profession. Mr Foster must have seen the omission and rectified it. You and I can understand that he was prompted only by the best motives. He knew his client's wishes. She was dead. Through a slip, her wishes were going to be defeated; he did what seemed to him the prudent thing. Unfortunately there were witnesses. I have nothing but sympathy for Mr Foster. But we must face the reality of the situation. His original mistake put my client in possession of his aunt's estate; the rectification of the mistake deprived him of it. Fortunately the money is available. It is in the hands of three eminent charities for all of which, by a coincidence, your firm happens to act.

"I don't know how my client will feel about a settlement. He has been a poor man for ten years when he might have been comfortably off, if Mr Foster hadn't deemed it necessary to cover up his own mistake. But Mr Haggard seems to be a pleasant fellow—I have only the briefest acquaintance with him—and he would have been lucky to have inherited an estate which his aunt was evidently anxious to deprive him of. I don't despair, at this stage, of a compromise; but if we take out proceedings and brief barristers, they will advise my client that he is entitled to every penny with interest. What did you say?"

Again Curran had opened his mouth and again words had failed him. Now he was under the arc light of those spectacles. He had to say something. But he had not only this overpowering person to deal with: he was overwhelmed by the psychic ubiquity of Woodhouse. Woodhouse was outside the door, about to climb in the window, waiting in his car in the street. Those spectacles, trained on him, were binoculars through which Woodhouse stared. That sewing-machine voice, with its undertone of chronic disapproval, came from a ventriloquist's dummy. The real speaker was Woodhouse.

Curtis was aware of the effect he was making. He was accustomed to dominate and enforce his will. It was what he intended when he realised that fate had delivered an essential witness into his hands. That Curran was hardly aware of him at all, that his influence was vicarious never occurred to him. He was trying to frighten a haunted man, as well might a tiger enter the room after a ghost.

Curtis now came to the conclusion that he had gained his point. He explained that he expected to have a consultation with Counsel next week, after which the running of the case would be virtually out of his hands. He must settle with Stephen before then. If Curran would be good enough to act as go-between it would save the necessity of letters and telephone calls. Stephen was to hear that Curtis was ready to receive him and to hammer out an agreement in confidence and secrecy. Curtis was even prepared, if a message reached him, to call on the older man. There was no limit to his magnanimity. But if his good offices were refused he was not to be held responsible for the consequences. The reputation of the profession and the peace of mind of an old friend and colleague—these were all he had in mind. These were very precious to him.

Somehow Curran was wafted to the door, pulverised by a smile, and left alone on a landing behind a door that had closed on a room in which he heard a telephone ring and a voice reply with a scream.

He wanted to go back. He wanted to say that he had admitted nothing. But he couldn't gather the courage to knock. He couldn't endure the screech that would follow it, the scrutiny down the long room of those spectacles or that unfathomable face.

As when he had at last got to bed after the evening with Woodhouse, he sieved his brains to discover on how many counts he had failed his master. He tried to estimate the harm he had been forced to do him by these demons. There was no going back to the office now. He needed comfort; he needed compassion; he needed help; he needed strength. Port and peppermint in the pub or a prayer? He chose the latter.

The church was crowded for a week-day and the afternoon. A retreat was in progress, and an old priest in the pulpit was lecturing a congregation, mostly of women. Curran stood at the back of the church; his eyes on the altar; not hearing the sermon. Dumb, he wanted to ask God to help him or to take him away and drown him in the deepest sea. He could feel himself falling gratefully into the healing waters. The infinite peace of it! All evil washed away; his soul as white and spare as a bone. He had ceased to hope that God would raise him up and call his soul to Heaven and to glory. He prayed for a watery Hell, a Hell without fire or fear. He was tired of being alive and afraid.

The words of the priest, a distant susurrus at first, had begun to penetrate his unheeding ear.

"And of all these sins, I believe infidelity is the most shameful. *How sharper than a serpent's tooth it is to have a thankless child.* Shakespeare put those words in to the mouth of the old pagan king; but how appropriate they are to most of us in our relation to God, whose children we are. Infidelity is all around us; it is growing; it has become the fashion. If husbands are unfaithful to their wives, wives to their husbands, children to their parents, priests to their vows, bishops to their Pope, servants to their masters—is it surprising that men should be unfaithful to the God who sent his son to die for their sins on the Cross? St Peter betrayed Christ; and when he betrayed him the cock crowed and Peter was ashamed. If a cock were to crow every time men in the world betrayed Christ the din would be so terrible that we could not hear one another speak. We are not so fortunate as Peter. No cock crows to call our conscience home. Our hearts are all we can rely on, and hearts can die. A man can walk around the world for years after his heart is dead..."

Curran thought the priest was looking at him. He edged his way out of the church, almost imperceptibly. Outside he ran across the road, deaf to a yell from a motorist, regardless of traffic lights. But he went unscathed; and, out of breath, he pushed through the swing doors of the pub and was spared the necessity of making an order. At his appearance a hand went up to a bottle of port on the shelf, and he had hardly sunk into his favourite corner, when a familiar voice said 'the usual, sir'. All, it seemed, that remained to him now was port and peppermint. He had three inside him when he mustered the courage to go home.

CHAPTER XVIII

THE BED WAS not intended for more than one, but Sonny had acquired the art of accommodating himself to many situations in which no place had been provided for him. In the present one—they were lying on their backs, watching cigarette smoke curl towards the ceiling —nature made a larger claim for the woman. Sonny was as thin as a radish. In spite of the fact that he was stretched, fakir-like, along the iron frame of the bed, he breathed a greater content than his partner, who had slipped into the hollow of the worn mattress. Their relative contentment might have been observed from the way each smoked his cigarette. Sonny wafted the smoke clouds upwards as if he were giving a lasso its preliminary twirls; Joan sucked at the weed like a famine child at the breast.

"I can't get it out of my mind it's a sin," Joan said.

"You only spoil it for yourself," he reflected. "After all it's not your fault the permission has taken so long to come through. If you have done wrong—and, mind you, I don't consider you have, the world being what it is —I'd put the blame where it belongs, on the Vatican; it is responsible if we do take an occasional frisk before we are under starter's orders. You must do something about this bed, by the way; it's cutting the back off me."

"Move over."

She shifted, but it was only a temporary displacement. Inevitably she must roll back in. He stayed where he was. Sin, or no sin, Joan was not so easily satisfied as he was, and he preferred relative discomfort to excessive propinquity. His demands on life were few and trifling, but incessant; and urgent out of proportion to their nature. He acted always on the prompting of the moment. In the present instance, he had urged Joan, against the objections of her fluttering conscience (not for the first, or second, time) to assuage an appetite that in proof fell short of her own. What he wanted, really, was to get his way, being relatively indifferent as to what his way was. Having, as on this occasion, prevailed, he would have waived the object of contention. In the act he had aroused her. Now he wanted only to smoke, and her inability to disengage bored him. He never wanted anything to go on for long. There was a perverse streak in his nature. If Joan had said, 'Let's lie here peacefully and enjoy our cigarettes', he would probably have been seized by an uncontrollable impulse, although it was dusk, to go out and find the cause of the rattle in his car that he had endured for a week without comment.

"I only want you to put your arms round me," she had said.

He tired soon of that. From some cause unknown, it made his back itchy.

Neither said anything for the next few minutes; later she would reproach herself for having wasted their time together in hopeless yearning. He was so difficult, as a rule, to pin down, and there was so much she wanted to talk to him about. On less intimate occasions he brushed her confidences aside, and hummed or whistled when she tried to get him to talk seriously. Whenever she finished, after talking at any length, he never kept the topic going when his turn came, but changed the conversation at once, as if his thoughts had been waiting impatiently at the back of a queue. But she needed him; she had nobody; he was her man; she loved him.

For him she was the mother he lost when he was fifteen and the dog that died when he was ten. She loved him; he trusted her. He made no emotional demands. The nearest to ecstasy he had ever been was in a car; and in his dreams he rode in steeplechases or piloted areoplanes with dash and daring. Even now, he was thinking of himself in a plane, plummeting into a bank of cloud as, ten minutes before, he had been riding over Becher's Brook and coming to grief at the Canal Turn. He never listened and never read; all experience had been at first-hand.

"I have something I have got to tell you," she moaned at last.

"Yes," he said, looping the loop.

"You will be mad with me."

What she said, vaguely heard, pleased him. He was going to be given his order of release. He could relax. He took a deep pull at his cigarette and sent a cascade of clouds aloft. The plane nosedived.

"It's the reason I seemed mean when you—well ... anyway ... I went to confession on Saturday."

He watched a circle detach itself from the mass of cumulus and float on its own, wraith-like, towards the naked electric bulb. His silence whipped her on; but it had no significance. There was a perfect blank behind it. If she wanted to go to confession, she could spend her life at it, so far as he was concerned, so long as it was not made an excuse for thwarting any plans of his.

"Not because of us, really. Oh, I know it's wrong but, somehow, I believe God will forgive that. It's the other thing. It preys on my mind. I feel we are going to be punished for it in some awful way."

"Now, Joan!"

"I can't help it. I told the priest and he said it was wrong to betray my employer unless I did it for a higher motive. For justice's sake. Not to please you. I said I wanted to do what was right. And he—"

"It will be all over the town."

"I was in confession, dear."

"I don't care where you were. Do you think priests don't talk?"

"Of course they don't. Have you never heard of the seal of the confessional? A priest would die at the stake before he would disclose a sin confessed to him."

"What do you think they talk about when they are sitting over drinks? After all he can do it with an easy conscience. You don't give your name, do you?"

"You don't understand, Sonny. There is no use in trying to discuss it with you."

"You know my opinion. The whole business is a cod that's kept up for old women."

"I couldn't live without it. It's all I've got. Except you. But if anything happened to you—how could I go on living? I mean, if there was nothing else, it would be so awful. When you think of a life like mine—anyhow you can't shake my belief. Nobody can. And I want to do what's right. The priest said—"

"What did the priest say?"

She hated his sarcastic voice.

"He was very understanding. He said I must not involve my employer in disaster. We have no right to judge him. He trusted me, and as I had waited all these years it didn't look as if conscience had much to do with it. So I must be suspicious of my motives. I told him I had called on Mr Stephen—"

"Giving his name?"

"Of course not. He said that was right and he wanted to know what Mr Stephen said. I didn't like to say he was going to ring for the guards, so I said he refused to talk to me."

"Where exactly does that get us?"

"He said I mustn't give up. So I went—now don't be cross with me—I went to see Mrs Henry Foster. I called on her when I knew her husband would be in the office. I couldn't think of anyone else to talk to. The Preston woman had thrown me out. I remembered Mrs Henry. She used to come into the office, and it often struck me that she was rather smitten by Mr Stephen. She gave me that feel somehow. I thought a woman would understand my position. It was foolish to have gone to Mrs Preston in the first place. I saw that afterwards. She is not in a position to help. I was desperate. Oh, *say* something."

"Go on. I'm listening."

"At first she was very sticky, but she listened. Then she asked me how much money was involved. I told her the place sold for forty thousand, but you would be satisfied if the charities gave you back half. It seemed reasonable when I said it."

"And what did she say to that?"

"She almost gave me the impression that she knew about it all. I told her about calling on Mr Stephen, and I said Curtis was handling the case now, and he meant business, and she said, 'Mr Foster won't like that. Why are you telling me?' I tried to explain and at first she kept on repeating, 'It's just blackmail'."

Sonny sat up in bed. He had kept on his shirt. He

looked like a corpse.

"What were you up to, Joan? You are working against me. I've a damn good mind to tell Curtis to go for the whole lot, every penny. Foster can pay. Why shouldn't he?"

"I thought Mrs Foster might approach the charities and explain the position. Mr Stephen is too proud to. If I did they'd suspect me. They wouldn't listen. She did pay attention. The idea of Mr Stephen having to pay out twenty thousand pounds didn't appeal to her. I suppose she sees it coming out of her family's pocket eventually. Suddenly she changed; she seemed to drop her hostility to me, and I think I can guess why. She saw an opportunity to get herself into Mr Stephen's good graces. By the time we had finished she was quite friendly to me considering—"

"Considering you had given the show away. Of course she will tell old Foster, and he will be encouraged to stand out when he hears your heart isn't in the case. You ought bloody well to be ashamed of yourself. What's Woodhouse going to say? Unless he puts up a thousand the case can't go on. You didn't think of that. You didn't think he had promised me the newspaper and tobacconist shop on the new estate. You didn't think of that. I must say you have a wonderful notion of how a wife should behave to her husband. You sell him up the river at the bidding of a priest. No wonder I kept off R.C.'s. You should hear Ernie on them. He advised me not to marry you if you didn't promise to drop the whole bag of tricks. He said I'd never have a moment's peace or be able to call my soul my own. I'm beginning to think he's right."

Sonny got out of bed. It was symbolic. There was nothing else he could deprive her of. She watched in tears while he put on the socks she had mended, the worn underpants she had washed, the terylene tie she had bought him.

"I think she is going to help, Sonny. Honestly I do. If you can get your money without any publicity, isn't that what you want?"

He stood at the end of the bed, looking somehow elongated in the half-light.

"Don't meddle any more. Do you hear me. Don't meddle any more."

He was not really put out. So long as money came, he didn't care how the miracle was contrived. Until he met Joan there was nothing in sight for him. His luck stemmed from that; but now he was involved with Woodhouse. His prospects were more splendid. He did not want the end to be achieved by one of Joan's snivelling compromises.

His show of indignation was a mere pandering to a liking for drama. He left, slamming the door, although he wanted to borrow a pound, and he waited downstairs for a full five minutes before he came back for it. With what pathetic eagerness she pressed two on him. He felt sorry for her. At heart, he knew, she was all right.

CHAPTER XIX

THE DAY OF the gymkhana loomed ominously. It had been raining all night, and water was slopping off the eaves. Sparrows wetted their feet cheerfully in the pools on the gravel. Rain lay on the roofs of the marquees and the tents for the side-shows. Everyone was cross.

"I wish the weather would make up its mind," Brereton Bramwell said at breakfast. Twice during the morning the black clouds had folded their wings and torn across the sky only to return and blot out the feeble blue that had encamped in their absence. It had not been possible to decide on a cancellation while there was a possibility of anything less than a downpour all afternoon. Gymkhanas are attended by enthusiasts who do not regard their sport as a mere entertainment. There are money prizes and competition is keen. However, a neutral grey had taken over at one thirty; it had turned into a cold, dank, but not intractable day. The gymkhana would probably take place.

Mr Woodhouse and his friend Mr Haggard, supported by a 'woman in a dirty blouse' (Mrs Bramwell's description of Joan) arrived at noon; but they found themselves without any function to perform. From now on the proceedings were in the hands of officials of the horse-jumping association. There was strict protocol. Any idea of Mr Woodhouse as a presiding deity had gone to the wall. Mrs Bramwell was inclined to snub him. She had more courage than her husband; but Julia fastened on at once to the unwelcome trio, brought them indoors, found whiskey in the sideboard and a box of cigars.

"What a kid!" Sonny said.

He sat on the dining-room table, waving a cigar, with a nonchalance that his status in the household hardly justified. Joan stood uneasily as if poised for flight, fingering the beaker into which the child had poured sherry. Mr Woodhouse put the cigar she offered him into his pocket. He took his whiskey neat. He was grinning in the corner.

"You are terrific," Julia said to him. He had handed her the official programme in which she saw her pony entered for the class for which it had been recently disqualified.

"I think I know the vet who has to measure them," Sonny said.

"Then have a word with him," Mr Woodhouse said.

"Better not say a word to the grandparents. They are frightfully sticky," Julia warned.

Mr Woodhouse's busy little eyes travelled round the room; his grin confirmed the result of that inspection. 'So I can see,' he seemed to say.

"I'll have another spot of that," he said, taking up the decanter. "Here, Sonny, help yourself."

"I think we ought to be going," Joan broke in. She nudged Sonny, who had all the appearance, in contrast to her apologetic stance, of having taken root. She was the only one to notice that Julia had bridled at Mr Woodhouse's air of taking possession.

"What's biting you?" Sonny said to his fiancée. "Take a pew."

Ernie emboldened him; Joan drained his confidence. After all, he was a Haggard, and these should be his neighbours. As if to emphasise the fittingness of his being here, he flicked his cigar ash on the table. The alternative was to let it spill on his suit. Mrs Bramwell came in and saw him do it. For her, as she was frequently to say when describing the incident, it was the last straw.

"What the hell are you people doing in my dining-room?" she said.

Sonny slid off the table at once. Joan began to mouth apologies and made for the door. Only Mr Woodhouse's demeanour remained unchanged.

"The young lassie invited us," he said.

Mrs Bramwell, so far from being appeased, seemed to resent the explanation more than their presence.

She wanted to say 'Miss Julia, to you'; but as she suppressed this anachronistic utterance the recollection of the folly that had brought 'this poisonous crew' round her ears, the ever-increasing resentment at the man Woodhouse's familiarity, his impertinence in proposing the gymkhana on her property in aid of a charity with which he had no connection whatever and in which he manifestly took no interest—the mounting irritation of months, pent up, now burst its dam.

"Get out, the whole lot of you. Get out of my house."

"Oh Granny! I invited them," Julia said.

An unhappy intervention. It reminded her grandmother that the desire to please this unresponsive, ungrateful and unattractive child had been the deciding factor.

"You shut up, miss. And if you are going to appear this afternoon you had better polish those boots."

"I asked Christine to."

"It's no part of Christine's duties to keep your riding clothes in order."

"Come on," Joan said, plucking at Sonny's sleeve. He wanted to take a parting shot at 'the old bag', but words failed him. His presence here was owing to the influence of Ernie Woodhouse; and in this situation he looked to his leader. But Ernie was quietly finishing his whiskey. He did not seem in the least perturbed. He left the room grinning. The most studied sally could not in the circumstances have been more infuriating. His grin could only have been answered with a blow.

"Come back here, Julia."

The grandchild was trying to make her escape with her confederates. She paused reluctantly on the threshold.

"I forbid you to have anything more to do with those people. After today, if I see any of them here, I shall order them off the premises. Do you hear me?"

"But Mr Woodhouse is coming to live next door."

Mrs Bramwell had managed to hide this from herself behind more pressing grievances. Spoken, it was a knife thrust.

"He can live where he likes. He doesn't come in here."

"He's going to turn the top fields into a cemetery."

She chose this as her exit line; but her grandmother pursued her and caught her on the stairs.

"Would you kindly repeat what you said downstairs, miss."

"I said that Ernie is going to turn the top fields into a cemetery. You and grandad won't let anyone make a road into them, so he says he will sell the County Council the land for a cemetery."

"When did you hear this?"

"Oh, I don't suppose I was meant to hear. He was talking to Sonny."

"Who's Sonny?"

"Sonny Haggard that you bawled out just now. His

aunt used to own the house next door. It should be his by right."

"You don't know what you're talking about."

But Julia was more than satisfied by her grandmother's appearance of discomfiture. She looked old and broken when she left her on the stairs. Not that she hadn't thought it infernal cheek on Ernie's part to behave as he did. But at least there was some fun to be got out of Ernie and Sonny. If it hadn't been for them she would have had an even more boring time than usual with her grandparents.

Mrs Bramwell had come into the dining-room for a last look at the lunch preparations. She expected some of the dignitaries of the Society for the Prevention of Cruelty to Animals and also a few selected persons from the horse-jumping world. The most distinguished of these —the Duke of Wellington, as it were—to whom all disputes were ultimately referred and whom everyone feared and respected, was Colonel Flaherty O'Flaherty, a cavalry officer in the British Army at some period so remote that younger enthusiasts, better versed in horse lore than history, said he had taken part in the Charge of the Light Brigade. Outstanding in the hunting field, narrowly defeated in the Grand National, a Polo player of renown and a regular winner at the Dublin Horse Show competitions before the war, Colonel Flaherty O'Flaherty's attendance at the gymkhana raised it at once to a superior level. Mrs Bramwell had no anxiety about her other guests, but she shared the general awe of the Colonel. At his place at the table all the appointments must be flawless, and it was the thought of his critical eye on them that made her send Julia back to polish her boots. The Colonel was known to be a stickler in these matters.

As a result of the fuss over lunch preparations, Mrs

Bramwell had only time to mutter quickly to her husband that she had heard evil tidings. The idea of a graveyard at her door was, she knew, more devastating for her than for him. He would be quite happy in a neat bungalow somewhere near a golf-links. To her, she realised now, this house and its surroundings were the cord that bound her to life. Her husband and she were the crew of a ship, and if it sank she would go down with it. He would take to the rafts alone.

With such thoughts in her distracted mind, a total failure in the mayonnaise, which Christine had insisted on making, and Julia's appearance at the table with her hair not done, Mrs Bramwell was not geared to beguile Colonel Flaherty O'Flaherty. At the best of times she was not a charmer, suspecting charm in others; and she prided herself on downrightness. It was one of the reasons why her social inferiors mistook her for a Protestant.

The Colonel produced further consternation by announcing that he was 'off his oats' and asking for bread, cheese, and an apple. For this the Bramwells had taken their best silver out of the bank's vaults, not to mention the hours spent in polishing.

Like many martinets in their particular field, the Colonel was mild when off duty; if the theory that he had served in the Crimea rested on no firm foundation, he was a serving officer before 1914. Mrs Bramwell found herself telling him about the graveyard threat. He listened attentively. The view from his own house had been ruined, he said, by the erection of a terrace of Council houses. He was glad to think he would soon be dead.

The graveyard became the subject of general discussion; a local woman, the doctor's wife, suggested the preparation of a petition which the people in the neighbourhood could sign; but before doing anything Mrs Bramwell should see the Parish Priest. He would have a say in the matter.

"You dig with the same foot," she added. "That ought to help."

Mrs Bramwell looked doubtful.

"If this Woodhouse man is prepared to let his fields be used for such a purpose, I can only complain about the inconvenience of funerals and the melancholy character the graves will give the view. It terribly weakens my case. What a ruffian!"

"Nobody wants a graveyard in his backyard," the Colonel said. "I'll have a little more of the Cheddar, if I may." He had tired of the subject. It rested with him to pronounce whether the weather conditions justified the cancellation of the gymkhana. He stepped out after lunch, smelled the air, and declared that there was no reason why the proceedings should not go on.

"After dragging myself down all this way," he added to himself; and Julia, who took a morbid interest in the behaviour of her elders and betters, and kept close to pick up what crumbs were going, overheard him. It was something else to tell Granny.

Realising that there were going to be words with her grandmother about her hair, not to speak of the controversy when it was realised that she was taking part in the event for which her pony had been recently pronounced unqualified, she tactfully disappeared and, when searched for, could not be found.

She had joined the Woodhouse party in the rain-sodden refreshment tent, where they were drinking beer and eating sandwiches in which the beef had a conscripted appearance.

Julia was anxious to conciliate them, and afraid that they would include her in any indignation they might be feeling towards her grandmother. However, her appearance was hailed as if there had been no set-back in community relations.

"Have a beer," said Sonny.

"I wouldn't mind a coke," Julia replied. She had an abnormal passion for that beverage to which her pocket-money couldn't reach.

Sonny ordered the coke; Joan handed it to Julia; Mr Woodhouse paid for it.

"What's the news? How's the quality getting on?" Woodhouse enquired.

"They were talking about the graveyard at lunch. Granny is frantic, and she is going to ask Father MacNamara to stop it. That's what she was advised to do; but she says your agreeing to it terribly weakens her case. She is mad at the idea. I don't blame her. I wouldn't like to have funerals passing our house all day long."

"Have another coke," Mr Woodhouse said. He went to fetch it himself.

"I suppose Father MacNamara will be with us this afternoon," he said to the young man behind the bar.

"I daresay he will. His reverence likes a bit of diversion," he added.

On Mr Woodhouse's return to the group, he insisted that they should concentrate on Julia's fortunes. Her competition was early on the card. She would have to take her pony in for measurement, what was to be done about it? Sonny blushed. He had boasted of acquaintances who were influential, but now that it came to the point he saw through his own too sanguine hopes. He was a hanger-on in so many circles that he found himself prone to exaggerate the strength of the tie that bound him to people who were vaguely familiar with his appearance, ignorant of his name, and unaware of his business. Even those who exchanged 'Hello, Sonny' for his own peculiar head jerk and greeting by Christian name were not so easy to approach when it came to asking them for something. In fact they tended to draw back, as if recognising for the first time that Sonny was a potential nuisance and regretted those passing exchanges of good-will.

"I thought you said you knew the vet," Mr Woodhouse said. "I have my cheque-book here."

"If its Des Magill, we are all right," Sonny said, mentioning a veterinary surgeon who practised in a remote part of Ireland and whom he had met six years before in the bar at the Curragh.

"We haven't much time," Julia said.

Sonny, miserably aware that this was one occasion when he was being asked to subscribe 'know how' to the partnership, said he would go out and reconnoitre. Joan went with him; though it occurred to her that the Bramwells would not be pleased if they heard their granddaughter was in the refreshment tent with Mr Woodhouse. But the possibility of yet another coke made the child reluctant to move.

"Trixie is in her stable. I don't want to bring her out into this muck until I have to," she explained.

Other competitors had been arriving for some time and were taking their mounts out of horse boxes.

Sonny looked round him vaguely. "I suppose there is an official tent," Joan suggested, anxious to be helpful.

"What the hell am I to do? I can't go up to some fellow and say 'how much will you take to let this pony through?' If Ernie thinks he can bribe his way here, he ought to do it himself."

"But you said—"

"I don't want to hear what I said. After the way that woman turned on us I don't know why we should bother our heads about the child. Who cares if she is disqualified?"

"It's not the child's fault, Sonny."

"Oh, shut up."

At that moment a face hove into view that Sonny recognised without being able to place, but he connected it with his gambling excursions and he jerked his head at it hopefully. The salute was returned. The man actually stopped.

"Have you a light?" he said.

Sonny fumbled in his pocket and produced a packet of cigarettes.

"Here, take one of mine."

The offer was accepted.

"This is my fiancée," Sonny said.

"Pleased to meet you."

He was, she saw, such another as Sonny, flashily shabby, brittle, without lining or foundation. A temporary structure.

"Any interest yourself in the programme?" Sonny asked.

"I just came down. Nothing else to do on Sunday. Bloody awful day."

"We have a pony in the first event."

"I didn't know you went in for this business."

Sonny opened his rain-sodden programme and pointed to an entry. The stranger obediently read: *Trixie. Miss Julia Briggs. Ridden by Owner.*

Sonny put the programme back in his pocket with the air of a smuggler who has made a successful passage through a douane. Joan, anxiously observing, saw the man's eyes travel from one to the other trying to understand. He had no idea of Sonny's identity and had been glad to think the programme would supply it.

"A nice class of pony. We got it in Kilkenny; but there

is some trouble about her height. It wasn't questioned until recently," Sonny said.

"May have grown. They do sometimes."

"I don't think so. It was a mistake on the judge's part."

"Try and get them to measure the pony out on the grass. On a day like today if you could manage to lean on her back, she would sink half an inch."

"You don't happen to know the vet, do you?"

"I might. I'll go up to the tent and see. Wait here for a moment."

"Nice fellow. I thought he could help," Sonny said, after the stranger had disappeared. He had to keep his end up, even with Joan. She said a little prayer. The happenings of the day had depressed her. She had always been hard up; but she had never known moral squalor until she met Sonny. His troubles, she had regarded as circumstantial. But the day with his benefactor, Mr Woodhouse, had begun to fill her with a new fear for the future. She had been mortified by the expulsion from the Bramwell's house. The others had treated the incident as if it were a fracas in a pub. And now she saw her fiancé asking favours from strangers. She had always had her pride. She paid her way. She didn't go where she wasn't wanted. But ever since she fell in with Sonny she had been doing things which were shameful as well as sinful. Somehow today was the most degrading of all.

The stranger returned. An objection to Trixie had already been lodged by a Mrs Escott, whose daughter was competing. He had had a word with 'your man', and everything possible would be done to defeat Mrs Escott, notorious for tirelessly campaigning on behalf of her brood.

Sonny thanked the stranger.

"For nothing," he said. "See you later."

"There are always fellows like that going round," Sonny explained, as they made their way across the muddy field. "They'd do you a good turn in the hope that you would do them a good turn. I might meet him at a race meeting when I had a winner. If I did, I'd give him the tip."

As relieved as if he had already discharged his obligation, Sonny went back to tell Mr Woodhouse the news. He turned to Julia.

"Who is the old fellow in charge? Tell him to get the measuring done at the bottom of the field. Say your granny insists. They are ruining her bulbs where they are."

Julia found Colonel Flaherty O'Flaherty confronting Mrs Escott in full spate. He was looking uncomfortable.

"Damned awkward when they have been good enough to get the show up," he was saying.

"They ought to know better," Mrs Escott said. "Why did they let the child enter the pony in the first place? I know my Margaret is competing. But I'm not thinking of her. It's the principle of the thing. What do you want, Julia?"

"Granny says the ponies are to be measured at the bottom of the field."

"I never heard such nonsense," Mrs Escott said.

But the Colonel was pleased to put her down.

"I think we ought to do what Mrs Bramwell asked us to do. It's a reasonable request. Go and tell the fellow who is using the loudspeaker that entries for all competitions are to go to the bottom of the field to be measured."

"There has been a mistake," Mrs Bramwell at that moment was saying to her husband. "Some damn fool has put Julia's pony into the wrong competition. What are we going to do now?"

"I'll go and see the Colonel."

He found the Colonel surrounded by angry officials.

Why, at the eleventh hour, had they to move their head-quarters. The bottom of the field was water-logged, was it a joke?

"Excuse me Colonel. Just a moment. There has been a mistake," Major Bramwell said.

"Ah, I thought so," said Mrs Escott, astonished at the source from which it appeared she was receiving support.

The Colonel began to snort.

"I can't talk to a hundred people at once. Look here, Bramwell, does your wife absolutely insist on the judges moving their tent at this stage of the proceedings?"

Since the Colonel put it that way, and Bramwell couldn't understand what he was talking about, he answered at once in the most conciliatory way: "Of course not. Do whatever you like. She will be delighted. The end of the field is a quagmire."

"Leave everything where it is," the Colonel barked.

All the trouble had been for nothing. Trixie was found to be of the right height; and after the effort to get her into the competition her elimination at the first jump—she disliked the pool at the take-off—was something of an anti-climax. It was watched by Sonny and Joan. Mr Wood-house was not to be seen. He had made a tour of the ground and stopped every cleric he met on his rounds until he encountered Father Macnamara, with whom he begged a word in private.

Huddled together in the corner of a tent assigned to grooms for the storage of buckets, he presented the startled priest with a cheque for a hundred pounds for the church building fund. He had seen the appeal, he said. He also let his reverence know that he was prepared to sacrifice his valuable building land for the purpose of a cemetery. "I hear one is needed, and I would like to do something for the people round here. Not that I have received much thanks for organising this gymkhana for the Cruelty," he added.

His behaviour was eccentric; but the priest had learned to judge men by their fruits. The cheque looked good.

"I thought the Bramwells ... I see ... I didn't understand. And did I hear you say you had bought Miss Haggard's old place. Yes. Yes. Of course. I think we should be moving. The rain is coming through the roof in here. I mustn't lose this cheque. A pleasant surprise. I'm very glad to meet you, Mr Woodhouse."

In fact he was somewhat taken aback at having to talk shop when he had escaped for an hour or two from parish duties; but a contribution is a contribution even if it is given at an inappropriate moment and in an unlikely setting. And the news about the cemetery was a miracle. It had proven very difficult to arrange for a site in the neighbourhood. Otherwise Father Macnamara hadn't taken very kindly to Mr Woodhouse. There was *something* about him—his grin, perhaps—that was disquieting. And he couldn't make head or tail of his reference to the gymkhana. Why was he giving it on the Bramwell's ground? Why not on his own?

Mrs Bramwell retired to bed in the course of the afternoon. The gardener reported that a stone had been thrown through the roof of the conservatory. Colonel Flaherty O'Flaherty had gone away in a temper after a vile-looking individual had offered him a ten pound note if he would allow Julia to jump again. The man was not drunk but clearly mad, and grinned like an ape. It was the last straw. A disastrous afternoon.

A disastrous afternoon; but not for Mr Woodhouse. Joan and Sonny, wet and depressed, huddled in the back of the Mercedes, while he talked over his shoulder to them. He had enjoyed everything: the rage of the 'old one' when she saw Sonny sitting on her dining-room table: the rage of the 'army character' when he offered him the ten pound note; the face of the 'greedy priest' when he gave him a cheque for a hundred—it had been a rich experience.

"And your shop is in the bag, Sonny," he said.

Sonny could not respond. He was damp in soul as well as body.

"I don't see what use a newsagent and tobacconist can be beside a cemetery, to be candid with you."

Mr Woodhouse laughed. It was meant for mirth; but he lacked the faculty of amusing.

"Cemetery? Who is talking about a cemetery? There won't be a cemetery there. I was told by a fellow in the Council that if I offered the land for a cemetery and old Bramwell objected, as he's bound to, the Council would buy it off me for houses and take over part of Bramwell's place to make an entrance. They have been longing to for years; but thought it would be locally unpopular. They are delighted with me. I've brought something new to the neighbourhood—a spirit of progress, they call it. I'd say it was just common sense. I've arranged to sell a site in front for a petrol station, did I tell you? It was a great day for Ireland when I came to Malahide to organise a gymkhana for the Cruelty."

Joan, timidly, took Sonny's hand. A current runs between the palms of lovers, she remembered from long ago. Or was her memory deceiving her? It was so long ago.

CHAPTER XX

MARGARET FOSTER, AFTER thirty years, was still curious to know *exactly* what her brother-in-law thought of her. She had never abandoned the theory—and confided it in friends and strangers, in the appropriate setting—that the tragedy in both their lives, recognised by Stephen, when it was too late, was that she had married the wrong brother. It explained why he remained a bachelor. And then the 'Preston woman' came along—how easily even the cleverest of men are taken in!—and Stephen was made captive—to all appearances a willing captive; but Margaret—apart from her 'deep insight'—knew Stephen and had watched him when her own tragedy was beginning to unfold. He had been stoical past belief; even when they were alone together he never hinted at the inner state of their feelings but—maddeningly at times—kept conversation on the most prosaic level. Whatever he might be suffering under Barbara's yoke, Stephen being Stephen, the world would never know. For a nature so romantic as Margaret's it was a tragedy in itself to have to live in alliance with Henry. Henry was as near to nothing as a man could well be. Whenever he said, 'I'll have a go at the grass with the mower this afternoon,' she was reminded of his approach to what she had once long ago seen beautifully described in an old novel as 'the sacred mysteries'.

Not that she was passionate. Fortunately for Henry. There had been flirtations—once or twice they threatened to become serious—but she had married Henry with her eyes open. There were certain substantial advantages. It was a tragic pity that in connecting herself with the Fosters her fate had been to attach herself to the junior partner.

She dressed with special care for her lunch with Stephen. She had thought it better not to invite him to come to see her at home; and in the office the interview would be conducted on certain lines. Stephen was economical of his time.

She had given great thought to this meeting; it was possibly more charged with significance than any in her life—the first opportunity in twenty years to confront Stephen with something that might call out into the open at last their mutual need. She was only concerned to be interesting. She had not thought of the repercussions for Stephen inherent in the very nature of the communication. Nothing to do with office life had ever assumed importance in her romantic mind. The office produced money, and not always as much of that as one had been left to expect. Apart from that it breathed only dullness, routine, and the worst kind of worry. If Stephen had been in some other kind of trouble; if he had slipped up with a woman instead of in a matter so prosaic as a will, all her interest would have been aroused. As it was, what occupied her mind was the drama. She had anticipated everything. At the very end Stephen would indicate—by a simple phrase, a pressure of the hand, a deep look from those impenetrable eyes, a note attached to a bunch of roses—by some gesture or speech out of the ordinary—how he had cherished the thought of her all these years. It would be the most beautiful incident in both their lives; and even if, on the surface, everything returned to its old place, there would still remain the recollection of that moment when the veil lifted.

Applying eye-shadow Margaret felt a dart of gratitude towards the old woman—whoever she was—whose will had been muddled. Venus must have presided over her testamentary act. She was ensuring that the mistake at a dismal death-bed would provide the means whereby twin souls would be forced to acknowledge the true nature of their buried feelings. Yes. That was it. Funny how beautiful thoughts and imaginings eventually crystallised in a truth a baby could understand: Stephen would have to give himself away after twenty cautious years.

She had sent a little note that had taken a long time to write, as little notes do—the first draft was prodigiously long and would have done as a preface to a history—saying simply 'Must see you. Alone. Not Office. Mags.' Funny thing: that signature was what had given her most trouble of all. He very rarely called her 'Mags'. But he used to when they had all been young. It was a subtle touch, and helped to lay the scene.

He had rung up, apparently oblivious to undertones, and in his loud clear voice asked her what the matter was. She couldn't speak on the telephone, she explained, and what she had to say would take time. Would he be at home if she called in the evening, after dinner? He hadn't jumped at this. So she suggested lunch. While he paused she had a revelation: he thinks I'm having trouble with Henry.

"I was supposed to be lunching with someone tomorrow; but it can be postponed. If you really have something urgent to discuss, I will meet you. What about the Unicorn at one, then?"

Margaret's heart dropped at that. She had expected him to choose a more glamorous setting. The Unicorn was good value. Lunch was at a set price. She would see, and be seen by, nobody. At the Russell, in her imaginary script, heads turned as she came in with Stephen, and everyone in the room sensed there was drama in their corner. (She was in a corner, inevitably.) At the Unicorn the diners sat cheek by jowl; some of them did crossword puzzles; some had regular tables and formed a sort of lunch club; they discussed the day's news at the top of their voices. It was the sort of place where people had coffee without brandy at the end of the meal.

But, then, if he thought she wanted to talk about Henry, he, characteristically, detonated the mine in advance. His wonderful sense of loyalty had been paramount. She was his brother's wife. If she told him a story of desertion and betrayal, the wasted years would cry for recompense. He had anticipated this, and made sure by his choice of prosaic surroundings that emotion would be kept in bounds. Wise Stephen.

"It has to do with you," she said.

"What has?"

"I can't talk about it over the telephone."

"Why don't you and Henry come out and lunch here on Sunday? I'll be by myself."

"Henry has gone over to Wimbledon."

"Of course. I forgot. Well, all the more reason why you should come then. The girls, I take it, will be able to get along without you for once."

"They certainly will. Now you won't go to any trouble on my account?"

"We will put another potato in the stew. None of your

182

Cordon Bleu nonsense in this part of the world. But you are used to me by this time."

Margaret smiled as she hung up. Stephen's table always reminded her of a nursery tea. In some respects he seemed never to have grown up. Then she sighed. In proper hands where might he not have got to? The Fosters—one had to face it—had never been gentlemen in the precise meaning of the word. No man had more to gain from the right wife than Stephen. Curious, that for all his legendary good sense he had made such a complete balls of his social life. Did he realise it? Had he turned to the Preston woman in despair. There had been one incident which kept recurring to her, especially at night. After a wedding—when one of the other dependent Foster brothers, the engineer who went eventually to Canada, married a rather dim girl from Bray—she had been alone with Stephen in the hotel garden. It was very shortly after her own marriage. The champagne had run out. It got cold—her frock was flimsy—and Stephen helped her on with her wrap. In the process he had lingered, to an extent that had aroused in her a fascinated apprehension. She was certain he was going to make a gesture of some kind, and the odd thing was that she knew, whatever it might be, she had not it in her to repel him. At that moment her sister-in-law chose to come round the hedge, and Stephen let the wrap fall into place.

That was all; never again was there any episode between them of a similar character. Did he, she often wondered, dwell on that moment in his inmost thoughts, too? It was impossible to believe that there had not been a telepathic communication between them. She couldn't have felt like that without sending out a wave, unless the wave (it must have) radiated from him. Life never allows a replay of these inconclusive encounters; the most tantalising questions are taken unanswered to the grave; but they provide fascinating exercises in hindsight. Margaret had never quite relinquished hope that Stephen might some day fill in the picture if she sketched the outline for him. She never seemed to get the opportunity.

That could explain why she set such store by her visit on Sunday. Henry was always with her when they lunched at Howth, and usually some other relation. Stephen could have arranged interesting luncheons, but he seemed satisfied to have his own family around him. Nothing ever changed. One Sunday at Stephen's was so like another that she was unable to distinguish between them. But this Sunday was different. Margaret was far from psychic, but something inside her told her that fate was at work. And if it was she was more than ready to meet it half way. Her hair was a problem. She had been tinting it for some years now, ever since she detected the first streak of grey. But as a result her face had grown away from it. Her fairness had been all over; now there was a hard line between hair and forehead. The effect was metallic. She decided to have a bleach and be done with it. When she was fifty she would have it made white. White was very becoming; but not yet. Not yet.

Her hairdresser expressed delighted surprise at the transformation in her appearance. He made a *risqué* joke about it. He was inclined to be familiar with all his customers; but he was so full of interesting gossip and such a screaming pansy, he got away with it.

The Henry Fosters went to church on Sundays unless they had something really interesting to do. They went for the children's sake. It gave them a background. They were, after all, Protestants, even if her own beliefs were nebulous and Henry never considered the subject at all. He liked the parson because he had played scrum-half for Monkstown the year they got through two rounds of the Cup. Neither of them would have liked the girls to marry Catholics: going to church was one way of helping to ward off this evil. Margaret's mother told her Catholics didn't wash. She could never get this out of her head. She had been brought up in Rathmines in a Protestant circle and only met young men from the other camp on rare occasions. She had had a flirtation with one and when he kissed her she had let her imagination carry her so far that she pictured him in her bedroom, broad-shouldered, white-skinned, with most fascinating humorous eyes and then—grubby feet. Once the idea got into her head, she couldn't get it out. The romance never prospered after that. Then Henry came along. She had no doubts about his feet, and she was awe-struck by his age. She never could get worked up about boys. It was strange.

She let the girls off Church today. They were going on a picnic to Brittas Bay with some Trinity students. They hung around, and couldn't get off, making her impatient. She wanted to be alone to get ready.

She had a new well-cut grey flannel skirt and a blue silk shirt. It seemed exactly the sort of rig that Stephen would approve of; but it was so terribly unenterprising. There was that crocheted dress she bought in the sales but had never had the courage to wear without a slip on. She had a look at that. It was a sort of cowardly compromise. After all, by what was the fashion now, the dress was demure enough. The holes were tiny. She tried it on again. She was so confused now that she was really incapable of making a rational decision. She left it on, without the slip.

As she drove out to Howth, giving herself plenty of time, she felt a strange excitement. She had entirely forgotten the purpose of her visit. It only occurred to her when she saw the roof of Stephen's house. It presented a sort of challenge.

He was working in the garden, the sleeves of his shirt rolled up. A pair of very old trousers and a quaint old hat had the appearance of a uniform. He nodded in Margaret's direction to acknowledge her presence but continued to clip the bush he was working on. However, when she crossed the lawn and stood beside him, he stood away to survey his work, inviting her tacitly to join in.

"That will have to do for today," he said, mopping his brow.

"I didn't put on my glad rags, as you'll notice," he said as they walked back slowly towards the house. Every now and then their progress was halted while he pulled up a weed or cut an errant branch. She knew that he had taken her in; the reference to his own garments showed it. He might have had the grace to say something about her appearance. He could pay compliments when he chose.

In the house he told her to take anything she wanted to drink, he was going to wash.

With two servants in the house she would have expected some preparations to have been made, but there was no tray of drinks prepared. She had to forage in the drawers of the heavy sideboard where, indeed, she found God's plenty.

She helped herself to sherry. If Stephen had attended on her she would have preferred something fussier, with ice and bits of lemon.

The dining-room table was set for two. There was cold mutton on a dish and some salad, and on the side-table a dish of rice decorated with tinned peaches.

Nowhere was there sight or sound of the precious pair who had left it in readiness. Margaret felt her protective instinct in the ascendant. It was shameful to see a man in Stephen's position being put upon like this. She experienced a sudden tenderness for him. He was really a great school-boy with a capacity for applying a cool head to other people's problems, and a child where his own interests were concerned.

When he joined her he had put on an old cricket blazer that harmonized with the picture of him that she had been drawing in her mind. He had changed his shirt and wore a bright blue tie that went well with his cripsy grey hair. She had an impulse to kiss him. But he carried a tumbler of beer in his hand, and, anyhow, she wouldn't, not without some encouragement. She did, however, take the well-chosen tie as a tribute.

Conversation hardly flowed. Stephen kept on glancing in the direction of the Sunday papers that had arrived as they sat down.

"I hope there's enough for you," he said. "I like to let my pair out on Sundays when I can."

And when they were half way through the cold meat he said, "I find I can't take wine in the middle of the day. But would you like some?"

"I would," she said, only to keep her end up. She had taken so much trouble, looked forward to this encounter so much. He was so determinedly prosaic. She wanted to do something to shake him into awareness.

He seemed quite genuinely upset about his neglect. He got up and searched in the sideboard, bringing out an opened bottle of claret. "Or would you like white?" he asked. "It's no trouble to pop a bottle into the fridge."

"I'll take what's there," she said.

As he poured the wine out she was conscious he was looking at her. He realised by now that she was disappointed by something. When he sat down he braced himself as if to give her a fuller share of his attention.

"I hope Henry's getting this weather in London," he said.

She nodded.

"We used to go to Wimbledon in the old days; but, somehow, I find watching other people doing things no longer has much appeal. I'd rather mess about in my little garden."

"You must have cursed me for breaking in on your peace."

She looked at her hands. She had gone to great trouble over them.

"I never feel that way when it's one of the family. One doesn't have to make an effort. You and Henry—and, indeed, the girls—are always welcome. But you know that."

"You Fosters have a great family sense. It's a shame you never married."

"I might surprise you all yet."

"We would all be delighted," she said, fighting against tears.

"Don't put too much money on it. What's the matter with you today Mags? You seem to be under the weather. Henry hasn't been beating you, I hope."

"I rang you up. Stephen."

"You did. I meant to ask you about it. I thought for a moment it might be trouble at home. But it isn't that, is it?"

"It concerns you. I told you that. That's why I wanted to see you. I thought it might be urgent."

Margaret waited until he looked straight into her eyes. He tended to avoid the concentrated glance that was one of her characteristics. One was being asked to yield up a secret that so often wasn't there.

"A woman called Joyce came to see me. About a will—
I found it hard to follow, but she wanted me to get in
touch with some of the charities I work for."

Stephen dropped his eyes and gave all his attention to
an unrewarding-looking slice of mutton (none of the
Fosters had kept their teeth). After the struggle was over,
he said, looking at her sharply. "I hope you told the lady
to run and to keep on running."

"I didn't know what to say. I was only longing to see
you. But when I rang you up, you somehow made me feel
that I had placed an exaggerated importance on the
visit. It was such a strange thing for anyone to do, I
thought."

"The lady in question has been trying to make trouble.
She's calling on everyone. If she comes back tell her
to come to me."

"You are sure you wouldn't like me to talk to any of the
charities."

"Quite sure. The only thing that makes me angry is to
find that anyone is discussing my business. I've had words
with Henry, you know. I had hoped that would bring all
chat to an end. Have some pudding. It's not very exciting,
I'm afraid."

He got up and waited on her. Her hand trembled as she
helped herself to the comfortless schoolroom food. She
brushed her eyes quickly as a tear dropped into the
Sheffield-plated dish in which the two half-peaches sat on
their ricey bed. Somehow it symbolised her life and the
failure of the day.

They ate up the pudding quickly. Margaret refused
coffee; then Stephen in a bracing voice invited her to help
him with *The Times* crossword. "I do it after lunch every
Sunday," he said. "So does Arthur Evans. We time ourselves. Though I shouldn't say so, I always win."

Crossword-puzzles bored Margaret, but as the un-domesticated enjoy playing house when away from home, she was glad Stephen invited her to help him. Not that it fitted in with her imagined picture of their day. But that lay in pieces anyway. She racked her brains, but couldn't be of any assistance. He had the ease of practice and surprised her by his skill. In an hour he had the puzzle done, but for two evasive clues. 'xxxxxxx and xxxxxx' was one. 'Sea against harm', the other.

"Come into the garden," he said. "I want you to see if there is anything you would like cuttings of in the autumn."

He was preoccupied as they strolled about. Suddenly he said, "I've got it! Lemons."

"Lemons?"

"Oranges and Lemons."

"Oh, the crossword."

"I must go and write it in. We are very conscientious about timing ourselves. I wish I could get the other."

Margaret followed him, her slack movements were intended as a protest against his exaggerated briskness. All this fuss about a crossword-puzzle. It was well nigh insulting. By the time she dragged herself back to the house he was back in the doorway with *The Times* in his hand.

"Someone's coming," she said, not concealing her satisfaction that the puzzle would have to be discarded now.

A woman's head and shoulders could be seen at the gate. A moment later she came into view, a woman of Margaret's age, dressed in a flannel skirt and blue blouse. They went well with her grey hair and happy eyes. She carried, as if in triumph, a scarlet rose on a long, straight stem.

"I've got it," Stephen said again and turned to his

190

Times. "Sea against harm. That's charm, of course. Silly of me."

Margaret looked up. He had pushed the newspaper back into his pocket and was looking towards the woman who was coming with the rose. Warmth, affection—a glow of sheer pleasure—radiated from him. She had never seen him look like that before.

"I couldn't resist it. I had to bring you my Uncle Walter," the woman said.

"It's not a patch on mine, Mary. Not a patch. Come and see."

"Oh, hello. I didn't recognise you, Mrs Foster," she said.

Margaret bowed to Mary Evans, but she couldn't screw her features into a smile. She felt suddenly cold and faded and lonely.

CHAPTER XXI

"Where's Curran. Mr Britton has been on the telephone demanding the key of his house. Curran must have brought it back with the deeds after closing the sale yesterday."

Brian Fagan was talking to the staff in the outer office; but none of them had seen Curran after he went out the previous afternoon; and he had not appeared this morning although it was now eleven o'clock.

"If he is ill, Mrs Curran will surely ring up."

Whoever said that spoke for everyone. Curran had never let the office down. Unfortunately he was not on the telephone, otherwise it would have been easy to clear up the mystery of his disappearance. He had not yet appeared when it came to lunch time, and Mr Britton, who liked to get his own way, had sounded definitely unpleasant when he rang up a second time to be told there was as yet no news about his key. Like other rich and successful men he could not brook delay even when, as in the present instance, he had no immediate use for the key. But he had paid for it; it was his; he would not rest until it was in his possession.

Brian decided to call on Curran at lunch time. He might have collapsed—perhaps in the street. He had been looking so unwell lately.

The Currans' house was one in a long row of small red brick dwellings, each with its bow window, varying only according to the owners' ideas about colour and the arrangement of curtains. The Currans' door was a very dark green, much in need of renewal. The curtains were old-fashioned muslin. Brian knocked. After due delay a woman's face appeared at the door, which she opened sufficiently to talk through.

"Is Mr Curran at home?"

"Are you from the office?"

"I am. Fagan is my name."

"Mr Curran is not well. He's in bed."

"I came to enquire. We were anxious about him. Has the doctor come?"

"He won't let me get the doctor."

"Do you think he is well enough to see me?"

"Is it about business?"

"Well, as a matter of fact, he closed a sale for me yesterday, and I was anxious to get the key of the premises and the title deeds. The house was in Ailesbury Road."

"Come in."

She was a bleak-looking woman, older than her husband.

The hall with its huge Victorian hat-stand and a print of the death of Lord Nelson, with brown damp stains on the margin, gave the impression that no change had taken place here for a century.

Mrs Curran led the way into the front room. The curtains let in very little light. Chairs in plastic covers were spotted round the floor. On the mantelpiece a wedding photograph, and on a black cottage piano, a picture of the Sacred Heart. In the grate there was a basket of coloured feathers. They looked no less dis-couraged than Mrs Curran.

"I'll tell him you are here; but he's not fit for business. He's killing himself, and if anything happens to him I'll come down to the office and tell Mr Foster myself. For he is responsible. He's given his life to the office, Curran has. And it would make you cry to see the way it has him now. It's all the thanks you can expect to get, I told him. Of course, being what he is, he won't complain. He will go on till he drops; but when he does the office will have me to contend with."

Her voice did not rise in complaint; she faltered; her defiance had come to an end. She had expressed her misery in the only way she knew.

"We want him to take a holiday. Perhaps he will now. We are all greatly concerned for him. I wish you would let me get a doctor. And when he is fit to move, you must both take a good holiday. I'll talk to Mr Foster about it. He thinks the world of your husband. We all do."

The dejected woman gave a depreciatory sniff, almost a sneer. But it was aimed as much at life in general and the prospect before her as at the people who were killing her husband.

"I'll go and see. Wait here," she said.

Brian felt too big for the room when he stood up. The furniture looked like toys. Sitting down he felt as if he was playing a solitary game of house. The room was never used. It was a certificate of the family's respect-ability. A declaration of insubstantial independence. From upstairs came mysterious sounds; Mrs Curran came down at length with a bunch of keys.

"These were in his pocket. He wants to see you. I wouldn't stay long."

The Currans' bedroom was sparse and spare. In clean

linen Curran lay looking like a corpse. His eyes were rolled back, which added to the impression; but Brian decided that in part this arose from embarrassment.

"How are you at all?" he said. "Giving us a fright like this. Everyone told you to take a holiday. And you are not coming back to the office until you do."

The man in the bed groaned.

"And you've got to see a doctor. But I'll talk to Mrs Curran about that."

Curran moved his head slightly. Perhaps the light was bothering him. Brian could not think what to say. It seemed coarse to ask about title deeds.

"I'm sorry to come barging in like this," he said at length, "but we were beginning to worry."

"The wife gave you the keys," Curran spoke very slowly.

"She did. Mr Britton was raising Cain about them. You know what he is like when he wants something."

Curran nodded.

"I'm going back to the office now. If you could tell me where the deeds are, I'll take them along."

Curran tossed his head about feverishly. Then he rested his sad eyes on Brian.

"I lost them. I left them behind somewhere."

Shades of Mr Britton's wrath closed in on Brian, but he must spare this wreck for whom Mr Britton's life, much less his deeds, had probably become an irrelevance.

"In Curtis's office, do you think? If you had I'd have expected them to ring up or send them over. Where else were you?"

Curran put up a spectral finger. It seemed to beckon. Brian came closer. He had taken instructions for wills from the dying. This was the way it was.

Curran's breath was quietly offensive, but he articulated

perfectly and he was concise for one who usually shot off at verbal tangents.

"They could be at Campion's in Leeson Street. I called in. Wasn't feeling well. Curtis came at me, about that will of Miss Haggard's, tried to make me say Mr Stephen didn't sign, said I told Woodhouse, said Woodhouse said I said. They are going to take an action. They will call on me and say I said—no they can't say that. Woodhouse has been at me. I daren't leave here. Look outside. Keep back from the window. Is he there?"

Brian, incredulous, looked out, but only to satisfy the misery in the bed. As he expected, the road was empty.

"No. He's not there."

"But his car is. A big white thing."

"No. There is only my car. A small black one. And further down I see—"

"Yes!"

Curran sat up; pitiable, pyjamas opened showing grey hair on a shrunken body; a Spanish picture of a hermit.

"A van. It has a name on it. Wait till I see can I make it out: TASTE RITE CONFECTIONERY. That's not Woodhouse."

He came over to the bed and put an arm round Curran's shoulders.

"Listen to me. We won't let Woodhouse persecute you. I promise you. I'll see Mr Stephen this afternoon, and if necessary, he will speak to Woodhouse himself. He can't do anything to you. If you are called as a witness nobody can force you to tell a lie. You must stop worrying. I will take over. You forget about everyone. And I shall tell Mrs Curran if Woodhouse calls she is to send him away on my instructions. Now."

Curran sank back on his pillows. He still looked frail, but his sepulchral expression had given way to one of puzzled relief. A pain that seemed perpetual had paused.

He couldn't accustom himself to the absence of that sensation. He expected it to come back. Nothing actively pleasant had replaced it. But the pressure was off. He could breathe. He even glanced around. Brian, interpreting, offered him a cigarette.

He was pulling at it untidily when the younger man left him.

"I think he's better," he said to Mrs Curran, not sure how much she knew, guessing not much. Curran was not the sort who would tell his wife about his work, and she did not invite confidence. He wondered at the possibility of a relationship so limited and yet enduring, like the damp-stained print in the hall in its frame of bird's-eye maple.

"I'll come again. But I would like him to see a doctor. He needs building up. Have you anyone, or shall I get in touch with a doctor for you?"

"Dr Kennedy comes to us. Not that we often need him."

"What's his address. I'll ring him up. It will save you."

"Ranelagh Road. I don't know whether Curran will see him. He doesn't hold with doctors."

"Put the blame on me. And if a Mr Woodhouse calls, say that I said he was to leave Mr Curran alone and see me about his business. You may be as rude as you like."

Mrs Curran gave no indication that the name Woodhouse had any especial significance. But she clearly liked the tone of the message.

Brian's anxieties returned as soon as the door closed behind him. Curran was out indefinitely, perhaps for ever. And Mr Britton's deeds were anywhere or nowhere. It would not do the office any good if that dictatorial individual were to spread the news round his lunch table. He could be observed any day laying down the law in the Army and Navy Club to the less successful tycoons who gathered in that former meeting-place for imperial officers.

Brian did not in the least want to encounter Richard Curtis's supercilious gaze when he inquired if his official clerk had by any chance closed a sale and forgotten to take away the deeds. Just like Curtis to retain them to rub it in. Anyone else would have dropped them back without fuss, if only to keep Curran straight with his employers.

The pub was too horrible to contemplate. Foster & Foster leaving clients' title deeds in public houses! Where else? Curran was noted for his darts into chapels. Perhaps he left the deeds in a pew. Brian decided to call first at Campion's; and exquisite was his relief when the proprietor came forward in person to explain that he had put the parcel away for fear that if he sent it to the office Curran might have got into trouble. He was expecting a call from him.

That was certainly something. Mr Britton could now be deprived of his grievance without delay. Not until that was done had Brian time to reflect upon his visit.

Curran was ill, perhaps mortally ill, and his chief cause of worry was not Woodhouse but something Woodhouse had made him say. And whatever it was Curtis knew about it because Woodhouse had told him. And Curtis was taking proceedings to upset the will and, most improperly, had taken advantage of Curran's presence in his office to trap him into giving evidence.

One thought nagged Brian unceasingly, like a bad tooth: Stephen's gratuitous reference to unspecified decisions that the head of an office had to take, which they could never tell anyone about (not one's staff, not one's wife, not one's barrister). He had not been able to give an example. Was he thinking of Miss Haggard's will?

Had he altered it after she died?—No doubt it was necessary to take the secret with him to the grave. What else had he done? How self-sufficient he must be to take the law into his own hands. How did he sleep at night?

Brian found himself quite unable to attend to business. He must talk to Stephen; but before he talked to him he wanted to come to a conclusion about the whole affair. Whatever the truth, he was fighting on Stephen's side. That went without saying. But he could not reconcile himself to the idea of feet of clay. And he couldn't decide, on the assumption that Stephen had done this thing, whether it revealed feet of clay or a mature compromise with the imperfection of reality.

It might be easier to act if he was face to face with Stephen. He tried to get in touch with him. He had been lunching with the Minister, his secretary said, and was due at the Department of Industry and Commerce at three. After that he was going to call on one of the banks; and then, presumably, he would return to the office.

He came in at six and said he had to go out again. The Taoiseach wanted to see him. A hurried chat was not Brian's idea of the way this should be tackled; he went into Stephen's office and asked if he could come out to his house that evening. He looked so solemn, Stephen—who was in particularly good humour—didn't ask the reason. At last they agreed that Brian should call at the Taoiseach's office, and wait outside. Then the two men would drive out to Howth together. "I'm sure they will have enough at home for both of us," Stephen said.

It was impossible, Brian told himself, to believe that the man he was talking to had anything on his conscience. He felt ashamed of his own disloyal doubts and of the time wasted while he sat paralysed by them staring at the pile of undone work on his desk.

At half-past seven he drew up outside Government Buildings and waited wondering vaguely what was keeping the Taoiseach at work so late and why he wanted Stephen with him at this hour after the Civil Servants had gone home. At eight o'clock Stephen appeared in the doorway. He waved at Brian in a curiously self-deprecating way he had. It was the gesture of a footballer who had made a wide shot at goal; then he came down the steps, eyes beaming—that, Brian decided, was his most attractive characteristic.

"I'm sorry about that. I hope you were not waiting too long. I simply couldn't get away."

But he wasn't complaining; he was bubbling over—in splendid buoyant confident form. The younger man found it infectious; so far from talking of the problem which he was bringing out to Howth he exclaimed at the beauty of the coast road.

"I was criticised for living on the wrong side of Dublin," Stephen said. "Everyone at that time was on what they described as the 'right' side of the bay looking at me, with the best view behind them. I stayed here where I had it in front of me. Now they are beginning to come. Soon the Hill will be a litter of bungalows. But what is one to do? Fair shares mean short rations; and that goes for scenery too."

Cold supper was laid out for them. Stephen's staff tended to lie low when he had visitors, which lent colour to the family view that they were a sinister couple.

"Help yourself," Stephen said, going out of the room. He returned with a bottle of champagne.

"This is in the nature of a celebration, Brian. Let me tell you why. But bear in mind that this is a confidence, not a secret. A secret is something people compete to tell. First come, first served. A confidence is in a different category. You choose your confidant. This evening the Taoiseach invited me to join the Government. All the work we have been doing has collapsed. I was to have been Chairman over a board entirely composed of workers. The Government has reliable information that once the organisation was set up I was to be told to resign or there would have been a strike in the concern, paralysing building. The next step was to nationalise the industry. That wasn't the Government's idea. The object of the whole operation was to co-ordinate labour and management on a new mutually trustful basis. A Minister is going to be dropped as a result. I won't bother you with details. But the Taoiseach has agreed to appoint me as Minister for Justice. He wants to introduce basic changes in the law and he has decided that a well-known lawyer without political involvements could succeed when a regular party man might fail. It means putting me up for the Dail at the by-election in the autumn; but it's a safe seat.

"As soon as I am named as a candidate—there will be a rumpus among the rank and file, by the way—politics is a closed shop—as soon as I am named it will be perfectly obvious what the Taoiseach has in mind. He will take over the Department until I arrive, and make his Cabinet changes now. I'm to think over the proposition and see him again in the morning. Now, what do you think of that?"

Surprise and a mixture of other emotions made Brian dumb; when he could find words he said: "I'm delighted for you, of course; but I thought you hated the idea of politics."

"So I do; but this way I can keep out of them in the ordinary sense. I can do a tremendous service to law and lawyers. I don't really see how I can refuse it and—I must confess—the prospect bucks me up no end. But it means more changes in the office. And this is why I am confiding in you tonight. I am going to tell the other partners that you are to have my share. They have all done very well out of me. Of course, I may come back. Anything may happen. But I can't be an active partner in the office when I'm a Minister. You will have to take on extra staff at once. I shan't lift a finger to get business for the office. I shall refuse all patronage; but business will come of its own accord. Ambitious people follow the sun. This is an organisation problem: you can handle it, but it would kill Henry or Tom. They will surely think I have taken leave of my senses."

The evening passed quickly. There was so much to discuss. Stephen made Brian feel that his prospects and their attendant responsibilities were of greater import than his own elevation. At eleven, Stephen produced a second bottle.

When he was out of the room, Brian's thoughts came down to earth. Forgotten in the excitement of the last two hours, the miserable business which had been the only purpose of his visit now emerged from its hiding place, introducing a discordant note of gloom. How was he now to introduce it? And yet it had become even more urgent in the light of Stephen's latest promotion. The Minister for Justice could not be exposed in the law courts.

Stephen, carrying the bottle like a baby, took in the altered picture as soon as he came in. Brian lacked resilience, he told himself when he looked at the young man's anxious ascetic face. There was nothing of the buccaneer about him. It was desirable that a solicitor should keep on the rails, but he must not be ceaselessly preoccupied with anxiety as to what would happen if he came off them. That way led to a paralysing caution, a self-regard which could militate against the interests of clients who, after all, consult lawyers to get their business done, not to be regarded as hazards in a professional mine-field.

Nothing was said while Stephen opened the bottle. He had served the wine in the beer mugs that stood beside the cold meats. Brian put out a hand to stop his filling the mug up. Stephen brushed it aside.

"None of that. Not tonight. I told them to make you up a bed. We can go into town together in the morning. Perhaps you had better ring up and tell them at home."

He had lost his ebullience when Brian came back. He had shrunk into himself and looked suddenly older.

"Tell me what was upsetting you today. More trouble with Curran? I have settled that once and for all. Back he goes behind closed doors to do his conveyancing in peace and quiet. He can keep the raise in salary. God knows he deserves it."

Brian recounted the day's adventures. "I spoke to the doctor. As soon as he is fit, I think the office should send the Currans on a good holiday. If he could get right away from the office and from Woodhouse, who has become a regular bogey-man to him, I think he will be himself again. I was thinking of Majorca."

"Nonsense. He'd hate it. And besides the Currans have some travel phobia, one or the other won't go by boat and neither will go by plane."

"Perhaps a good hotel in some place like Bundoran."

"Just as bad. The Currans go to Arklow every year. They don't enjoy it; who could? Anything else would upset them completely. But I quite agree; off to Arklow they must go. We can give out any conveyancing that is held up to one of the young chancery chaps. Have you tried Willis? He did a very good piece of work for me lately. I promised his father I'd try to give him a leg-up."

But Brian had not yet told all the story. "I think we

must tell Woodhouse to take his business away. He is up to some very shady deal over the Haggard will. Most of Curran's worry comes from that. He thinks Woodhouse is trying to trap him into giving evidence. I must tell you what happened when he was closing a sale for me with Curtis."

Stephen listened, counting the bubbles on the top of his wine, watching them blink and disappear.

"Now is that everything? You haven't any other shot in the locker?"

Brian shook his head. He felt enormously relieved. Not that he wanted to add to Stephen's troubles; but somehow they seemed to be more manageable when they were in his keeping.

"I'm not surprised at Woodhouse. As the man is a blackguard to his wife and to everyone, why should I be exempt? Besides he will hang himself eventually. But you do upset me by what you say about Curtis. I can't believe Curtis, for all that he is as ambitious as Lucifer, would act against me in a matter like this. He has everything. He has only to wait and he will be the Father Christmas of the profession. He won't ever be that if he tries to buy time by burying me. They won't stand for it. Dammit. The only advantage I have is ten years' seniority. If he could take that from me, I'd willingly swop places."

"I don't suppose he deliberately wants to hurt you or anyone. But the trouble is his vanity which forbids him to refuse any business. It's not the money—there won't be much in this for him—it's the feeling of power. If he ruined you he would be the first to pension you out of his own pocket, and not tell anyone either."

"That's very good of him. I still find it hard to believe he could do this to me. Of course he will expect me to settle now. He has only to issue a writ at this juncture of my affairs, and I must go with my tail between my legs and say 'How much?' and pay up and look pleasant. Afterwards he will say how glad he was to have been able to keep me right. I can see the score. A child could read it."

"How much is involved?"

"The old lady had a life estate in a trust. That went when she died to a cousin in Canada. All she had to dispose of was the place in Malahide. It sold for forty thousand pounds. The nephew could ask for that and interest on it, too, I daresay. But can you see any court listening to the case?"

"Is Curran to be trusted? Suppose he breaks down. Even if he did not support the evidence of the typist, he could give the impression that he was concealing the truth. It could affect a jury. He is drinking; and Woodhouse has some magnetic influence on him. Svengali."

"Am I to be blackmailed because one of my employees wants to get money for her husband for nothing and the other has taken to the bottle? Suppose my present secretary accuses me of making improper advances to her; am I to buy her off because I can't afford to have a whisper against me? What's to stop you all taking every penny I have by the same routine? I'm damned if I'm going to crawl to Curtis. Let him take his action."

"But don't you see he won't be anxious to take proceedings against the Minister for Justice. It would be a mad thing for any lawyer to do, like flying in the face of Providence. I'm sure he would persuade the nephew to settle for a few thousand pounds. It's a very risky case at the best. Why not let me see Curtis and make a settlement? Then we will tell Woodhouse to get out of the office and stay out, and get on with our business."

"Leave Mr Woodhouse to me. He will go when I send him. At the moment I see a possible advantage in leaving a channel of communication open. It's no use, Brian. Nothing will persuade me to barter my reputation. It's my life's work. The money doesn't matter. I could settle the case at any time if it were only a matter of a cheque. Now, let me fill up your mug. I'm not going to leave half a bottle of champagne to die behind us."

CHAPTER XXII

BRIAN CALLED ON Curran again. This time he was out of bed. The doctor had come and ordered 'a bottle'. Curran believed only in doctors who ordered bottles. He visibly grew in his chair when he heard that Stephen knew everything and so far from holding his errors against him was prepared to pay for a holiday. He needed one. And Arklow was what suited them best. They were accustomed to the boarding house where they knew the proprietor. The food was exactly the same as at home, but Mrs Curran hadn't to cook it. There was Bingo for her. And he liked to take walks in the neighbourhood. Sometimes they hired a car and went as far as Avoca.

Brian produced a letter for Curran to sign. It was addressed to Richard Curtis:

Dear Sir,
    You mentioned to me when in your office on the firm's business on Thursday last (July 31st) a will case in which you had received instructions from a Mr Haggard. I am writing to say that I shall only give evidence if summoned to appear. Any evidence I can give will not assist your client's case.
                              Yours faithfully.

Curran read it over carefully. "Who drafted it?"

"Mr Stephen."

"In that case I'll sign. Very like Mr Stephen. So simple. You or I would try to do something clever; but Mr Stephen is so simple always. Curtis wanted me to call him in for a talk. Now he won't know for certain whether I've mentioned it to Mr Stephen or not. I don't suppose he will have the nerve to issue a summons now. It was the best way to deal with him."

Brian kept Stephen's confidence, but he felt entitled to tell Curran that he was going to be allowed to return to his back room activities and need never see Woodhouse again. "Anyhow, I don't think we will be keeping that gentleman on our books for very much longer."

Mrs Curran was called in by her husband to be told about the holiday. She was not, Brian observed, given any other information.

"I'm not going to allow Mr Stephen to pay for my holiday," Curran said.

"We have always paid for our own holidays and are not going to be beholden to anyone," Mrs Curran added in her lugubrious voice.

"She loves the Bingo," her husband said *sotto voce*.

"I haven't much," she added.

Curran asked for forgiveness with his eyes, forgiveness for his wife's ingratitude, understanding for his plight.

A life devoted to the drawing up of transfers of property was not a cheerful picture; but Brian could see, as Mrs Curran accompanied him to the door, how it might provide a stimulus that Mrs Curran, even flushed from Bingo, could never bring into the greyness of his existence.

*   *   *

Curran read the news about Stephen in the *Wicklow People*; he was standing beside the statue of Father John Murphy outside Arklow Church, into which he had gone on his way home to tea in the lodgings. To him it meant that his employer had arranged to be conveyed to Heaven in a fiery chariot. He was dazed. He stopped again on the way to read the announcement once more and consumed, at the same time, a port and peppermint. It did not, for one moment, occur to him to criticise so radical a decision. "What does a man at his age want with going in for politics," Mrs Curran would observe without interest or reverence, but her husband saw it as yet another sign of and tribute to the wonderfulness of Mr Stephen.

Mr Woodhouse saw the headline and, as his habit was, borrowed a copy of the newspaper from the vendor at the street corner, read the item slowly, and handed the paper back with a short expression of thanks. He made a point of not hearing the remarks the newsboy made aloud on these informative occasions. Stephen's decision surprised but did not upset him. At once his powerful mind set to work on the simple question: what use can I make of this? It engaged him all morning.

Richard Curtis read the news in the back of the car in which his wife drove him to his office at precisely nine o'clock every morning. It affected him strangely. Not only did he forget to address his spouse, he hurried so fast into his office when the car stopped that he forgot to shut the door behind him. Curtis was creating his own legend; and one item in it was this morning drive. There were various interpretations of his motive in sitting behind while his wife drove; those who disliked him said the arrangement was made by her; but the more general view was that Curtis would not allow his thinking to be interrupted. He had been seen in the theatre busily reading law papers between the acts; and he was said to have been observed making notes on his palms during a sermon.

He ran up the stairs and put a call through by the direct line telephone on his desk to a young barrister asking him to drop in on his way to the law library; then he began at once to dictate a summary of the facts in the Haggard will case. Nobody, he prided himself, could do this better; full and yet precise, his English was impeccable. At school Richard had won prizes in every subject, and he had never forgotten it.

The memorandum was taken by his typist at half past nine, and was ready for counsel when he called half an hour later. To be sent for by Curtis was a milestone in a lawyer's life. He had his trusted advisers whose brains he picked assiduously: young men were used in a case like the present where he knew exactly what he wanted and required it to be done quickly. The young man, who had shaved with extra care in getting the morning telephone call, would draft these proceedings during the day and deliver them in the evening on his way home from the library. Anticipating his call, Richard wrote to Foster & Foster.

Adeline Haggard deceased,
4th July, 196–

Dear Sirs,

We believe you acted for the executor in this matter. We are instructed by Mr Stephen Haggard, the nephew and next-of-kin of the deceased, to proceed to have the probate of the will recalled on the ground that the will was invalid and never legally executed. Will you accept service of these proceedings?

Yours faithfully,
Curtis & Co.

He then took out his pen and wrote a letter in a small and elegant hand.

Dear Stephen,

I am more than sorry at such a time as this to add to your worries. This business of Miss Haggard's will must be a horrible bore for you. My first impulse was to refuse to have anything to do with it, but I considered and decided that it would be better to keep it among ourselves than to let it fall into the hands of one of the wild men of the profession. I have never taken any case with so little enthusiasm!

I am sending you this note as a friend and without prejudice to the formal one that accompanies it.

Yours ever,
Richard.

The letters had been delivered when the barrister was shown in. He had never met Curtis before and tried not to look in awe; it was flattering to have been sent for, and encouraging; but disconcerting not to know to what test he was going to be subjected. A brief in the post would have been a more acceptable introduction to this influential office.

Curtis set him at his ease, and thanked him profusely for putting himself so thoroughly out, implying that the young man had a great deal in hand.

"I want you to help me by drafting the necessary summons in this case. Read this. It may be sufficient for you. I hadn't time to prepare a proper case. I hope you will forgive me."

The barrister took the memorandum, knit his brows, and began to read. He whistled when he came to the end of the first page. And when he finished his face wore that pleased expression of the unsophisticated when they are allowed to peep behind the scenes.

"You saw that he is running for the Dail."

"Is he? I suppose the Government want to bring him into the Cabinet then."

"But not as Minister for Posts and Telegraphs, surely."

"There will be a shuffle. He will either get Industry and Commerce or Justice."

"It wouldn't do to take proceedings against the Minister for Justice, of all people. Can't it be settled?"

"Do you not think that the appearance of a summons in Mr Foster's office might lead to that?"

"He certainly couldn't allow this to go forward. Have you seen the witnesses? I'd like to talk to them before we begin. One would want to be absolutely sure of one's ground, in fairness to him. He is so very highly thought of."

"We might be a long time before we could have a consultation. I think the Curran man will not be in a hurry to come to one."

"Very awkward for him. Did he volunteer the information?"

"No. But he admitted it to me and to a friend of the plaintiff."

The barrister looked reluctant. It seemed to him more important to complete the preliminary investigations than to rush into proceedings.

"If we act at once he will settle. He will not want there to be any talk," Curtis said. He was looking at his desk, which meant he wanted the interview to end.

"But it's bound to get out. Your client will tell his friends. I can't see how this Curran man can continue to work in the Foster office after he has given his employer away. If I were Stephen Foster I couldn't go into my office if I had to face him every day. The whole thing has a nasty smell. I'm sure the court will think so. Ten years pass and nobody disputes the will, then a typist wants to marry Haggard, and he hasn't any money. It doesn't look very nice to me. The evidence would have to be very strong. Frankly I don't see your client getting away with it."

"My dear boy; the case will never get to hearing. Stephen Foster is a wealthy man, and a bachelor. I don't suppose it would cost him a thought to pay Haggard the whole amount. As it is, if our client stays in his present frame of mind, he will settle for half. If we delay matters, his ideas may enlarge; he may insist on the full amount. In Foster's own interests—and Stephen is a very old friend of mine—I think a quick settlement will be cheapest for him. Needless to say, I won't let him pay me a penny costs."

"Haggard can do that."

The solicitor began to play with a pencil; if this young man did not get up, go out, and do as he was told, this was the last case he would ever get from Curtis & Co.

The significance of the pencil was lost on him; but he was sensitive to atmosphere. He had made a stand, showed his mettle: Curtis would see he was not a mere stooge, someone to push around.

He got up, and the smile with which this was greeted told him he had chosen well.

"I'm enormously obliged to you," Curtis said, before he could change his mind, "And you are so quick on the uptake. What a relief that is. Drop it in downstairs this evening, will you. I hope we will be seeing one another very soon on a more cheerful occasion."

He would write the young man a personal letter of thanks, he decided; he would pay him a special fee for this early morning consultation; he would leave him with a good taste in his mouth.

Later in the morning Curtis strolled from his office in Dawson Street through Molesworth Street (without looking up at Stephen's window) and into Kildare Street. He had decided to call on Arthur Evans, the President of the Law Society. His appearance in the office caused a flutter among the typists; he noted the air of importance with which the telephonist announced his unexpected arrival to her employer.

"Mr Evans is with a client, but he is coming down to see you," she said.

Richard remembered as a youngster sitting in this office when it was run by Arthur's father. He had been impressed by that portly figure, and wondered would he himself ever attain to such dignity. How long ago was that? Thirty years. It seemed like yesterday.

Arthur Evans, genial as always, came bustling in. "Listen, old man, I have an old lady upstairs that I simply can't hope to dislodge for hours, what is it? Can I ring you up later?"

"I dropped in on chance. Just a word in your ear."

Evans took the hint, and the two men proceeded into the hallway.

"You saw the news about Stephen," Curtis said.

"I did. But he told me about it yesterday."

Curtis winced.

"Of course you live very close.'

"In one another's pocket. My wife and he are deadly rivals. Rose-growers."

"Don't you think his senior colleagues ought to give a dinner for him. It's a tremendous step for him to take. I suppose he has been promised a seat in the Cabinet."

"I didn't ask him. I was so surprised. Stephen in politics! I'd have thought he had more sense at his age."

"I think it is a wonderful example to the country. Especially at this time. We complain about the Government, but we don't do anything to help. You may take it, Stephen wouldn't be going forward unless he had been promised a Ministry. It will be a tremendous thing for the profession to have someone of his calibre in the Government. I think we ought to show we support him."

"The best way to do that would be to send him a few quid for his election campaign."

"I take that as a matter of course. But Stephen, as you know, is intensely human. I think a dinner given by just a few of us—the ones who love him as we do—I think that would be a gesture he'd appreciate. Would you think it over and let me have your ideas? We ought to ask the C.J. and some of the bar. You will know his friends there. Half a dozen, say. Keep it intimate."

"Certainly. It's a nice idea. Come and lunch with me at the club tomorrow and talk about it. I must go back to my old lady. She will think I've dropped dead."

Mollified, but not glowing as he had expected, Curtis returned to his office. Evans, going up the stairs, wondered if he had been unfair in the past about Curtis. Was he really a good fellow underneath? It was thoughtful of him to have put aside his work at once and planned this for Stephen. He felt ashamed that someone who was not close to Stephen (he had looked quite offended when he heard he wasn't in the secret) should have had this pleasant idea. Arthur had been satisfied to send fifty pounds and a message of good wishes.

When he came into his room his client sat with her head down in silent dignified rebuke.

"I am sorry about that," Arthur said. "One of our colleagues has become suddenly famous, and I have been called upon to help to celebrate it. Stephen Foster; I am sure you know him."

Nothing in the bowed head suggested that the interruption was justified or the excuse accepted.

"Now, where were we?" Arthur asked. His client, looked up and resumed in a hurt voice. Arthur tried to make up for his neglect by looking almost ludicrously attentive. His face was not built on earnest lines. He was excellent at encouraging, at blowing away cobwebs of anxiety with the bluff wind of common-sense; but he was out of his element where solemnity reigned. Curtis would have worn the appearance of one about to pierce the seventh veil; Stephen would have suggested a wise judge; Arthur brought to mind a lovable spaniel waiting for a lump of sugar.

"I was saying that it was only after we had agreed to the idea of the wretched gymkhana and found ourselves involved with horse jumping associations and pony clubs that we discovered he had bought Miss Haggard's old place. It was too late then, and the I.S.P.C.A. had leaped at the idea, naturally. He had nothing to do with them at all. It was a complete bluff. He wanted to get the right to come and go, and, of course, he was able to make local contacts. Father Macnamara was abject when he heard about it. He, of course, assumed we were all hand in glove. In the end I lost my temper and ordered him and his dire friends out of the house. The pity was I didn't act on intuition and do it the day he first put foot in it."

Arthur, never quick at taking a point, was trying to piece together a narrative the telling of which had held him prisoner for nearly an hour.

"Is there any hope of getting the idea of the graveyard quashed. I must say it would make life gloomy for you both if they were to go on with that."

Mrs Bramwell sighed. "I thought I told you at the very beginning that the graveyard idea was a ploy. The County Council sent in an inspector yesterday to examine the right-of-way. He told a girl who works for us that the Council is buying the Woodhouse man's land for building and intends to run a road through our field."

"I say. Can't we stop that?"

"That's what I've come to ask you about."

Arthur stopped looking attentive and tried to look wise. How did one prevent a County Council from acquiring land to which it had taken a fancy? These matters were covered by Acts, and it was too much to expect a busy man to carry them all in his head.

"I'll see Counsel about it at once. There would have to be some sort of acquisition notice, first of all. We can lodge a protest to that, and then, I think, an arbitrator is appointed."

"And by that time it will be too late."

Arthur tried to look sympathetic and resourceful; the effect was as if he had been suddenly attacked by a bad headache. But his expression was suitable to Mrs Bramwell's mood; at least he was alive to the nature of her problem.

"We have sacrificed everything to keep the place as it was. It's far too large for us and we have never been able to bring the house up to date. And after all that we are to find ourselves the centre of a rural slum?"

"Once a notice is served by the Council you will have to

tell any future purchaser about it and it will make a sale of your own place impossible. Is there not something to be said for cutting your losses and putting your house on the market at once, before the rumour spreads?"

"If we do that, the awful Woodhouse man will buy it. He has the County Council in his pocket, I'm told."

"At least he will have to pay for it. We can try to make sure that he doesn't get it at his own price."

"I must say I'd do anything to deprive him of it. I'd rather sell direct to the County Council. But have we come to that? Why should people like this Woodhouse man have all the influence nowadays? And decent people have none?"

"It's the way the cat has jumped."

They sat brooding over this historical judgment. Its truth was not in question; its consequences had been brutally exemplified in the present instance.

So perfect was their communion that it was several minutes before it dawned on Arthur that his rôle as a fellow-sufferer at the hands of social revolution was no recommendation as a pilot through the shoals and quick sands of the turning tide. Curtis got a lot of business by being reputedly 'in' with the new establishment. Mrs Bramwell would not be the first of his clients to turn to Curtis in her present dilemma, believing he could grasp official elbows. Suddenly he thought of Stephen. He was in the know nowadays if anyone was. And you could ask him to help in a crisis like this where you wouldn't put yourself under compliment to Curtis, who would make it quite clear that your client's trouble arose from not having consulted him in the first place.

"I think I know where I can get the lowdown," Arthur said. "Leave it to me."

Mrs Bramwell left, feeling a little better for having

unloaded her misery to someone. She had caught her husband looking at advertisements for bungalows, confirming her suspicion that he regarded Woodhouse's schemes as blessings in disguise. He lived for golf.

Joan Joyce read the newspaper in the office. It was one of the perquisities. When she saw the paragraph saying that Mr Stephen Foster, the well-known solicitor, who resigned last week from the National Building Organisation of which he was to have been Chairman, had been chosen to contest the vacant seat in County Dublin on behalf of the party in power—a safe seat, according to the reporter—Joyce felt as if the office floor had heaved violently. She had to put down the paper to steady herself. Why the news should affect her like this she couldn't have said. It was the feeling that the water she had thrown herself into had suddenly become deeper. She was contending with unmeasurable forces. If only she could find some other solution. If Mr Stephen would get Sonny a good job. That would be best of all. If he got into the Dail he could certainly do this. It was to a great extent what Dail members were for. It was the reason why a Government fought so hard to retain power. When it went out of office another lot came in and they had the giving of jobs. That, from all she had ever heard, was the process by which the State was governed.

To attack Mr Stephen now would be an act of pure madness; but perhaps Mrs Henry, who had promised to approach him, might bring about a change of tactics. She would surely be welcome if she could say that the case had been dropped. And what about a job for Sonny? Of course, she would not put it in that crude way. But she was a lady; she would know how to say it.

But this required further effort on Joan's part. She

hated her rôle; she hated to have to expect to be treated as a near criminal—Mr Stephen had threatened to call the police. It was bitter humiliation for one who had always done what she thought right. She had thought it right to tell Sonny; the priest had since put doubts in her mind; but now it might all be settled. Some sort of job that kept him outside, not an office job—that would not suit Sonny. An inspector of some kind. He got on well with people, and he was very observant.

The telephone rang then. The call came from Curtis & Co. Would she please get in touch with Mr Haggard and tell him to go in as soon as possible and see Mr Curtis?

The message calmed her down. It meant that the solicitor was thinking along her lines. Perhaps he might see Mr Stephen and make the suggestion himself. It would have to be very confidential, of course. But these men could trust one another. Mr Stephen had only to wink.

CHAPTER XXIII

HAVING MADE HIS bed, Johnny went to the letter-box to see if the newspaper had arrived. He looked at it while the kettle was boiling. The headlines were all he asked for, and the births, marriages and deaths. He then put the newspaper on Barbara's tray, part of a ritual that he enjoyed because it annoyed her to find him always first with the news. She had talked of installing a radio to forestall him; but he had kicked against that; and, anyhow, she was always in a doze at that time in the morning. It wouldn't have worked.

He read the news about Stephen without taking it in. When eventually it penetrated his consciousness he laughed. Barbara never looked at the front of a newspaper. The information that she sought would not be there. He had only to keep his mouth shut and she wouldn't know about Stephen until someone told her. He laughed all the way upstairs. She knew he had been laughing at her; the aftermath danced in his tricky eyes. She wondered what had occasioned it; but she didn't take up the paper until he had left the room. Then she turned at once to the paragraph about Stephen and read it quietly and carefully. He had called to see her yesterday to tell her. Johnny had been so obnoxious at dinner, she decided to teach him a lesson by leaving him out of the secret. She was surprised he hadn't seen the news this morning. She had arranged her face to hear it from him when he came in with the breakfast. But he must have been too taken up with whatever was causing him to laugh to have read the paper. Now, someone in the office would tell him. He would ring up. She would say: 'Stephen told me; but naturally I kept it as a secret.' That would make him laugh on the other side of his face. He would have to ring up pretty soon or he wouldn't find her at home. As soon as she had finished breakfast, she rolled out of her bed and dressed without bathing. She had a full morning ahead. She had come into her own. She had people to see and things to do. Stephen had taken up existence again at a new point of departure. So would she. Politics had never interested her, and the sort of people who went in for them nowadays were seldom much catch socially. But they were more exciting than the legal crowd, at least they were in the newspapers. Law was a back-water. If there were a divorce court in Dublin there might be some advantage in being intimate with a leading lawyer; but Stephen's cases, apart from the fact that he never discussed them with her, were of not the least interest to the average person. A doctor provided more occasions for a stimulating chat; people's diseases, mistaken diagnoses—there was usually something to be in the know about. But in the legal sphere, the one exciting incident for so long as she could remember was this will business; and her cheeks still smarted at the recollection of how brusquely Stephen had told her to mind her own business about that. She wanted to make up for her miscalculation, and now she had a chance.

She had seen in an advertisement a house in Shrewsbury Road for sale. It had two large drawing-rooms and would make an ideal setting for large social gatherings. Stephen must have a salon. She must run it for him. It had sometimes grated a little on her that he had never suggested that she should move to a rather more fashionable address. Except for Miss Joyce, on whose account she had been led into the little farce of mistaken identity, there was nobody of any account on the terrace. But Stephen justified what looked like economy by his professed preference for a simple sharing of their family life. He always put his foot down when she offered to entertain for him, as she would have loved to do, provided he paid for it. Now his excuse had gone. He had deliberately chosen to enter public life. He must allow her to be of real practical use to him. And to be that she must call on all her resources. Her first call was to Sybil Connolly in Merrion Square, into whose sympathetic ears she poured her story. She must be armed for the fight. There would be periods when an appearance every afternoon and evening would be expected of her. On each of these she would have to make a renewed impression. Gone were the days of one dress for best. Now all occasions were best occasions.

She would have to lose a few pounds. But that could be done and allowed for in measuring.

From the couturière she went to the house agent. Twenty-five thousand pounds was the price asked for the house. A bargain, he said, owing to temporary credit restrictions. Barbara mentioned her present house. What did the auctioneer think that might fetch? Without examining it he thought about eleven thousand pounds. That left fourteen thousand to find, and then there would remain decoration and a great deal of furniture. But it was an investment. And it was a way of rescuing some of Stephen's money from the clutches of his sister-in-law. She would be mad when she heard about it.

The auctioneer was very friendly and helpful. Barbara bound him to secrecy before telling him why she wanted the house. He agreed with her plan. He thought Mr Foster would appreciate the wisdom that lay behind it and the concern for his political welfare. All Barbara had to do was to sign the Conditions of Sale that lay open before her and pay a cheque for £6,250 as a deposit, and the deed was done. Mr Foster, no doubt, would get his firm to look into the title; but he would find it perfectly in order.

Barbara hesitated; the little girl in her that had never completely died was atremble with excitement, but experience of Stephen—his opposition to show, his invincible ordinariness—warned her. His recent rebuke intimidated her. It was a tremendous hazard to embark upon alone. And yet the excitement lay precisely in that, in her devilment. If Johnny were any use—but he would be no help at all. He might even urge her on for the fun he would get out of it if the plan miscarried. That would give a fresh impetus to his awful laughter.

She was a diver on a very high board with no one to watch her except a young man busily working out what percentage of a percentage he could count on if the silly woman signed. She had struck him as being silly.

"Damn it. I'm entitled to a little fun after all these years," she said to herself. To the young man in the dark suit she said: "Where am I to sign?"

Barbara could not remember when she had felt so excited; but the enormity of her act frightened her in retrospect. She had planned to go from the house agent into the decorators and choose a scheme for the reception rooms of the new house—stripes, she thought, remembering a picture in *Country Life*; stripes would make a good background to gatherings where Ministers of States and diplomatists exchanged secrets, and the eyes of their wives wandered, seeking whom they might devour—but she found her spirits suddenly collapse and, instead, she went into a bar at the top of Dawson Street and ordered herself a large brandy.

Once, as a child, she joined in a conspiracy to burn the school down in order to enlarge the holiday. The school looked black and huge and sinister under the moon; and as she and her fellow-conspirators approached with their bottles of petrol and matches, the impression grew that the school was watching them and collecting itself to strike back in some awful way. She could hear the beating of her own heart and her companions' breathing, otherwise the universal silence, like the building, was closing in, surrounding and threatening them. One of the girls stood on a dry stick; it snapped. With one accord the others turned and ran. Barbara was never good at running; she came back last; but she was the best at explaining to her parents' satisfaction where she had been. All the other girls got into trouble.

Now she was alone; there was nobody to run away with. She longed to spread the burden of her secret; and if Johnny had appeared at that moment she would have told him, although she had enough imagination to picture the scene. Johnny would laugh; he would be delighted to find her once again dreading an encounter with Stephen. He might also cut up nasty at the threat to his own peace of mind. Their house to be sold to go towards paying for another at more than twice the price! Should she go ahead and present Stephen with a *fait accompli*? She tried to picture the scene when she led him—blindfolded playfully on the threshold—into his faery surroundings and then removed the handkerchief. It would be the high point of their relationship which, until now, had been remarkable principally for its uneventful consistency. It would add the touch of magic that only she could bring. Stephen didn't deal in that commodity.

On the other hand—and one had to prepare for the worst —suppose he refused to respond; suppose for one ghastly moment that he cut up rough. What then?

The question was too much for her; she ordered a second brandy. It went down, warming her inside agreeably, but as ever she failed to discover in alcohol as substantial a solace as the reason for taking it required. A genie armed with a cheque-book would never come out of the bottle, and that was the only alternative to an interview with Stephen.

If worse than the worst happened, if Stephen told her to get herself out of her problem: what then? Presumably she could sell the house again. But would she get so good a price? Were there not auctioneers' expenses? What a mess she might be in! And with no one, absolutely no one, to stand beside her if Stephen cast her off. It was a deplorable situation for any woman to be in.

In the end she compromised. She went home and told Johnny, having taken more care than usual over the preparation of his dinner. It was not so much that she expected him to solve her problem, but there was a measure of relief in hearing herself tell it aloud, measuring the awfulness of the sound.

For once, he didn't laugh. His laugh was a safety-device; it expressed and concealed his feelings about her. Now he took the catch off and aimed his contempt at her direct.

"You've done it this time, you fool. You stupid bloody fool."

Not a select arrangement of epithets, nothing remarkable in the way of vituperation from one who did so much miscellaneous reading; not, for the times they were living in, coarse. But, after a quarter of a century of restraint, he needed nothing more. Into each of these tired words he poured such pent-up emotion that they flowered again, answering the passion that called them up. Their very ordinariness lent them added force as an artist sometimes gains effect by bold simple strokes.

Barbara was frightened. She expected nothing from Johnny; she hardly ever thought of him. He was like a dog that had somehow become attached to the family but which nobody cared for sufficiently to claim, and which lived on leavings. She was accustomed to despise him, and when she thought of him at all, pitied herself on account of his inadequacy. What he thought of her never crossed her mind, because, like his opinion of anything, it was of no interest to her. That it should be so powerful a feeling, a contempt so much greater than her own, a hatred such as she had never felt for anyone, frightened her. It opened up such terrible possibilities. She had known life to be boring, she had pictured it empty; but not frightening, not threatening. Stephen, she remembered suddenly, would be sixty-one on his next birthday.

"I'm not going to get my nose bitten off this time. You can go in and face Stephen; and I'll be very much surprised if he doesn't pitch you into the street. Do you not know the man by this time? He isn't lavish. He doesn't spend. He hates show. The fact that he is full of money is neither here nor there. Why at this moment in his career did you choose to make the maximum nuisance of yourself? He will see you now, if he hasn't already seen you and looked the other way, for the stupid bloody fool you are."

The three short words lost nothing in repetition. They exactly suited his mood. He left then, and drove out to Milltown, repeating over and over, "Stupid bloody fool, stupid bloody fool."

Barbara woke up ill and sent for the doctor. He pre-

227

scribed a sedative and said she was 'probably doing too much'. From that she derived a little consolation. But it was miserable being in bed. The boys did nothing to help. Mrs Dunne brought up an occasional reluctant cup of tea.

Eventually Stephen would discover; but he didn't ring up every day as once he used to. Sometimes three or four passed; and the thought struck her in the endless time she had to assemble the details of her present life in order in her unhappy mind that it was more often than not she who made the contact now. It would be informative and might be painful to see what happened when she remained passive. He might give no sign until he arrived on Sunday, as usual, at seven.

He would find her in a darkened room when he came and she would take the occasion to rid her mind of her testamentary intentions. He was to have a choice among her possessions of any memento he liked. She hoped he would choose something that recalled a particular occasion, a happy day somewhere—the little picture of St Francis with the birds, he bought her at Assisi, perhaps.

But he did ring her up. He rang up on the second day. He was coming over to see her, he said. That was all he said, and she could not interpret his tone. He had a strong unaffected way of speaking always and did not indulge in subtleties of tonality. There was a time when Barbara used to haunt the cinema, particularly when Charles Boyer was acting. Sound and splendid as Stephen was she could not help feeling that life would have been richer and memories more fragrant if Stephen had had a little of the Frenchman's air of mystery.

Bracing, that was one of the adjectives that summed Stephen up. He took good health for granted. Barbara got up when she heard he was coming and met him downstairs. She moved towards him affectionately, but he brushed past her into the sitting-room, so that she had to follow him in and be greeted by him in her own house. She had not planned it that way.

The greeting was disagreeable.

"Barbara, I want a plain answer to a simple question. Did you sign a contract to buy a house in Shrewsbury Road?" When she hesitated he added, "Come on, I want to hear: yes or no."

"It was for you, Stephen. When I thought about you and wondered what I could do to repay you for your goodness to me and to all of us, I decided to devote myself to your career and place you in a proper setting. I knew you, and knew that you would refuse to make a fuss on your own account or allow me to. But entertaining is tremendously important for anyone in public life and this pokey little house simply wouldn't do, not for a Minister of State. You must put your colleagues in the shade in every respect."

"And where, may I ask, was the money to come from?"

"Well of course we would have to sell this house. I haven't really thought out the rest. I would have to tell you sometime and I thought you might get the office to arrange—these things can be arranged can't they? Loans. Mortgages. Oh, you understand all that side of it! I kept imagining what it would be like when I showed you what I had done for you. You haven't a wife, Stephen. If you had she would have seen to this and left you free to think about affairs of State."

She smiled up at him as she had done that evening when they met at dinner and she had thought what a splendid-looking man he was and wondered what it would be like with him after Johnny. He was just everything that Johnny was not. Large, successful, assured, simple. And he had such capable hands. Johnny's were like a monkey's. But time apparently had effaced the impression from Stephen's mind. He banged the fireplace with his fist.

"I have enough on my mind at the moment without fool-acting and mounting up expense. It's time you grew up. I seem to be surrounded by silly women. Will you please get it into your head once and for all that I have stopped making money, that I've given most of my money away, that I want to live quietly. Can you not understand that? If I have to entertain in the future I am well able to arrange it. There are places for these tiresome occasions. I don't intend to change my ways in any respect. If you or anyone else try to interfere with my plan of life, let me assure you it will be the worse for you."

She cried, cried silently and wetly as if she had been whipped. She felt herself a little child, and did not see what he saw. A fat woman of over fifty cannot be cast as Little Nell, nor can her performance, however sincere, strike a sympathetic chord in an audience.

"Oh, stop blubbering," he said. "At your age a woman shouldn't be such a bloody fool."

"You are all against me. What am I to do? How can I get out of it now? I meant to please you. Oh, Stephen, tell me what to do."

All his life people had been asking him to tell them what to do. She could not have hit upon a happier phrase. It was the only appeal to which he was irretrievably conditioned to respond.

"Go into the office and see Henry about it. I haven't time. You may be lucky. If someone else wants the house you can slip out of your contract. Fortunately the house-agent rang me up. What am I going to do with you Barbara if you keep on making trouble for me?"

"I don't want to make trouble for anyone. I'll take

myself away. Johnny doesn't need me. The boys are provided for. You have grown out of my reach. You don't want to be reminded of the old happy days. I'll find work. I'll make myself useful. Nobody need worry his head about me."

Seeing that she had returned to her usual form, Stephen went away, making that gesture with his shoulders which Barbara had noticed lately, as of someone bracing his back for the renewal of a load.

CHAPTER XXIV

Sonny got the message from Joan and went at once to Curtis's office where he was kept waiting for an hour. But he was used to this and expected it. His life for so long had been one of applications rather than application. Time was all he had, and it was the only commodity in which he was richer than the people he called upon. He had time to think and reflect, but it was possibly a natural aversion to both of those occupations that kept him sane. He had usually one thing in his head, one thing that he wanted; and he concentrated on this. It might be a spare part for the worn-out car he still managed to drive about in or, even, a cigarette. It was by thinking only of the need of the moment that he was spared a view of his life as a whole. Never had he had anything of the significance of his present claim. He could hardly believe in it himself and expected to wake up some morning and find it had been a dream. One aspect of the matter engaged all his attention while he was kept waiting: what was he going to say if Curtis demanded a thousand pounds? He had mentioned the matter to Woodhouse, but so far he had not shown any disposition to write a cheque—Joan put up the twenty-five pounds that Curtis had required as a preliminary. If Woodhouse had not parted with any money as yet, nevertheless he conducted himself as if the case was his own. He had left no doubt in Sonny's mind that he was going to exact a reward for his services. Up to now they had consisted of brow-beating Curran. Now, something more substantial might be called for. A thousand pounds was nothing to Woodhouse, but it was not easy to see why he should be interesting himself in the case. It would be as well to have it down in writing what he was to get; but how did one get anything in writing from Woodhouse? Should he consult Curtis about it? After all the man was making sure that he did well out of the case, and taking no chances. It was mean of him to ask for costs in advance, knowing, as he must, that Sonny would be put to the pin of his collar to raise any money.

Sonny found it encouraging to have a grievance; so he worked one up against Curtis. It helped to dissipate the awe he felt entering his enormous room. But today the solicitor was a different being. Instead of looking like an inquisitor, he put his arm round Sonny's shoulders and led him to the window.

"You saw the news about Foster in the paper. You may regard your case as settled. He must approach me now; and I have made it easy for him. Quite honestly, I would not like to have had to take your case all the way. Our best witness is suspect because of her connection with you. It's a pity that she went to such pains to make that known to the other side."

Sonny winced. He had forgotten that Joan was the originator of his gold rush. He saw her now as one of the obstacles in his path. He sighed. He wanted the solicitor to sympathise. Was all this talk going to end up in a demand for his thousand pounds?

"I've given it all the most careful consideration, and if I can get you anything above fifteen thousand pounds I think you should allow me to take it."

Twenty thousand pounds had become somehow fixed in Sonny's mind as a sum certain, his own property. It seemed that he was being asked to give a quarter of it away, and he wasn't in a position to afford to be so lordly in his gestures. But he was in this man's hands. If he left him how could he ever summon up the necessary energy to begin all over again?

"And what about your costs?"

"I can't ask Mr Foster to pay those. I'll have to look to you, I'm afraid."

"I can't pay you now."

"Wait until your ship comes in."

Relief made Sonny's thin face light up as if it was an angel's on a cathedral window—relief at not having to find money, relief at not having to look to Woodhouse. Afterwards did not matter. His approach was more akin to that of a bank robber than a litigant; and he expected to have to share the spoils.

By less than a sheer coincidence—the morning paper had set everyone's wheels in motion—Mr Woodhouse arrived in Curtis's office while Sonny was closeted with him. Solicitors arrange for the arrivals and departures of their callers on the principle established by French bed-room farce. Sonny going out did not encounter Mr Wood-house coming in.

The latter was not a client of Curtis's; and according to strict professional etiquette he should not have been see-ing him; but he squared his conscience by the considera-tion that Woodhouse only called in reference to Sonny's business. And Sonny was a client. If Stephen knew that Mr Woodhouse was not only calling on Sonny's account but discussing the transfer of his own business, he might question the propriety of Curtis's manner of handling the case. But Stephen, so far as Curtis was aware, did not know. He would be told in good time.

Mr Woodhouse was also greeted in a less formal manner than usual. He was rubbing his hands. But he had not called about the case; he wanted Curtis to act for him in another transaction. He was to write to a Mrs Bramwell in Malahide and offer her thirty thousand pounds for her estate.

"Does Mr Foster know you were going to instruct me?"

"He does not; and it is most important that he shouldn't know. You must not disclose who you are acting for. If I make an offer through Foster's office, the Bramwells will guess who it comes from. Man alive, there's no reason why I shouldn't give you this case. I know men who distribute their legal work through half the firms in Dublin. It's a great way to get costs cut. The competition is so keen; but it does mean that your business is known to everyone. And yet they say there's safety in numbers."

Richard considered the propriety of this. He was being asked to act in one specific matter. That was not the same thing as taking Woodhouse away from Foster. Anyhow, when the deed was done, he would write and explain. He was rather complacent about his ability to make all well with a well-phrased letter after he had done what suited him. Not every practitioner had this art. Hence the number of misunderstandings and bickerings between rival firms. Curtis very seldom heard the complaints that were made against him.

And a new case always cheered him up. Were it not for these aspects of novelty, a solicitor's life would be drab indeed. Then and there he dictated a short letter to Mrs Bramwell making the offer on behalf of an undisclosed principal and saying it was open for forty-eight hours.

Curtis was relieved at not having to discuss the Sonny Haggard affair. He guessed that Woodhouse might not be gratified to hear that it could be settled without any further help from him. Curtis was in fact more relieved than he admitted to himself. He had accurately assessed the situation, and knew that Woodhouse was the only source from which Sonny could obtain his costs. Now Woodhouse did not look like the sort of man who made interest-free loans or was content at the current rates of usury. No doubt he would ask for a share of the swag; and that was an offence. It might have been necessary to hint to Sonny that any arrangement between himself and his patron was not to be known to Sonny's lawyer. It was dangerous knowledge.

Now that their business was done he smiled his valedictory smile. Never one to take a chance, Curtis had arranged for a call from the outer office inventing an appointment if Woodhouse showed a disposition to linger. The ruse was superfluous. Mr Woodhouse could hardly wait. Curtis, pleased on every count, returned to his work satisfied. But he should not have been. He had only to look out of the window to see with what unusual celerity Mr Woodhouse went round the corner into Molesworth Street.

He always made it a rule to ask for Stephen when he came into the Foster office. By doing so he registered his permanent grievance that the senior partner no longer attended to his business. When he was told Stephen was out, he asked for Curran. Curran, he learned, had gone away. He was ill. Mr Woodhouse said he was sorry to hear it. Who, he inquired, was supposed to be in charge of his affairs? He was directed to Mr Brian Fagan, one of the partners. He had met Brian in the office and meditated upon his significance. This was his rule, because he never knew when he might have to use people; it was necessary to know about them in advance and, if possible, know something to their discredit.

Brian looked confident and reasonably prosperous. Something of a stickler Mr Woodhouse decided, not a man who would lend himself easily to a proposition that required native cunning. He decided not to let him share the matter in his mind. And to the business-like question: "What can I do for you?" he replied: "Write to Mrs Bramwell in Malahide and offer her twenty thousand for her place on my behalf. Say I want a definite answer before the end of the week."

Brian then began to ask the sort of technical questions that Mr Woodhouse found immensely tedious. Did he know how the Bramwells held the property? Was it freehold or leasehold? Was it settled on Mrs Bramwell? Were there trustees to be consulted?

Mr Woodhouse's opinion of Brian went down with each of these superfluous queries. He disliked all this pedantry; it was a transparent excuse for running up a bill of costs. But he could afford to smile. He never paid costs, so the point was academic; and this young man would never hear any more about Mrs Bramwell's property. She would receive the letter from Curtis & Co. and, perhaps, resent it; but as soon as she got the letter from Foster & Foster to say that Woodhouse was after the property and offering ten thousand pounds less for it than the Curtis client, she would accept that offer at once. In time she would discover to whom she had sold. And this prim young fellow would discover it too. Her rage would be wonderful to witness. His disapproval would be a treat in its own way. But by then Ernest Woodhouse would have cut his connection with Foster & Foster; and as for Mrs Bramwell: she could go and—Woodhouse laughed aloud at the happy pictures in his mind of the old duchess trying to do it.

Brereton Bramwell was often heard to say—it became a staple part of his familiar conversation—that he was thankful he had done nothing to induce his wife to accept the offer for St Anne's that came from 'the solicitor chap, Curtis'. He had advised her to discuss it with Evans. But she couldn't wait. She regarded the bid, that came on Woodhouse's behalf as a personal insult. She positively enjoyed being able to reply that she had accepted 'a much better offer'.

CHAPTER XXV

"ANY NEWS IN the office?"

Margaret always asked Henry that question, and then cut him off when he responded. By news she meant something else than the gobbledychook which he came out with.

"The Preston woman has done it again. Stephen's in a rage."

"Done what? Tell me."

Margaret was irritated with him for having waited until she asked the question. He should have come running in with this story. Henry's sense of timing was like all Henry's other senses.

"I don't know how Stephen can stand for it. She went off and signed a contract to buy a house on Shrewsbury Road for twenty-five thousand. Not dear as they go at the moment; but this one is full of dry rot."

"What came over her? I suppose the prospect of future glory went to her head. But I did think the woman was too cute to run him into that sort of disaster."

"If you ask me the woman is a bloody fool. Her excuse is that it was to be a wonderful surprise for Stephen, a palace in which he could entertain. She sees herself as

Madame de Pompadour."

"As if Stephen's principal aim won't be to keep her as much in the background as possible. It didn't matter until now; but I can see her as something of a liability from now on. Funny to think of Stephen as Parnell."

"He will keep her in her place. I should think she has learned her lesson now. But it's going to be quite a job getting rid of the house. However, the neighbourhood is excellent. The whole operation may cost Stephen a few thousand. He won't like that. He's generous, tremendously generous, but he hates anyone to try to take him for a ride. I never met anyone quite so obstinate when his heels are dug in."

Henry was in good humour. He shared to the full his wife's pleasure in Barbara's discomfiture. But he was satisfied to feel mellow, to enjoy his dinner, to relax and think of nothing except vaguely to consider whether it would be more advisable to go up to Milltown Golf Club after dinner or stay at home and watch a football game on television. As his plans never included his wife in them he did not have to communicate with her, and did not notice an unusual intentness in her expression or realise that her brain was working with unwonted vivacity.

They were at coffee when she said: "Henry, this gives me an idea. Someone will have to help Stephen with his entertaining. Why shouldn't it be us?"

"Stephen hates anyone making a fuss over him," Henry said. Recognising from the way she moved her hips that his wife was settling into her chair like a hare into its form, he decided to go out. He hated long discussions.

"There will be no fuss. Stephen will know nothing about it until the time comes and we can show him that we have everything ready for him."

"I don't know what you mean. Stephen is welcome to the use of the house whenever it suits him. He knows that. Look here, I must be off. I said I'd meet a few fellows at the club."

"They can wait. Sit down there, Henry, and listen to me. We have all taken, taken, taken from Stephen. None of us has ever attempted to give."

"I don't agree with that. I've worked for every penny I got."

"And what about the settlement on the children?"

"Stephen would have left them something anyhow. Don't think I'm not grateful. As a family we have always stuck together; but I don't see really why we should behave hysterically because Stephen has decided to go into politics. If you ask me, people will laugh at us and say we want to get into the act."

"Who is behaving hysterically, may I ask?"

"Well, you sounded as if you were going to work yourself up into one of your enthusiasms. I'm not saying it's a bad idea, but I do think it's quite unnecessary; and what's more I am sure Stephen will only be embarrassed."

Margaret looked sharply at her husband. Even now he couldn't assert himself and stamp off to his wretched club. She knew his excuse was a lie. He had forgotten that she had heard him say he might stay at home. The sudden recollection of an appointment was a ruse to avoid discussion. He had got up as if to replace his coffee cup on the tray; but she knew his tactics, he would edge closer and closer to the door and then attempt to slide out of it while keeping a conjuror's patter going to cover his retreat. 'I must fly': that would echo in the hall, and the door would slam before she could follow him.

A noble fellow this husband of hers. Her lips curled. He had seen this gesture before, and resented it. What particularly irritated him about her condecension was the underlying assumption that she was a superior class of being. He had no frills. The Fosters never had. She made no secret of her belief that Stephen was the only member of the family to answer to her own pretensions. If there was one thing on which Stephen and he saw eye to eye it was in their contempt for swank and show.

"I told you about the mess the Preston woman has got herself into. Stephen didn't say very much; but I knew from the way he told me to get her out of it that he was thoroughly fed-up and disgusted. I can't think of a worse moment to embark on a show of our own on the same lines."

"Let me tell you what is in my mind. I have it all worked out. We can turn the billiard room into a dining-room. Nobody seems to use the table. It's taking up a lot of useful space. Then we can break through the wall between the dining-room and the drawing-room and make it into a reception room. There is a window on the garden; we can open it up in summer and let the guests go outside. That cupboard space off the dining-room is large enough, if cleared out, for a band, if we gave a ball. The advantage of the billiard room as a dining-room is that it will be easy to open a hatch close to the kitchen instead of having to cart food across the hall as at present."

"It would cost a mint."

"Not necessarily, not if I supervise the work. Besides, we were saying it was high time the house got a clean up. We have only done it up once since we married. I feel quite ashamed of it when people with an eye look round."

"It's good enough for anyone, in my opinion. Your scheme won't leave any change out of five thousand. Where am I to get that?"

"This is little-minded of you, Henry. Can't you see that

the Preston woman's folly has given us a chance to show Stephen where he should look for support. I'm not a prude; and I don't grudge Stephen anything he has managed to get for himself. It's little enough in all conscience when you think what he has done; but he will have to think about his position now. He can't be seen everywhere with that woman. It will give his critics a handle."

"But at his age."

"That won't stop them; besides it invites ridicule. I was looking at her the other day. She won't dress her age, and she is in danger of becoming a figure of fun, if she isn't one already."

"Stephen will know what to do."

"No doubt. But he will be very grateful when you show him what we have done without calling on him for a penny. And what is more natural than that I should act as his hostess? Whatever arrangements he made, he was not, I assume, going to receive guests with that woman beside him and her curious little husband hanging out of the chandelier. I shouldn't be surprised if Stephen didn't broach this to you himself. I'd like him to find we had anticipated him."

"I'd like to think about it."

"Well, think fast. I'm going over to Mona Taylor to borrow a book of standard colours she has. Have you your own key?"

"I'll stay in. I had a latish night last night. Don't tell the Taylors about your plans, whatever you do, unless you want them all round the town."

"What do you take me for?" Margaret blushed. Henry shrugged, and went into the sitting-room. He would doze through the programme until the news at ten-to-nine and then doze again until the match came on.

If Margaret insisted he would let her go on with her

scheme; it would give her something to think about; she was too high-powered for him, and the alternative of complaint and bickering was worse than a capital outlay. He was quite snug. The children were provided for; and there was something in Margaret's point; if Stephen did want to throw the odd party he might be glad to do it in his brother's house. His own place was too small, and he was not the sort of man who hired hotel rooms. He hated the impersonal.

Margaret knew she had won the day. "It's as good as settled," she told her friend, Mona Taylor.

CHAPTER XXVI

STEPHEN CAME BACK late to the office. Everyone had
gone home. He did this very often nowadays, and sat
dictating at his table until nearly midnight. Then he took
a taxi home. He found he could get through more in the
quiet than in twice the time during the day with tele-
phones going and innumerable interruptions. He had
thrown off his bad temper with Barbara; and was feeling
sorry for her. He compared her with Mary Evans whom he
had seen dining with Arthur to celebrate their silver
wedding. They were as close and affectionate as a newly-
married couple, and he had enjoyed the few moments
that he had sat with them and drank their health. Arthur
was a kind, honest, very limited man, and he had been
blessed with this charming wife. She surrounded him with
an affectionate gaiety which embraced everyone who came
into its orbit. And when she was with him he reflected her
joy in life. As always Stephen left her feeling on better
terms with the world. And for her sake he pardoned
Barbara, who had never seen the smiling face the world
turns on the attractive.

It did not occur to him to pity himself when he compared the women in his life with Arthur's good fortune.
Having the Evanses as friends and neighbours was what
kept him in love with his house. For her sake he struggled
with rose pests; they had roses in common. It was some-

how appropriate; he thought of her whenever he looked at a rose; and added one to her collection every autumn. She had come into his mind and was pleasantly distracting him from attending to a proposal to increase the working capital of a bottle manufactury when the stillness was interrupted by a loud knock at the door.

It sounded like a policeman's knock. He must have seen the light on upstairs and wondered at it in a building which was deserted at night.

Stephen came downstairs. At first, when he opened the door, he saw nobody, then he became aware of a figure in the shadow of the porch.

"I saw the light. Is it convenient to have a word? I was driving past."

"Oh, Mr Woodhouse. I didn't recognise you. Come in."

"You keep hard at it," Mr Woodhouse said, following Stephen upstairs.

"I have a job I must finish tonight."

Stephen motioned his visitor to a chair.

"A nod is as good as a wink," he said, sitting down as always on the very edge of the seat. He grinned at Stephen; the grin covered his amusement at interrupting the lawyer's work as well as his own smartness at picking up the hint to make his stay as short as possible.

"What do you want to see me about?"

"It's something that cropped up today. I couldn't talk about it to the young fellow you've put in charge of my business. I can never remember his name."

"Fagan. He's my partner."

"And a very smart gentleman, I've no doubt; but this is out of his line. I was with my accountant today and when I told him I had drawn a cheque to pay for a certain property I bought the other day, he nearly went up the pole. I've already paid for the Haggard place this year, and this on top of it means I've drawn fifty thousand out of my number two account. My idea was to keep number one clear in case the income tax people asked to see it. The accountant is a young fellow and he has rather lost his head. He says I had no right to do this, that I got the over-draft for building work and the bank refused to finance any more land purchase. I don't see how it's the business of the bank what I spend the money on; but there it is. The accountant says the bank will insist on my refunding the money. If I do this the Income tax people will want to know where it comes from. You'd expect an accountant to be able to keep you right; but this fellow goes on as if he was in the mess himself. I used to employ another firm that knew how to get me out of these troubles, but you said the Revenue didn't accept their statements. I thought if I took on a young man he'd do what I told him; but it seems to me that all these fellows think they are working for the Revenue instead of for their clients."

"I've never involved myself in your accounts, and I can't tell you what to do. After all you are coming on pretty well, and it is asking rather a lot to expect to get it all tax free."

"I pay tax. Don't run away with the idea I don't. I draw fifteen hundred a year from the firm and I'm taxed on that. I never see any of the rest of the money. It's always locked up in land. The trouble with the Bank arises from my buying two more places when I had already used all my credit on other purchases. I've too much on hand, they say."

"You haven't told me yet what you want me to do."

"It's simple. I can't make the bank happy without changing the whole set-up of my business; if I do that the Income Tax people will come down on me for ten years arrears and more. It would ruin me. I'd have to sell this

Malahide property just when I see my way to turn it into a gold mine. You know the fellows at the top. A word from the Minister of Economic Welfare to the Inspector of Taxes to leave well enough alone in my case is all I need. I thought you might fix this for me. Everyone says the whole crowd of them is eating out of your hand. They want you in the Government to save their faces. Nobody trusts the present lot. They have done too much feathering of their own nests. I don't want you to go out of your way; all you have to do is to give a wink to your man, and he will tell the Inspector to go easy. He has my accounts. He needn't go behind them. They are the same as last year's and the year before. No trouble at all."

Mr Woodhouse couldn't see Stephen's face; and the silence that followed his plea might have been simply rumination.

"I didn't know you had bought more property," Stephen said. "My partner didn't mention it. He usually keeps me up to date about your business."

"Only in the last few days."

"Where is it, may I ask?"

"It's the place beside Miss Haggard's, belongs to old fogies, name of Bramwell. One property was not much use without the other, but the two together make an ideal estate for development. Lovely. I got it for a song."

"Did we put up the deposit this time? You haven't let me have the other one back yet, by the way. I meant to remind you we have to pay interest on the money to our bank."

"I'll make that up to you. Don't worry."

"Where did you get the deposit this time?"

"I wrote a cheque for the whole amount. That was the condition on which the sale was made. I put in an offer of twenty thousand under my own name. I knew the old

248

pair wouldn't touch that. They don't like me. Then I made another offer—without letting on who it came from—for thirty thousand, spot cash. They fell for that."

"You worked a trick on them. Did you make these offers through us? I don't think Brian Fagan would have lent himself to that transaction."

"I put one offer through your people."

"Without mentioning your plan?"

"That's right."

"Did it occur to you that you might have won us a bad name in the process?"

"Ah, how could I do that? You were as innocent as the babe unborn. I might as well come clean and tell you I got Curtis to make the other offer. I thought that would put them off the scent."

"And did you tell Mr Curtis that you were instructing us to make another offer for you?"

"What do you take me for?"

"As you put the question, and as I have been a long time awaiting the opportunity, I'll avail myself of it to say 'the shabbiest scoundrel I've had the pleasure of meeting in a life spent in the law'."

"That's not nice. That's not the sort of language I'd expect from you, Mr Foster. I've put a great deal of business in your way, business other people would have been glad to get. You thought so little of it you handed me and my affairs over to a tuppenny ha'penny little clerk who spends the time he isn't praying in chapels drinking port and peppermint in pubs."

"As you mention Mr Curran, I think I ought to say he is a most experienced conveyancer, and if you find his equal in Mr Curtis's office you will be lucky."

"Who said I was going to Curtis's office?"

"As you are leaving mine, and as you have become a

familiar figure there, and as he is an excellent solicitor, I can't think of anywhere else I could recommend you to go."

"Now, I didn't say I was leaving."

"No. But I did. I want every one of your papers out of this office tomorrow and a letter from Mr Curtis undertaking to pay the costs due to my office."

"Costs?"

"I daresay you owe us quite a lot."

"I never thought you'd treat me like this. To talk of costs! It's not worthy of you. I always said you were a gentleman. That's why I gave you my business in the first place."

"I'm sorry it is going to be so expensive to learn the truth about me. By the way, Mr Curran is on holiday. His health gave way. You were persecuting him about Miss Haggard's will. I am writing to Mr Curtis to say that if you persist in this, I shall have the matter brought to the attention of the court when the time arrives."

Mr Woodhouse brought a hand down on his knee.

"Now that's something I wanted to talk to you about. Curran and this Joyce woman, who used to work here, are going round the place saying you played tricks with Miss Haggard's will. This Joyce one put the nephew up to it. They think you will pay to keep the case quiet. They also think they are going to get the costs of the action out of me; but I won't touch the business with a barge pole. I was sorry for Sonny Haggard. He found me easy game. But when I heard that he was prepared to drag you into court I decided I'd have no more to do with him. I thought, as between friends, I might get you to give him a share of whatever you got from the charities."

"Would you repeat what you said just now about charities?"

"I thought you might—seeing as how Sonny wanted to get married and no luck had come his way—I thought you might agree to split whatever the charities gave you for writing them into the old lady's will. After all it was thirteen thousand each and they wouldn't have had a penny if it wasn't for you. I guessed they couldn't offer a man in your position less than twenty per cent."

"I see. Well I'm glad I lived for this moment. I thought I had exhausted your possibilities. And now I must ask you to leave my office."

Mr Woodhouse looked sheepish.

"Get out."

He had intended no offence.

"Get out."

Stephen rose. Behind the lamp he loomed enormous.

"I'm going. Don't worry," Mr Woodhouse said. His mood had changed. He was genuinely puzzled. He believed he understood everybody; and he had names for the six types into which all humanity fell. Stephen had moved from 'Honesty is best policy' into the 'Dark Horse' bracket. Now he seemed to qualify for another. But which?

Stephen sat down and, when the street door slammed, tried to concentrate again on his problem. He was so well versed in work of this kind that he could do it almost mechanically, but he knew that he was not giving the whole of his mind to it; the bottle company at that moment seemed irredeemably irrelevant. This, a warning device experience had implanted in his brain told him, was a moment of danger. He might easily overlook something, and confronted with a problem in the future wonder how he could ever have made some elementary mistake. Faced with it in after years he would forget that it had been conceived on the evening when he saw Woodhouse wholly for the Caliban he was and experienced the catharsis of telling him what he thought of him.

The desire to get him out of his system was strong; there was a limit to fortitude—the forgotten virtue, and the only one he laid a claim to—and the telephone, like the cities of the plain, tempted him to free himself from the burden. He had only to pick up the receiver and dial Curtis's number. He could anticipate the sequel. "Is that you, Richard: this is Stephen Foster. I've been very busy lately or I should have got in touch with you about a certain matter. I'd like to talk to you about it. Could I drop in on you anytime?" And Curtis would say, "Not for the world. I'm not going to have you calling on me, I'll pop over whenever you give me the word."

And he would say something self-deprecating and suggest that Curtis drop in on his way to work. "It won't take us long, I fancy."

A cheque (for what?) would settle the matter. Perhaps twenty thousand pounds. He could sell the shares he was given when he helped to float the tinned meat company in the midlands. They had gone up to ten times their original value. The income from them went in tax. He would not miss it; and he could go to bed and wake up in the morning without that persistent drag on his spirits, the smell of a dead rat under the boards, sometimes dormant always liable to poison the air; and for which there was no remedy but to tear up the floor and get rid of the offence.

The telephone gleamed on his desk, reflecting the lamplight. He had only to stretch out his hand. It gave a click, and rang. He looked at it fascinated, but afraid to pick it up. It continued to ring.

He grabbed it to stop it and said, "Stephen Foster speaking."

"Oh, Stephen, this is Arthur. We have come out of the cinema and I took a chance on finding you still there. You've done more work tonight than is good for anyone. We will be round in less than two minutes."

He was standing on the kerb looking, Mary said, like a lighthouse when the car drove up.

He sat in the back; Arthur said little, and Mary did almost all the talking. For the most part it consisted of a parody of what had evidently been a tedious film. Stephen enjoyed listening to her; but he thought he detected under her fooling a note of effort, the last thing he associated with anyone so wholly spontaneous as a rule. There was tonight a determined quality about her cheerfulness as if there were a necessity to keep the spirits of the company up. She would be like this, he thought, if Arthur were ill.

When they arrived at the Evans's house, Arthur invited Stephen in for a night-cap, and Mary went up to bed. This was unusual. Stephen felt cheated. What he liked best about his late night visits at this time of year was to sit in the garden-room with both of them. Mary's leaving took the light away. Stephen realised—and felt guilty—that Arthur, by himself, was rather heavy-going.

The men went into the dining-room and Arthur fetched whiskey from the sideboard. With its oak panelling the room was more appropriate to their subdued masculine mood.

"That's far too much."

Arthur had filled half a tumbler; then he poured a stiff one for himself.

"We might as well sit in here," he said. Then he began with an obvious effort, "I very nearly came over to see you today, Stephen. But I am never sure when I can catch you in the office. I'm worried to death."

He was accustomed to telling Stephen all his troubles.

His partners were supposed to be not a little jealous of the fact that his closest confidant was a professional competitor. But they all benefited from the friendship. Whenever Stephen had business to pass on, he sent it to the Evans office.

Now Stephen understood the constraint that had been in the atmosphere.

"Tell me about it. Get it off your chest. You could never be in disgrace, Arthur; and that's the only trouble that is ever too big to bear."

"I don't know how to tell you, Stephen. But you must bear with me. I could save myself trouble by keeping my mouth shut, but if I did you would be entitled to say I was a very poor sort of friend."

"Let's hear it." Stephen looked into his glass.

Without his scrutiny Arthur fared better. "There may not be anything in it; but the talk is damaging. It's got to be stopped. We had an old pair to dinner last night—the Bramwells. I've known them for years and they come to me with their business. Her people were called Hall. They've lived for centuries in Malahide. The house beside them belonged to an old Miss Haggard. Now do you know what I'm talking about?"

"Go on," Stephen said, still looking into his glass.

"It seems that the Haggard place has been bought by a ruffian called Woodhouse; and he has been plaguing the Bramwells with the object of getting hold of their land. The two properties were mixed up in a most extraordinary way. I suppose orginally they were one. He tried to buy them out. But they accepted another offer without consulting me, largely to spite him. I think they were foolish. If they were going to sell, the place was worth much more to Woodhouse than to anyone else. They could have held him up to ransom. Anyhow, that's not my trouble. Mrs

Bramwell is one of those people who tell their advisers how to advise them. She is heartbroken at having to leave. This Woodhouse man drove them out.

"In the course of telling us about this—it wasn't very interesting for Mary—your name cropped up. The Bramwells didn't realise that we were friends, and they told us a long saga about a will. You should have seen Mary's face when Brereton Bramwell said that you had doctored Miss Haggard's will after she died. Woodhouse is backing her nephew who says he can upset the will. I don't see how. The old lady is dead and buried for years. But that's not the point. We can't have people talking about you like this. Mary said 'That's a lie' with such emphasis that old Bramwell nearly choked himself with his false teeth. But if they are saying it to us they are telling everyone else they meet; and from what I could gather Woodhouse is a really sinister figure. I must say we roared laughing at the account of a gymkhana he landed them in for, pretending he was interested in the prevention of cruelty to animals. Like a great many people who haven't much use for their own species, Mrs Bramwell is a great lover of every other sort of animal. Brereton is a jolly old boy and glad enough to get away from a house which is too large for a pair of old people to keep up. He made the incident as good as a play. It was only after that your name came up. We stopped laughing then. Stephen, something must be done. Tell me what lies behind the story, and if I can help to put a stop to it, I will."

Stephen began at the beginning, with the call at his home by the typist whom he had forgotten. He ended with the events of that evening. The scene with Woodhouse had taken more out of him than he realised until then. He felt his voice lose control. He had to stop. This had never happened to him since he could remember. Arthur's

255

honest face, mystified, unhappy, suddenly took on the expression of a decent schoolboy outraged at some act of signal injustice.

"You mean to tell me Curtis has issued a summons. Curtis! Why he called on me to suggest the dinner in your honour. He never said a word. If some of our friends hear about this they will flay Curtis alive. How could he? How *could* he have done it? I never liked the fellow. But I put some of that down to my own petty jealousy. He had got on so incredibly fast. I knew he was ruthless; but that he could stoop to this! By God, I'm going to have something to say about it. And why have you been keeping it under your hat, Stephen? You know if I were in your shoes I'd have been across that garden wall to let you hear the story before I moved an inch. What are friends for? I'm put out. I feel you've let us down. You know that Mary and I are fonder of you than anyone in the world. We make no secret of it. When I die she says she will propose to you at the funeral."

Bald, stout, approaching fifty, Arthur in his concern looked like a dismayed baby.

"You have a heart of gold," Stephen said.

They talked long into the night. Arthur wondered to himself why Stephen, so pragmatic as a rule, did not put an end to the source of the trouble by writing a cheque. But he accepted his explanation: it would relieve the pressure, but it would, whatever agreement was reached or words used to express it, be an admission of guilt.

A strong man faced out his blackmailer. Only by doing this could he look at himself in the mirror every morning. Arthur agreed; but a few people talking was one thing; the general public reading the newspapers was another. They would see the allegation and come, as they always did, to the conclusion that the matter would never have gone to court if it wasn't true. Some people were found guilty; some got off. It was all luck; it had nothing to do with guilt or innocence. Such was the popular opinion.

"You must think of the office, Stephen. It won't hurt you politically, I suppose. But it couldn't come at a worse time. You are going to be the best Minister for Justice we ever had. We can't let you begin with a dent in your helmet. I'm going to see Curtis myself. I suppose he will have some regard for the President of the Law Society. And if he doesn't see reason, I'll call a meeting of the Council. You're too important to us all. Besides our more worldly brethren will agree that it would never do to antagonise you when you have powers of life and death over the profession. Curtis will be lynched if he doesn't behave himself."

Arthur walked with Stephen as far as his house, and Stephen came back with Arthur to his door. They repeated this three times until Stephen yawned 'Good night'.

He was not given to demonstrations. And Arthur would have been embarrassed by any show of it.

But on parting Stephen said: "God bless you," which was unusual for him. And Arthur said: "I can't tell you how much better I feel."

They waved at one another. Both suddenly shy. Then Stephen, who had put his latchkey in his door, came back to where Arthur was standing, waiting to see him in.

"Tell me," he said. "Do *you* believe I did it?"

"I couldn't believe you would ever, in any circumstances, do what wasn't the right thing to do."

"Thank you," Stephen said, and turned away.

Arthur, walking slowly home, sobered by the silence of the indifferent stars, trying to recapture the exact tone of Stephen's voice when he thanked him, gave up at last.

CHAPTER XXVII

RICHARD CURTIS ALWAYS arrived at his office early:
and there was chronic anxiety among his staff, none of
whom could make up his mind which was worse, not to be
there when he appeared or to have to be present at the
ceremony: this consisted of two complementary bangs,
not so loud but not less dramatic than thunder. The first
meant that he had come through the street door, the
second that he was in his office. There followed a pause of
varying length, broken eventually by a scream down the
telephone. Work had begun.

When that scream came—it was usually a call for his
secretary—any vital message had to be communicated
against clucks of impatience, very alarming to new staff;
and even those who were growing old in his service found
it a trial.

On this day he was told that Mr Evans and Mr Woodhouse were waiting to see him.

"You may go up," the telephone girl said to Arthur.

Curtis came out on the landing to meet him; he still
paid court to long-established members of the profession.
He had their respect; he wanted their love. They were not
convinced that he did not also want their clients. He had
not yet, for all his success, got to a place of trust in the

estimation of his colleagues. They were strictly polite with him.

"I won't keep you a moment, Curtis. I'm sorry for barging in on you like this."

"It's an honour to see the President on the premises," Curtis replied, but not in the opening key. He was already discouraged.

"Look here, Curtis. What's this about your serving a summons against Stephen Foster? Have you taken leave of your senses?"

Curtis turned away. He had anticipated an informal word about dinner preparations. His general idea had been taken up; but he sensed a reluctance to give him the credit for it. He was grudged a proper acknowledgement of his good-nature. He did not expect an attack.

"I've taken no proceedings against Stephen." He spoke with his back turned.

"He says you have. We were talking about it last night."

Curtis, looking very precise, spoke deliberately: "You are probably referring to a will suit I was instructed to take. Stephen is involved as the executor of a will. There are no proceedings against him personally."

"Come on now. It's not quite so simple as that. The action is to prove that Stephen cooked the will. In plain language, is that not the whole of it?"

"The person entitled to the property in the event of an intestacy is disputing the execution of the will. Are you here as President of the Incorporated Law Society? Is it an offence to question the wills prepared by former presidents?"

Arthur did not like sarcasm. It was not his mode. He was for bluntness.

"Let me put it to you as a reasonable man. Stephen stood over the will. He witnessed it. Are you going to call his honesty into account? Did he benefit by the will? Is there any suggestion the old lady intended your client to benefit? Has any injustice been done? Has your witness a motive? Doesn't she want the money for herself and her husband? I'm asking these questions to clear the air before I come to the point that concerns not only me but the profession as a whole. Are you going to allow such a flimsy business as this to prejudice Stephen at this point in his career? He is going to be Minister for Justice in the near future. He will be the best we have ever had. When the profession sees that you have chosen this moment deliberately to call his honour into account, to do your level best to ruin him—well, all I will say is, you will not have a friend on the Council. I shall never talk to you again; and I think I can speak for my colleagues. I don't want to threaten, but if you go through with this we will oppose you when your time comes for the presidency. I will keep nothing up my sleeve. You know I'm a man who speaks his mind."

"I am not going to be insulted in my own office, even by the President of the Law Society."

The words were measured, but Curtis was trembling. To be disliked by Evans was a very bad mark.

Now he had exceeded himself as people do who are unversed in abuse. He saw that Curtis was upset. To leave him in possession of the field was no victory to either.

"I'm sorry, old man; but I thought it better to let you have it straight in the face, than to be damning you behind your back. I haven't spoken to a soul. I came to you in the heat of the moment. I wish you would consider your position quietly; and if I can help, I will. The great thing is to nip this business in the bud, for your sake as well as Stephen's."

Curtis sank into a chair. He had never anyone to sustain

him. He was always his own guide, his own judge; and against unspoken criticism, which he was not insensitive enough to be unaware of, he presented the armour of his self-esteem. He had never remembered a time when life did not consist of competition. His first temptation to steal was when another boy topped his collection of cigarette cards. He had always to be first.

His rise in the profession had been the wonder of Dublin. There was very little left to attain; but to lose that little for the sake of a victory over Stephen Foster: that was madness. He prided himself on the fearless thoroughness with which he fought a client's cause. Haggard could not be in better hands; and for nothing would he let Haggard down. But Haggard had no moral rights and a shaky case. Obviously the desirable end in such a dubious matter was compromise. He had intended to advise one; and if Foster had only come to see him it would have been arranged. Instead, he had complained; and now he, Curtis, was in the dock. For what? For simply doing his duty.

But his plan had misfired. There was no point in being obstinate. He had too much to lose.

"What am I to do? Haggard knows his rights. He is determined to get as much as he can."

Curtis had dropped his priest-martyr tone. He looked dejected. He was asking for help.

"I can see that. It's a horrible position. Makes you realise what a tight-rope we walk every working day. My God, what would I do if someone tried the same game about the wills I've drawn! One should always make note of what happened for the file. It's useful. But I don't always remember to. I'm sure you do. You are such an efficient bloke."

"If as you say the profession will feel it is affected, why shouldn't the Council subscribe the sum among themselves? Haggard would settle for twenty thousand."

"What! Seven hundred a skull! I don't think most of our members would feel the honour of the corps was worth that! And why the hell should they be asked to pay? They didn't start the proceedings."

"What do you suggest?"

"I think you ought to settle with this ruffian yourself."

"I'm not going to allow a client of mine to be called a ruffian, even by you."

"Well done! Point taken. But honestly, old man, I'm afraid you've landed yourself in for this. Your judgement was astray. No one in his right mind would have taken this on without going to see Stephen first. Did you?"

Curtis blushed. The interrogation of Curran was on his conscience. It had been an unworthy resort. He didn't like to recall, much less to recount it.

"I didn't as a matter of fact."

"You hadn't the nerve. You knew you couldn't after Stephen looked you in the eye."

"I'm not unduly in awe of Foster."

"Not when your conscience is clear. Come on, Curtis. Pay up and look pleasant. We must all pay for our mistakes, and you can set it off against the last bit of good luck you had. Thank God you can afford it."

"I really don't see why I should have to pay Haggard because of the way Foster messed up his aunt's will."

"Stephen stands over the will."

"I know but—"

"*But* nothing. As between him and any crew you can assemble, my vote goes to Stephen. So will everybody's."

"Then why not let the case go on."

"Because the world is full of people who believe that anything they read in the newspaper must be true. You don't want to see Stephen in the *Sunday Mirror*, do you?"

"It's not my fault."

"It is; and everyone of your colleagues will think so. As for the politicians they will see it as an opposition move to discredit the Government. You will be regarded as a tool of the opposition."

"Will you leave me to think the whole business over. I won't be rushed into anything."

"Quite right. I hope you won't misunderstand my intervention. Don't take it personally, like a good chap. But you must try to keep the good-will of your colleagues. I think I have it, and it sweetens the toil. On the whole they are a very decent lot of fellows."

Arthur left; his blood-pressure had taken considerable punishment; but he felt he had exercised himself to some purpose. Curtis might well decide to make the gesture. It could be an exhibition of the strength of his resources. He was vain.

The dinner was on Saturday night. It was now Wednesday. If Curtis were going to face the company on Saturday he would have had to settle the case between now and then. If a diplomatic illness kept him away that meant that Stephen would have to put his pride as well as his hand in his pocket. In the last resort Arthur could even contemplate making a whip round his colleagues. Anything was better than the publicity of the case.

The telephone girl in the Curtis office could not have been expected to know what had passed at the interview. If she had she would have hesitated before ringing up her employer after Arthur left to remind him that Mr Woodhouse was still waiting. The cry of sheer pain it produced pierced her ear-drum. But, after a short interval, a less frantic call came through to say Mr Woodhouse was to go up.

He came in grinning to be met with a stare.

Curtis found his visitor particularly disagreeable at this precise moment as he held him in a great measure responsible for his recent embarrassment. He was pushing Haggard on, and he decided not to use him as an intermediary now. He would see Haggard and his fiancée together. This man must be kept out of the picture. Nor did it lessen Curtis's dislike of him that he was sure he wanted to share the spoils. If he had waited to be paid his costs before acting, as he originally intended, he had no doubt where they would have come from. It was illegal to maintain a suit with the prospect of sharing in the result. On this his conscience was not quite clear. The sooner he got rid of this wretched case the better. It began with a question mark against Stephen Foster. It looked as if it would end with several against himself.

When Curtis disliked a visitor's business he let him open it and gave no help.

Mr Woodhouse liked to begin with a little friendly chaff. When he met with no response he was at a loss; he, too, liked the other to begin. He enjoyed mystification.

He was coming as a patron and he expected a patron's welcome, not to be made feel small. Kicked out by Foster the night before it was galling to unload his treasure in these discouraging surroundings. However, he had to start.

"I've decided to give you all my business in future. I was very pleased with the way your firm handled the Bramwell purchase. I was glad to get that property. It's a bargain. The old couple will be dancing mad when they discover who the purchaser is. I have plans ready for the development of the two estates. It will be a little city. I want you to look after the leases as soon as the plan goes through."

This was not what Curtis had expected. He was not too

blasé to recognise that this was a substantial case. Wood-house was a great acquisition. But, before melting, he felt it incumbent to say: "Do your former solicitors know you have taken your business away? I must keep right with them."

"I told old Foster I was going to leave him. He doesn't give me any of his attention, and I'm tired of being handed from one clerk to another as if my business was done for charity."

Curtis had forgotten for the moment that Woodhouse was a client of Stephen's. The news took all the pleasure out of what should have been a red-letter day, the acquisition of yet more valuable business, a further step towards El Dorado, where everybody's business would be done by Richard Curtis and every solicitor would be working for him. The final solution.

He pointed to the map in Woodhouse's hand.

"Perhaps you'd leave that plan with me," he said.

He would scrutinise it carefully, then hand it to Delaney and tell him to get on with the work.

"This copy is for you. My architect lodged the other for approval with the County Council before we had the Bramwells' place. I took a chance. I had to get my oar in. There was talk of acquiring some of the land for Council houses; but I believe they will drop that now. This scheme will suit them. I have a friend there." Mr Woodhouse winked.

He did not expect Curtis to wink back, but a fastidious half-concealed grimace was an approximate equivalent.

"Well, we can't do anything until the permission comes through. Meanwhile I must go ahead with the completion of the purchase. By the way, into whose name am I to take the conveyance of the Bramwells's property? You remember we did not disclose your identity when we put in the bid for you."

"I'll have to think about that."

Mr Woodhouse winked again. Curtis made one of the signs that his other clients understood to mean that the interview was over and time pressed. It was a sort of general fluttering as of a bird disturbed in the nest. Mr Woodhouse ignored the signs.

"Do you know anyone in the Government?" he said.

"I've met some of the Ministers. I often have dealings with the Minister of Industry and Commerce. I know the Minister for Economic Welfare."

"That's the man."

"I don't quite follow."

"I want you to drop a word in his ear. I'm in trouble with the Income Tax over my purchases. You'd have to see my accountant to understand. It means they can open up my returns for ten years, and I don't mind telling you that that wouldn't suit me."

"I'm afraid I can do nothing of the kind."

Curtis felt suddenly angry, not only at the suggestion. This man must have asked Stephen to do precisely this, and been refused. Now he was offering his business as a bribe, thinking that he, Curtis, had lower standards. It was too much. Stephen. Stephen. Stephen. Stephen. Stephen. Was he going to haunt him?

"Did you ask Mr Foster to intervene? He is in those circles you know."

"There's no use asking that old fellow to do anything. He's past it, if you ask my opinion. The Government wants to put him up like an ornament on the mantelpiece. He won't have a say in anything, if you ask me."

Curtis was mollified to hear what might be a representative view. But he was not going to encourage its development.

266

"If you want me to take over your income tax problem I shall. It's a line of country in which I have considerable experience. But I want to warn you it will cost you quite a lot. It's time-consuming, and I expect to be paid for my expertise."

"Oh, I'll pay."

"Very well. Leave me your accountant's name and I shall get in touch with him. Then I'll be able to tell you where you stand. But, remember, this is not a case of whispering in Ministers' ears. I don't work that way. Do you understand? And I would not like to think any Minister would be influenced. Are we quite clear? The reputation of my firm is all that concerns me. And we do our business in the full light of day. If you want it done in any other way, please take it away. I certainly don't want it. I've more to do than I've time for as it is."

Mr Woodhouse winked. He liked what he heard. Curtis was covering himself. It was providential that he had discovered this man at such a critical moment. He had been cheating the Revenue successfully for years. He had over-invested. He could become a millionaire. He could be reduced to his beginnings. It was as critical as that.

"I want a cheque for two thousand pounds on account of my firm's costs," Curtis said.

Mr Woodhouse was hard to startle; and his complexion had the tenacity of French polish; but he paled.

"I haven't my cheque-book with me."

"You can post me the cheque. I will see your accountant as soon as I hear from you. You understand it means putting other important work aside."

It was not the amount that staggered Mr Woodhouse. Had Curtis asked for a great deal more to bribe, say, a Minister, he would have cheerfully written the cheque. What outraged his sense of propriety was the idea of paying—and paying in advance—merely for professional services. But the enormity of the demand convinced him that he had made the right choice. This was a man to respect. Anyone who could get costs out of him in advance could breach the walls of Jericho. And that was what he wanted. He took a cheque-book out of his pocket and wrote without practised facility the order on his bank. Curtis examined it, put it in a drawer and nodded.

Never had a miracle been witnessed with less awe; diffidence of this order was a miracle in its own right. Dumb, Mr Woodhouse withdrew.

CHAPTER XXVIII

MARGARET FOSTER CONTEMPLATED the salon she had created. The white walls, dove grey fitted carpet and blue velvet curtains were her own idea. It followed faithfully a set she had been charmed with in a London comedy. The heroine was an actress with three men in love with her. In the last act she sent them all packing and remained with her good solid husband. Cecil Parker had played that part perfectly. It was a most satisfactory evening; and she often thought of it nostalgically.

Mona Taylor had questioned the white walls. They would look, she said, too like a hospital. She had a way of saying things like that and comparing small things to great. But would it not have been well to have listened to the decorators who suggested mixing a touch of red in the white? She had seen it as yet another attempt to prevent her from getting exactly what she wanted, and stood her ground. Now she was doubtful.

"Henry, what do you think?"

Her husband, looking out of sorts, had just come in. Glancing with eyes of misery at his wife's extravagance, he could not bring himself to consider it in detail.

"Think about what?"

"Are the walls too white?"

"They couldn't be much whiter, could they?"

"Oh dear! Do you find it too glaring?"

"I was quite happy with the place as it was. No use asking me. Ask your friend, Mrs Taylor. She's well up in all this sort of thing. But then Charley Taylor has a ton of money. She might cover their walls with five pound notes and he couldn't care. I was looking for my corkscrew. It used to be in that drawer; but the house is upside down. I can't find anything. The smell of paint makes me sick. When are the painters getting out?"

"They couldn't work any faster. It took Mona six weeks to get their bedrooms done up. We have only been at it for three; and there was the knocking down of the walls to be done as well. I think Mr Farmer has been wonderfully quick."

"I hope he won't be as quick about sending in his bill. Have you any idea what it's all going to cost? If in the end I have to ask Stephen to let me draw capital out of the office, I'll look pretty foolish. I wish we had left things as they were. I liked the house. What was wrong with it?"

"It's hopeless trying to explain anything to you," she said. "You're too wrapped up in your own concerns. I am left to battle on my own. Do you ever think of your daughters? Can't you see the advantage of a setting like this for them. Mona tells me Anne has been seeing the Coleman boy again. She spotted them lurking round the golf course. I shall have to speak to her. Why should the whole weight of life rest on me?"

Henry, measuring the curtains with his eyes while his wife delivered her soliloquy, decided that there must be at least thirty-two yards of material at about four pounds a yard.

"I've something to tell you," he said. "Stephen is giving

his share of the office to the Fagan boy. He showed us a deed he has drawn up. When he goes into government we are all three to share profits. He will take nothing. But eventually Fagan is to have all his present share."

"I suppose it's Stephen's to do what he likes with."

"I think it's unfair. Fagan is a stranger. We don't know how he will turn out. Suppose one of our girls were to marry a young solicitor: it would be galling to find there was no place for him in one's own office."

"You are not suggesting that you and Tom Murgatroyd could run the office between you, are you?"

"We could take on staff. I don't think Stephen treated me fairly in this matter. He pretends to consult us, but he knows damn well he is always going to get his way."

"I'll talk to him," Margaret said, conscious of new power. "We must get the painters to hurry up. I want it all to be a surprise for Stephen. When he sees what we have done for him, he may look at the office in another light. He may see the necessity of emphasising the family connection. You will have a new importance when people get into the way of coming here. It is bound to increase your influence."

He has even asked Arthur Evans to include Fagan in the dinner. Naturally they invited Tom and me; but I thought that it should be strictly for contemporaries. It will go to Fagan's head; and it's swollen enough as it is. Arthur showed me the list today. He had been over it with Curtis. If Curtis had his way there would be only himself and the Chief Justice. I can see myself down at the bottom of the table with young Brian Fagan. I'm longing to see Tom Murgatroyd's face when he hears. Do you think the corkscrew might have found its way into the kitchen?"

"Oh, you and your corkscrew," Margaret said.

It was the only word of his discourse she heard, symbol of the whole. While he had been talking to himself she had made a lightning decision. An extra coat of paint in which a little red was mixed would not take long or cost all that much. It would be a pity to stop short of perfection.

She had settled on a gold dress, suggestive of a Roman portrait, for the first official reception. It would be beautifully set off by the decorative scheme. She was glad she had swallowed the price of the Bossi chimney-piece (she hadn't yet told Henry). She would receive her guests standing against it. The mirror overmantel would aid the effect. *'Au Bar de Folies-Bergère.'* She did not look wholly unlike the girl in the Manet picture. A well-bred version, as became the difference of the setting.

CHAPTER XXIX

SONNY WAS GLAD enough when Joan suggested she should accompany him to the interview with Curtis. The solicitor intimidated him—he never liked lawyers anyhow—and it was annoying to be employing a man and have him behave as if you were imposing on him. Not that Joan was much of a prop. She ate humble pie as if she had been reared on it. But there was some comfort to be derived from her presence. They could divide the awfulness of the occasion between them.

But Curtis was quite different today. He seemed to have all the time in the world at his disposal, and he remarked that Joan looked as if she needed a complete rest. She was grateful for that. It led him into the subject they had come to discuss. The case must be settled, he said. The time had come to grapple with it. Stephen Foster would soon be Minister for Justice. As such he would not tamper with the law; but somehow cases against Ministers never got to the courts; and, moreover, there was a fatal weakness in this one.

For the first time Curtis mentioned Curran's letter. It was a strategic move, he said, and Stephen must have been behind it. If they had to call Curran and his evidence was unsatisfactory, he would not be subjected to a cross-examination. He was their witness, not Stephen's. He had said his evidence would not be helpful; and everyone knew it was fatal to have to rely on reluctant witnesses. His being in Foster's office had always been a disadvantage.

Sonny, not liking the direction in which the solicitor's monologue seemed to be heading, interrupted.

"But we have Joan's evidence."

"She will be regarded as a most suspicious witness. Cross-examination will bring out her engagement to you. And the silence for ten years never helped our case."

"It's perfectly understandable," Sonny said. He seemed to have to defend himself. On the last occasion Curtis had been full of fight.

"I agree with Mr Curtis," Joan said. "You ought to settle, Sonny."

Sonny kicked her ankle and took over.

"Has the other side made an offer?"

"Not formally; but I know I can settle."

"What will they give?"

"To be quite frank, I very much doubt now if I could get them up to more than a couple of thousand pounds. I suppose Foster would pay that to be finished with the matter."

"Oh, take it, Sonny," Joan cried.

He ignored her. "That's a come down from twenty thousand."

"I know, but I have given the matter careful thought. I've had a consultation with counsel. He thinks you are bound to lose."

Joan attempted to intervene. Sonny silenced her with a look. But before he could speak, Curtis resumed.

"I may be able to help you to make up your mind. A German client of mine bought a farm near Mallow.

You know the strong feeling there is at present against foreigners owning land. I have suggested to him that he finds a suitable couple to live on the farm and act as if it belonged to them. My client is a very knowledgeable gentleman. He will come over occasionally and direct operations. But nobody need be the wiser. You will have a nice house to live in, and we can arrange for a modest salary. Say ten pounds a week. If Miss Joyce wants to augment that, she will have no difficulty in finding work in Mallow. The town is three miles away. What do you say?"

"Take it, Sonny."

"But this is no skin off Foster's nose."

"We will get, as I said, two thousand from him. Indeed to get the whole matter out of our systems, I'll write you a cheque myself if you will give me an authority to discontinue the case."

"I won't take two thousand. I won't take a penny less than five," Sonny said.

When it came to haggling he was no longer out of his depth. Years of bargaining over second-hand cars had bred in him a certain confidence. There were areas in which he was more expert than Curtis. This, he realised instinctively, was one of them, just as he sensed that Curtis wanted to settle this case and had become the antagonist.

"Not a penny less," Sonny repeated. He stood up and beckoned Joan to do likewise. She clung to her seat, alarmed. Her prayers had been answered; and now Sonny was going to spoil everything by his obstinacy.

Curtis opened his drawer. His eye lit on Mr Woodhouse's cheque. Thanks to the wretched specimen of humanity in front of him, he had collected an unpleasant but remunerative client. To that cheque for two thousand pounds would soon be added the fees for perhaps a thousand leases of new houses. Very good business. Perhaps the money this little pair were looking for, which meant so much to them, would be well spent. He must settle before Saturday. He must be able to tell Arthur Evans that the case against Stephen had been bought off at his expense. And Stephen must know that he owed his peace of mind to Curtis's unexampled generosity.

Put in its crudest fashion, five thousand pounds was not a great deal to have to pay for Woodhouse's business. If Sonny were to take a percentage off that he would, in a few years, collect five thousand pounds several times over.

"Even if it has to come out of my own pocket, I'll see it is done," Curtis said, and he drew out his cheque-book.

"Thank God," Joan said.

Sonny, prepared to settle at the last—expecting the other to say, "Will you split the difference?"—expressed his relief in another way. Taking out a packet of cigarettes, he offered it to Curtis. A symbol of submission. The solicitor brushed the offer aside with a hand that continued to write.

"Will you please sign your name here," he said to Sonny.

He had resumed authority.

CHAPTER XXX

"WHO SUGGESTED THE ZOO?" Tom Murgatroyd asked in his complaining voice.

"Arthur, I think. He's a bigwig on the Council," Henry replied.

"I thought it might have been Curtis."

"It's very pleasant here at this time of year. Much better than a stuffy restaurant or some dismal club."

"I was only going to say that it was an odd place to choose."

The partners were walking from the entrance towards the lion house, near which the restaurant was to be found.

"I remember coming here as a boy to see swimming races in the pond," Henry said.

Murgatroyd looked at a goose on the path.

"Pretty dirty for that, I'd say."

"Never occurred to me at the time."

"You looked on the bright side of everything in those days, I dare say."

Henry was brooding over the implications of the remark when a voice behind them closed the ranks. With the same expression of outrage on their lined faces they acknowledged the greeting from their most recent partner.

"I have very bad news," Brian said before he had seen the signal. "I dropped into the office on the way and the telephone was ringing. Mrs Curran was looking for Mr Stephen. Curran died suddenly this afternoon. I said one of us would go and see her in the morning."

"We must keep the news from Stephen," Henry said. "It would ruin the evening for him."

"He was very fond of Curran," Tom agreed.

"But did the worst thing possible when he moved him up," Henry said.

"We all make mistakes," Tom said, looking at Brian.

"This will mean more confusion, more change," Henry said. He also looked at Brian.

They wanted to peck him, he thought. All over the gardens nasty birds were probably enacting similar scenes. It was not the mood in which to begin a dinner.

But now they had joined the other guests. Curtis, looking grave, stood a little apart. Arthur, in the centre of the group, spread geniality around him. He came forward to greet Stephen's partners. "I had a word with Stephen on the telephone. He has been summoned by the Taoiseach. Some crisis apparently; but he told him about the dinner and the great man has guaranteed that he will see he is delivered here on time. Very appropriate that he should come in a State car. I've told the others. And, for your private ears, I had a call from Curtis just before I came out. He has settled that will case. He was rather anxious to go into details, but I cut him short. I will drop the news into Stephen's ear before dinner."

"That's something," Henry said.

The Haggard will case had not been discussed in the office, but everyone knew that it spelled unpleasantness. Brian broke away from the company. His partners depressed him. To all these others the occasion was merely one of curiosity and good-will; but for him it was an evening that he would never forget. There was something of nightmare about poor Curran's death, and the dropping of the Haggard will case came too late. A relief for Stephen; but if Curtis had acted otherwise, if that 'wicked man' Woodhouse had not interested himself, Curran might still be alive. He contrasted the scene in the gardens—the peacocks parading on the close mown lawns, the pink and white of the flamingoes at the edge of the lake, the last rays of the sun throwing the shadows of the trees across the broad path—with a picture it was all too easy to conjure up, of Mrs Curran in her grim house, which death could not make more drear.

This dinner marked for him the great step forward meeting Stephen had given to his career. He had drifted into law, would have preferred a University life, but had the misfortune to strike a year in which a brilliant student deprived him of the first place that would have been his had he been younger or older. When Curtis took him into his busy office, it looked as if he had justified his choice of a profession. But the three years in that office had been bleak, and whatever Curtis planned for the future, he took nobody into his confidence. It was not an encouraging atmosphere. In a few months with Foster & Foster he had leaped ahead. Stephen, with an impetuosity that seemed quite out of character, had virtually adopted him. And when tonight colleagues were toasting Stephen's departure from the profession they were celebrating his own leap to the top of it at the age of twenty-seven.

The thought of Curran gave a hollowness to the laughter that came from the men standing in groups under the trees, their white shirt-fronts making them look like penguins. Nor did the spectral appearance of Curtis console him. He would have to say something before the evening was out to his former employer and receive his 'I hope you are keeping well' in exchange.

And then the scene changed, as if in a play. The guests had to leave their cars outside the entrance to the Zoological Gardens; but for a State car the gates were opened, and a shining black saloon had silently appeared in their midst, before the assembled lawyers were aware that it was coming.

Stephen stepped out beaming. Arthur came forward to greet him and they hugged. Then he looked round and saw Curtis, who had not rushed forward with the others; he went over and put a hand on his shoulder. Curtis looked pleased and uncomfortable at once.

Henry and Tom Murgatroyd, looking sheepish in the light of vicarious eminence, shuffled in towards the centre. Like two goats tethered together, they could neither leave nor love one another. The whole evening would pass in a wrangle about the World Cup or the probable composition of the Irish Rugby team in the coming season. But they were unable to make the effort to make conversation with outsiders. And, anyhow, it would probably be some kind of shop talk if they did, unless by happy accident they found themselves beside sports-lovers.

Stephen sat between Arthur and the Chief Justice. Curtis beside him, and another Judge, a friend of Stephen, sat at Arthur's left-hand. Otherwise there was no placing of guests. The vain moved towards the top or, resentfully, stood at the bottom, hoping, as the Bible misleadingly taught, that they might be called up if they took a sufficiently lowly seat.

Stephen was certainly in splendid form. A bigger man above than below the waist, he towered over his neighbours sitting down. Brian noticed how his good-humour lit them all up. But not Curtis. His smiles were wintry concessions. He spoke very little.

"Curtis looks as if he was off his oats," Murgatroyd confided to Henry. Inevitably they had sat down together, almost spitting at each other as they did so.

"I'm not surprised," Henry said. "I thought Stephen was mad to kick Woodhouse out of the office; but ever since he left us other developers have been crowding in. The word has got round. None of them will give business to any office that works for Woodhouse. Curtis lost three of his best clients to me yesterday."

"You must hand it to Stephen," Tom replied. "He always seems to do the right thing."

"Except with Curran."

"Isn't it typical of you to bring that up now? I'm glad you didn't come to my wedding."

"I can't recall that you invited me. I gave you a clock. I do remember that."

"We have it still. It's in the dining-room. It doesn't go."

"You forget to wind it, I expect."

Brian sat at the end of the table beside a very deaf and silent practitioner, who only looked up from his food at intervals to repeat the same question and nod with huge satisfaction at the same reply. Brian was content, he was enjoying the spectacle of Stephen.

The menu said there were going to be three speeches. Arthur, in his official capacity, was giving the formal toast of 'Ireland'; then Curtis was proposing Stephen's health, to which Stephen would reply.

There was a general expectation that he was going to let the company into a secret. He was not the man to have driven up in the Prime Minister's car merely for show. He had been closeted with him on some important business; and he was going to let this group of admirers know what it was. You could detect a buzz of excitement in the air. It added to the sense of occasion. They would preserve the menus of Stephen's dinner.

Then Richard Curtis stood up. He looked, Brian thought, like a priest in Lent. Distinguished. There was no denying that. A high forehead, a remarkable skull, long sensitive hands. His thick glasses added an impenetrability that was his most impressive feature.

"I hope he doesn't go on for too long," Henry whispered to Tom (who pretended not to hear).

The speaker had a small bundle of notes in his hand, which justified Henry's fears. Brian, too, felt a sinking at the heart. This was Stephen's night. Was Curtis going to try to steal his thunder and spoil the evening for everyone? The man was so vain.

He had a high thin voice, as penetrating as a drill. His style was dry; but he had taken trouble to be humorous. Stephen Foster, he reminded the guests, needed no memorial. We already had Stephen's Green and Foster Place, one the chief recreation grounds in the city, the other in the very centre of its financial power. Who could doubt that to future generations these, whatever their origin, would be connected with Stephen Foster, the great man they had gathered together to honour, not simply as a genius in his profession, but as the friend to whom every solicitor, young or old, turned to instinctively in time of trouble.

At this there was a roar of applause that must have startled the animals, locked in their cages for the night. Brian felt a tightness in his throat. He was afraid to look at Stephen. Absurd to feel so sentimental about an elderly solicitor. But, there was no other word for it, he loved the man.

At this moment, Arthur pushed a note under the

speaker's nose. He glanced at it. Then he picked it up. Whatever the message was, the consequences were fatal to the speech. He lost his thread. He rambled. He repeated himself. And then, as if despairing of recovering, he gave the toast rather summarily, and sat down.

There was a silence, then a buzz of conversation. Some had seen the note pass. Others had not. One group were surprised to find that so able a man could be blown off course by an interruption. Others put his collapse down to illness. But when Stephen rose up and the cheering broke out again, Curtis, deep in his chair, staring in front of him, was forgotten.

Stephen stood there, beaming, twinkling, benign, exuding good-will.

No notes for him. He had a word for everyone. Brian noticed that he glanced down at his menu before he referred to his 'young friends and my partner, Brian Fagan. I don't want to think that it's only the old fellows who would turn to me in their troubles. Not that any of you look as if he ever had a trouble in his life'.

Henry drew attention to himself by laughing too loud. "A dig at you Tom," he said.

The speech was exactly right. Friendly and funny, and free from the least note of complacency—a perfect beginning. But everyone was waiting to hear the end.

"You may have wondered," he said, "how I managed to acquire such a grand-looking limousine this evening. I'll let you into the secret. It's not mine. I'm only one of the taxpayers who supplied it to the Government. It was the Taoiseach's car. He asked me to call on him this evening because he had something very important to discuss. You will read about it in your newspaper in the morning; and I want to tell you what it is now. I'd like you to hear it straight from the horse's mouth. When it was announced that I was running for the Dail some of you must have said to yourselves 'Stephen Foster is out of his mind'. I wouldn't blame you. It's a long story. I won't bore you with details; but I was asked to stand because the Taoiseach thought it would strengthen the Government if I were to come into his Cabinet. I said I would if I could be made Minister for Justice. If I were to go into politics I was determined to use the opportunity to do something for law and lawyers. They have been my whole life."

Someone clapped, and others followed; but there was too much curiosity to prolong the interruption.

"He agreed. He had to put it to the Cabinet and they agreed. It was a compliment, and I took it as a compliment to the profession. Tomorrow is the day for nominations, and what the Taoiseach wanted to see me so urgently about was a threatened split in his party. Perhaps I shouldn't say that; but I've said it. He had recently rid himself of a Minister, not a very important Minister in the public view, but a man with a large following in the party. Today that group put it to the Taoiseach that if he went over the head of the local branch by running me at the by-election there was a certainty that the breach would widen. They want to put up the widow of the deceased member. It is a tradition that is not always followed. There has been a tendency recently to try to break with it. In this case the widow is a housewife with six children. She married at nineteen, and her contribution to parliamentary discussion is unlikely to be memorable; but there is a General Election in prospect; the leader of the party cannot have internal troubles at this time. To make a long story short, the Taoiseach asked me to help him out of his difficulties. I didn't hesitate. I said, 'I have never forgotten that I was taught "ladies first" when I was in the schoolroom. I'll stand down'.

"Now I will tell you something that may surprise you. I have never in my whole life felt such a sense of blessed relief as I did when I realised that I had been let off that string. I am married to my work. I'm too old to be transplanted. I have only one regret, that I am not to get the chance to do something for all of you. Perhaps I should apologise. Are you going to say that I had a dinner from you all—and a damn good dinner it has been—on false pretences? I don't think so. I'm vain enough to believe that tonight has been an expression of friendship. For my part the proudest moment of my life was when I looked round this table and told myself that I can't be altogether a failure if I have such friends. Thank you, Richard. Thank you, Arthur. Thank you, Chief Justice, for joining us. God bless you, every one of you."

"No need to ask what was on the note Arthur passed on to Curtis," Murgatroyd said to Henry. They left together.

CHAPTER XXXI

STEPHEN INSISTED, WHEN he heard on the following morning about Curran, that he should visit the widow. Brian met him at the office beforehand and offered to go as well. He was apprehensive about the encounter. The Currans had taken a month's holiday. He had been restored to his old work at an increased salary; but, still, the widow would probably attack Stephen for having upset her husband by changing his routine.

"I'll face her," Stephen said. "Before I go I'd better see if he left any instructions in the office about burial. And he may have left a will. I'll look in the safe."

"Let me go," Brian said.

"I'll do it myself. I know the way."

It was a Sunday morning, and except for themselves the office was empty.

Stephen was out of the room for some time; he returned with an envelope in his hand.

"Brian. This is very awkward. The poor fellow made a will on the day he went away. He got two of the girls here to witness it. He left everything to me."

Brian, thinking of Mrs Curran and that gloomy house, said nothing.

"I suppose he did it as a gesture of some kind. He

286

thought he had made trouble for me. It was the only way he could show his feelings. Oh dear! I wish he had spoken to me. What shall I do?"

"You won't take it."

"Of course not. He has probably saved a little through the years. It can't be much. I seem to remember that she had a shop of some kind when they married. And the house was hers. Curran's fortune won't make much difference. He had probably thought it all out."

"I don't believe he told her what he intended to do. Not from what I gathered when I called on them. She was not at all happy about the office."

"I dare say."

"How will you break it to her? I suppose it won't matter much if she hears at once that you are renouncing the will in her favour."

"It's not the money, Brian. They have been married for thirty years. They had no child. She is a singularly joyless creature. This will be the last straw, a final kick in the teeth. And she will dread what the neighbours will have to say."

"We can tell her that there will be no publicity. Curran's will won't attract attention. I suppose you must take out Probate."

"None of that matters, Brian. What matters is her feelings when she sees what her husband did at the end. It's a judgement on their marriage."

"I suppose she must see the will?"

"She is entitled to insist."

"Of course."

"Brian, will you do something for me. I left a bank book in the strong room. It has Curran's name on it. Stupid of me. He left it with the will. Get it for me, like a good fellow."

Brian found the bank book. When he returned Stephen was going through other papers. Some he put on one side, others he tossed into the grate.

"Now," he said. "I'll go and face the music."

"Are you sure you wouldn't like me to come with you?"

"Quite sure. Before we go we might as well clean up. Put a match to those bits and pieces in the fireplace."

Brian took a petrol lighter off the desk and lit it. Then he bent down and applied the flame to the bundle in the hearth. Circulars, envelopes, newspaper-cuttings, bills—they burned slowly. Damp perhaps. One paper as it caught fire took on a skeletal emphasis. The lettering made a last brave show before the flame consumed it.

Brian read: "This is the will and testament—" He gave a cry and put a hand into the grate; but the paper had turned into ashes and was sailing gently up the chimney.

He looked up, shocked and startled, but grateful that Stephen, not he, had made the fatal blunder.

Stephen came and stood beside him, looking into the fire, his hand on Brian's shoulder.

"Do you remember in one of our first conversations I told you that sometimes a solicitor had to do things that he couldn't tell his barrister or his staff or, even, his wife? You asked me to give you an instance. I couldn't at the time. Well there is one. You have burned Curran's will. You will tell nobody. You must not tell anybody. Nobody must ever know."

Brian felt the pressure of the hand on his shoulder. He was being comforted. It was like the loss of innocence, the knowledge that the world would never look the same again.

"What does the enemy have to say?"

Stephen had taken out his watch.